GOODBYE MY LOVE

GOODBYE MY LOVE

Jack Fox

The Book Guild Ltd
Sussex, England

This book is a work of fiction. The characters and situations in this story are imaginary. No resemblance is intended between these characters and any real persons, either living or dead.

This book is sold subject to the condition that it shall not, by way of trade or otherwise, be lent, re-sold, hired out, photocopied or held in any retrieval system or otherwise circulated without the publisher's prior consent in any form of binding or cover other than that in which this is published and without a similar condition including this condition being imposed on the subsequent purchaser.

The Book Guild Ltd
25 High Street,
Lewes, Sussex

First published 1999
© Jack Fox, 1999
Set in Baskerville
Typesetting by Keyboard Services, Luton

Printed in Great Britain by
Bookcraft (Bath) Ltd, Avon

A catalogue record for this book is
available from the British Library

ISBN 1 85776 451 X

CONTENTS

Part I	The Village in the Valley	1
Part II	Marseilles	25
Part III	Ashover	51
Part IV	The Threat of War	61
Part V	War	99
Part VI	Peace	239
Epilogue		256

ACKNOWLEDGEMENTS

To my wife Nancy for her patience, encouragement and understanding

To Glenys Goodwin for the art work

To Gina Boulton for proof reading

To Wendy Davis for typing

PART I
THE VILLAGE IN THE VALLEY

1

Ashover was like a bit of heaven the world had left behind, a kind of Shangri-La. It was a small hamlet nestling in a long fertile valley through which flowed the Amber, with its musical tinkling as its waters meandered and cascaded over its boulder-strewn path along the valley, to join the Derwent at Ambergate.

The village itself was the focal point of the farming community, which was scattered along the valley. It consisted of a cluster of inns and small cottages constructed in locally quarried sandstone and dominated by a spired church.

Ashover's only claim to fame was the intrusion of the King's Cavaliers in 1646, who rested themselves and their horses around the church and quenched their thirsts at the Crispin Inn nearby.

This picturesque hamlet was pretty well self-contained, with a few quaint shops which sold the basic requirements of life. Below the church, and centrally situated, was owd Jack Straw's blacksmith's shop. Apart from shoeing horses and the odd bit of scroll work, Jack Straw could turn his hand to almost anything. He'd mend saucepans, clocks and watches, and during his slack moments he'd even slip a basin on your head and give you a quick 'short back and sides' and maybe a shave. He treated animals for their many ailments and aspired to relieving humans of their petty afflictions, such as constipation, aches and pains; and for earache he'd stuff in a little hot onion. He had been known to draw his cut-throat razor across a troublesome boil, then slap on a hot bread poultice. This, however, was not the full extent of Jack Straw's enterprise. Oh no, not by a long chalk! His assistant, Willy Blossom, when not striking for him on the anvil, could be seen in a corner, busy making corn dollies, wreaths or bouquets. There was never a dull moment in the blacksmith's shop, and no problem was ever turned down. Jack Straw's ingenuity had no bounds.

Last but not least was Prospero De'ath, the undertaker, who stretched his tape-measure up and down his clients with lightning speed, his face as grave as an old crow's.

It was along the valley, by the stream, that owd George and Sara Pipkin and their two children, Robert and Mary, farmed a few acres. Slippery Edge Farm was about 2 miles from the village, or 'nowt but a stone's throw', as owd George would say.

It was 1918, and the four long years of war had just ended. It had been four gruelling years for the Pipkins, though it must be said, four successful years. In spite of everything, the farm had prospered and the bank balance was healthy. It was at this point that Mary's brother Robert was demobbed. He had joined the army prior to the war, going through Sandhurst, where he trained to be an officer. Robert, being a 6-feet-plus giant of a man, on passing out with honours, and having a penchant for horses, had joined the Household Cavalry. Later he saw action in France, with the Guards Brigade. Now, with all this action, and the ghastly war behind him, he rejoined the peace and tranquillity of the Pipkin household at Slippery Edge Farm. He retired from the army a colonel. The only reminder of his former career was the title, which lingered on. Out of respect, the locals deemed it right and proper to address him as Colonel Robert or Colonel Pipkin.

During the war years young Mary Pipkin had taken on much of the farm administration, lifting some of the strain off the shoulders of her ageing parents. In spite of her heavy workload, Mary nevertheless had found time to train in overseas post-war relief work. It kept her in touch with life beyond the farm and, perhaps, in a strange way, was a form of relaxation.

Now, with Robert's return, it seemed the appropriate time for Mary to 'do her bit', as she put it. Her assistance was now needed in France. She duly answered the call, and found herself dealing with the homeless – organizing soup kitchens, distributing clothing, generally assisting, and guiding the unfortunates into the various channels to suit their needs. Meanwhile Robert gradually took on the running of Slippery Edge Farm, much to the delight of owd George and Sara Pipkin.

With a few months' farming experience under his belt and the reins firmly in his hands, Colonel Robert Pipkin looked to make improvements in the running of the farm. Having a sizeable pension helped to facilitate his ambitions. He commenced by employing another cow hand, to take some of the strain off Benny, who had worked hard and long over the years. Benny's time became more flexible, and allowed him to oversee other work that had to be done. He liked the idea of moving around the farm, more in the role of foreman.

Owd George Pipkin, with the weight of the farm lifted from his shoulders, felt like a new man, and became imbued with a new flush of energy. He wasn't altogether off the hook though, and would never want to be. His job now was to deal with the buying and selling at the markets. This delighted owd George, who was never happier than when he was meeting his market cronies. Market day to him was the highlight of the week. He enjoyed the hustle and bustle of the market place, where he relished a good chinwag and haggled to the last penny of a bargain, and was over the moon when he got one.

With an extra cow hand, Robert suggested that his dad could take Benny with him on his market trips, if he liked. This chuffed owd George no end, and Benny felt highly honoured too.

Most farms seemed to have a Tom, Dick or Harry who skipped school whenever possible to hang around the place. They were usually frowned upon as being slow on the uptake, strong in the arm but weak in the head, or just plain stupid. Slippery Edge Farm had one such person in Sammy Mottishaw. He wasn't stupid, he just didn't like school! Who did? He hovered about the farm so much that Benny christened him 'Sammy the Ghost of Slippery Edge'. All Sammy's interest was centred on farms and animals. He was never happier than when Colonel Robert or Benny found him a little job to do, be it sweeping the yard or taking Clare, the pony, to the water trough. Sammy would do anything, from digging up potatoes to cutting the lawn.

The Colonel took a shine to Sammy and said to Benny one day, 'Sammy has become part of the farm. I don't know what we would do without him. He's left school now. I think perhaps we ought to take him on. What do you think, Benny?'

'Well, sir, we seem to depend on Sammy to do all the odd jobs, and that's what farming is all about. He's almost indispensable. He'll be chuffed, I'm sure.'

Sammy's job was far-reaching. He'd be digging potatoes one minute, the next he'd be grooming Clare the pony. Sammy was content to try his hand at anything. When busy, he was as happy as a pig in shit.

Slippery Edge Farm and Sammy.

2

It was Saturday, and owd George was just telling Benny to have the gig ready early on Monday morning for their trip to Bakewell market. Benny was all excited in anticipation of his introduction into the hustle and bustle of market life.

'Don't worry, George,' he said. 'I'll have everything ready for seven thirty, like tha' said.'

'By the way,' said George, 'put something decent on. We'll be going out to dinner, tha' knows, an' I don't want thee stinking o' pig shit.'

'Never fear, George,' he retorted. 'I'll be squeaky-clean and smelling all scenty, like a poof.'

'Great, but don't overdo it! I don't want some owd randy farm-hand following thee around.'

Just then a young couple turned up to buy two young pigs.

'See to them, Benny,' said George. 'You know the price?'

'Right, George. Leave it to me!'

The young pigs were eight or nine weeks old, and ready for selling off. To sell privately, one could expect a better return than sending them to market, and less trouble. Benny opened the sty door and the sow, proud as punch, brought out her litter into the yard, ten in all! She was a big sow, all of 20 stone, a very good mother, very protective, and on occasions inclined to be aggressive.

The couple picked out the two they wanted and paid cash. It was plain to see that grabbing the two piglets was going to be no easy matter. The sow was desperate to get to her two separated off-spring. In her anguish, 20 stone of pig lunged at Benny, knocking him off balance. Benny called frantically to

Sammy, who, as usual, was hovering in the background ready to pick up any useful tips on pig handling from Benny.

'Chase this bloody sow down the yard, while I catch these two little buggers,' called out Benny in exasperation, pointing out the two in question. Now this was asking a lot of Sammy, who was more for patting and scratching their backs than shooing them off. Give Sammy his due, he always did his best, no matter what. He chased the sow down the yard, beyond the dung heap.

Benny grabbed the squealing piglets, while Sammy, arms outstretched, tried to forestall any attempt by the sow to reach her squealing progeny. Sammy positioned himself in front of the dung heap, between the sow and piglets, but was hardly prepared for the onslaught that followed. The sow charged forward with surprising speed, straight between Sammy's legs. Sammy fell forwards onto the back of the sow, grabbing the only thing to hand, which was her tail. Sammy, shouting at the top of his voice, was carried along in a flash

Sammy and the sow.

to the dung heap. There, the sow suddenly jerked to one side to avoid it. Sammy was not so lucky. He was flung spreadeagled, and landed with an almighty squelch right in the middle of the glutinous mess. It was so comical, it was impossible not to laugh. As Sammy staggered out of the quagmire, festooned in shit and straw, the three of them rolled about in uncontrolled hysterics.

'Oh bloody hell, Sammy,' said Benny, trying to keep a straight face, 'Tha' looks like the scarecrow that's fallen out wit' muck spreader! Tha'd better go an' get thi' sen cleaned up.' As poor Sammy squelched along, somewhat down in the mouth, Benny added, 'An' tha' walkin' like a bloody scarecrow too.' Regretting his remark a little, he continued, 'Don't rush back, Sammy. There's nothing spoiling.'

Just then Sara Pipkin left the house to look for her husband George. She took one look at Sammy, clamped her hand over her nose and dashed back indoors.

Benny and the young couple laughed until they cried. Later, Benny declared to Sammy that the young lady had laughed so much that she had wet her bloomers. This remark helped Sammy to see the funny side of it, which brought on a roar of laughter.

'Tha're a one, Benny,' he said, holding his side. 'Well, it was funny really, wasn't it?'

'It was that, Sammy. But I bet thi' mam didn't think so!'

'Tha' reight there! She threw buckets of water over me, and scrubbed me off wi' t' yard brush. Then I stripped off and bathed myself.'

'Come here, let's see if tha's washed behind thi' ears.'

'Ge'r off wi' thi', Benny.'

That evening, Sara Pipkin was sitting quietly in the lounge answering her daughter Mary's letter. George was stretched out, sleeping soundly in his chair. His paper had slipped through his fingers and now lay scattered on the floor. Flash, the sheepdog, was recumbent, with his head resting on George's shoe, and Cuddles the cat was curled up purring peacefully on a cushion.

Mary had moved to Marseilles, helping refugees wanting to return north to their families. It was a mammoth task trying to reunite scattered families, but a wonderful heart-warming experience when successful. She liaised with the press, searching through lost persons columns, hospitals, even prisons. It was an endless search.

Mary was a good correspondent and kept the Pipkin family well informed. She always left the personal, exciting bits to the last. During her searches she had come across a certain Monsieur Brodeau, a nice, young, very intelligent Frenchman who, through circumstances, was reduced to earning a crust on a small farm. Formerly he had worked for a large international firm which made and sold farming equipment and machinery. During hostilities the firm had been turned over to war work. Now that the firm was in the process of reverting back to its former business, Monsieur Brodeau was hoping to rejoin it. The good rather startling news was that Mary had fallen hopelessly in love with this charming man. He had swept her off her feet and had asked her to marry him.

Sara wrote back in some trepidation, as would have most mothers in such circumstances. 'Are you sure you know what you are doing, dear? He's a foreigner, you know, with different ideas! They eat frogs and snails, squid and lots of horrid things. Do be careful, dear! Where would you live? Where would you be married? He'll be a Roman Catholic too, don't forget!'

Sara, after pointing out all the stumbling blocks she could think of, finished off by giving Mary a little bit of credit for common sense. 'By what you say, dear,' she wrote, 'he must be a nice kind man and I trust your judgement to do what is right. I hope you will bring him home on your next leave. He will be made welcome and made to feel at home.'

Sara poured out her concern over Mary to George. 'What do you think of our Mary marrying a foreigner, George?' she said. 'I always thought she would wed a local lad. I know one or two fancied her. Jack Straw's lad was very keen, always inviting her tut tanner hop, though he couldn't dance to save his life.'

'Hey lass! Stop thi' worrying. Our Mary's got her head

screwed on t' right way. She'll make a good choice, never fear! Anyway don't let's jump t' gun. It may never happen!'

'Tha's reight, George. Tha's got some good common sense in that head o' thine. I think Mary takes after thee! Anyway, what's Robert doing today?'

'Oh, he did mention something about branches trailin' int' river.'

Perhaps Colonel Robert was just trying out Sammy, or perhaps his confidence in Sammy was a little over the top, but that morning, he asked Sammy if he could saw a heavy branch off a willow tree which was overhanging the stream and denying the cows easy access to water.

Sammy was thrilled to be asked to do such an important job. He had never been trusted to do more than saw up a few logs. He patted himself on the shoulder and thought, This is indeed a step up the ladder of success.

The Colonel pointed out exactly what he wanted. Sammy climbed along the branch to about halfway. 'That's fine!' said Colonel Robert, stretching out to hand the saw to Sammy. It looked a bit awkward but Sammy straddled the branch and commenced to saw. 'That's the idea, Sammy,' called out the Colonel. 'I'll leave you now to get on with it, but be careful.'

'Righty-ho, Colonel Robert,' replied Sammy in a show of confidence. He set to work with a will, but the sawing was harder than he had first thought. As the saw bit deeper into the branch, so the friction on the blade became stronger, finally sticking. Sammy pondered. What was needed was a bit of weight on the part of the branch to be cut off, to open the cut. Sammy at last cottoned on to the idea and pressed hard on the part to be cut off. The saw slipped back and forth with ease, so long as the weight was applied. It was awkward and a little bit too complicated for Sammy's mind to grasp, then his activity ground to a halt, while his mind grappled with the situation. Suddenly the penny dropped! He kicked himself for not thinking of it sooner. Why don't I sit on the other side of the branch? My weight would keep the cut open, and free the saw blade, and allow me to saw.

To Sammy's mind that was the answer, the logical solution to his problem. Sammy didn't seem to have the ability to look further ahead, and really put his back into the sawing. This is easy now, he thought. Suddenly there was a terrific crack, followed by a resounding crash, as the saw, the branch and a surprised Sammy disappeared for a second or two into the murky water. No one was more surprised than Sammy! Dragging himself out of the water, he looked around; no one was in sight. He grabbed the saw, and made a wide detour of the farm, popped off home and did a quick change. Nobody would be the wiser, he thought, and he wouldn't let on to anyone. But he hadn't reckoned on Colonel Robert, who had been watching Sammy from afar. He too didn't let on, and quietly congratulated Sammy on his resourcefulness.

There must have been another pair of eyes watching, because that evening in the Crispin Inn someone was heard to say, 'Has tha' heard about owd Sammy Mottishaw sawing himself in tut river?'

'Really!' came the reply. 'Bugger me! I thought he had more gumption than that.'

It was hot news, news for an hour. Luckily Sammy wasn't there that night. Probably still drying his clothes!

3

Over in Marseilles, Sara's advice to Mary must have got squashed among the amorous embraces, for events quickly took control. Love had overflowed, creating a delicate situation in which the heart overruled the head. Mary and Charles Brodeau decided it would be prudent to marry as soon as possible, if only to forestall friends totting up on their fingers. The news of the immediate marriage culminated with the Pipkin family's lightning dash across the Channel.

The wedding went off smoothly. Apart from the language difficulties, the two families got on well together. They parted with lots of hugs, kisses and promises. The couple were showered with presents, but the best present of all was the news that Charles had been reinstated with his former company. The couple's future looked rosy, which was heartening news for George, Sara and Robert, and allayed one of their fears. After seeing Charles and Mary together, all their fears and anxieties were dispelled. They returned home happy and contented in the knowledge that Mary had made a good match. Sara, always a jump ahead, was already thinking of needles, wool and colours.

Slippery Edge Farm quickly returned to normality. The Pipkins settled down to await the happy event which was sure to follow. Sara had made a provisional note of the day of the expected arrival of her grandchild.

Benny had sold the litter of pigs, and Cuddles the cat had had kittens on Sara's nightdress in the airing cupboard. They were doing fine, but Sara didn't think much of it, and soon turfed them out into the woodshed.

The next evening after dinner, George and Sara were relaxing in the lounge. George had got his feet up, to relieve his swollen ankles. He was enjoying his usual glass of beer and a quiet smoke. Sara, wasting no time, had already bought wool, and now her needles were clicking rhythmically in time with the old grandfather clock.

'You've soon got going!' observed George. 'Suppose it's a girl? You'll have t' start from scratch again.'

'Oh, it's goin' to be a boy. I can feel it in mi' bones. By the way, where's Robert off to, all poshed-up like a dog's dinner?'

'He's goin' t' see Timmy Titmarsh down on Squirrel's Dray Farm. At least, that's what he says.'

'I'm sure there's more to it than that. I'll bet my bottom dollars on it,' replied Sara, with a knowing nod.

'Tha're reight there, lass. I reckon if he told that to a donkey it would kick his brains out. I reckon he's set his cap at Sally Titmarsh, the daughter. She'll be a good catch for somebody. She's a shapely wench with a nice round –'

'That's enough,' cut in Sara. 'You don't miss much, do you? Particularly if it's nice and round. I'll have to keep mi' eye on thee, George Pipkin.'

'Well, I think it's time he dipped his wick! I wonder sometimes if he knows what to do with it,' quipped George.

'If he doesn't, tha's been failin' in thi' duty. Tha' knew all about it before tha' were fourteen. Remember owd Joe Shaw's haystack?'

'Ay, I do that! An' it was thee who egged me on. Anyway, he could do worse than rompin' in t' hay wi' her.'

'It sounds to me as if tha's been castin' a wicked eye in her direction.'

'Nay, lass! It's just natural observation. There must be somethin' in it though, because Robert is talking about joinin' t' choir. We both know who the soloist is, don't we?'

'I've been wondering, George, why Robert has suddenly turned religious.'

'It all fits in, doesn't it, lass?'

'Happen tha' reight, George. We'll see. Time'll tell.'

* * *

With advancing years, time slipped imperceptibly by for George and Sara. Autumn, bright and colourful, came and went, and now once again the magical carpet of coloured leaves had given way to the first heavy flakes of winter snow.

George, with a bit of a shudder, added a few logs to the dying embers. Sara lit a taper and reached up to turn on the gas and lit the gas-light, then drew the curtains to shut out the heavy grey snow-filled clouds that bore down like a blanket along the valley. Pushing her chair a little closer to the fire, Sara remarked more to herself than to George, 'That's better.' George put his stockinged feet on Cuddles the cat for extra warmth. His feet were playing him up a bit, and Cuddles didn't seem to mind. 'How about a cup of tea, George?' hinted Sara.

'I'll put the kettle on,' said George. 'We need something to cheer us up in this bloody cold weather. I'll put a tot of brandy in. That should liven things up a bit.'

'Tha're a good 'un, George. I don't know what I'd do without thi'. Are tha' going down tut village tonight?'

'Not bloody likely! It's not fit to turn a dog out.'

'I thought tha' wanted to see Jack Straw about making a foot scraper? It would save traipsin' in half the garden every time tha' comes in,' grumbled Sara.

'Oh, I'll pop down an' see him tomorrow. I'll mention it to him,' called out George from the kitchen. He brought in two big steaming mugs of tea laced with brandy. 'Here tha're, get that down thi' an' stop thi' whittling.'

Now that winter had arrived, the farm work would be more concentrated. All the cattle were undercover. There was ample silage, hay and straw, and the ploughing was under contract. With a good team of workers, there were no foreseeable problems.

Letters flowed regularly between Sara and her daughter Mary. Sara had knitted a pile of socks and garments ready for the baby. The stress of waiting in a state of expectancy gave one the impression that it was Sara who was pregnant rather than Mary.

Each letter that dropped on the doormat was seized upon eagerly.

'I shall be glad when it's all over! Are tha' sure that tha's got thi' dates reight?' George asked.

'Course I'm sure. It's any day now, Grandad, an' tha'd better get a bottle or two in ready to celebrate.'

'Oh ay. If I forget, I'm sure tha'll remind me.'

'Well, George, I suppose he'll arrive in God's own good time.'

'That's it, lass. Forget about it, and let's get on with our own lives. We have plenty of other things to see to. We had better concentrate on having the right amount of poultry ready for Christmas. Orders are coming in now, and we ought to be thinking about buying in a few more goslings, before they are all snapped up. I'm not looking forward to all that plucking and dressing. I wish someone would invent a machine or something to do it.'

'Now there's a thought, George! You've got the idea, now put your thinking cap on and fathom out the details. Why don't you have a word with Jack Straw about it? He's a mine of ingenuity. I can see we shall be millionaires before we've finished. Just think, George. I can see the hoarding now: "George Pipkin's Mechanical Plucker" marketed by Farming Tools and Machinery International.'

'Oh, stop thi' blitherin' an' finish thi' breakfast,' retorted George.

Impatience was finally rewarded, for the very next day, Sara snatched up the long-awaited letter almost before it reached the doormat. She eagerly read it. Then with whoops of joy and a bit of ballet round the kitchen table, she presented the letter, with a majestic flourish, to George. 'Read it! Read it, George,' she said, brimming over with excitement and thrusting the sheaf of papers into his hand. 'My premonition was right! It's a boy! Little Pippikins has arrived! Isn't it exciting, Grandad!'

'Yes, and about time too. This calls for a celebration, Granny. I've got a bottle of champagne, all ready and waiting.'

As if by magic, Robert arrived on the doorstep. 'You're just in time, Uncle Robert,' called out Sara excitedly. 'Pippikins has just crashed in, and Dad is just rustling up a bottle of bubbly to celebrate.'

Happy and relieved, the three raised their glasses, and Robert acclaimed the latest addition. 'Here's to Pippikins – Brodeau, may his life be long, happy and war-free.'

'Amen!' said George and Sara as one voice.

Sara spent the rest of the day writing a nice long letter to Mary, and making up the parcel of clothes for Pippikins.

4

During breakfast the following day, Sara noticed that Robert seemed absent-minded and smiling to himself. Several times he seemed on the point of saying something then suddenly changed his mind. Sara knew Robert inside out. She knew something was revolving around in his brain. She watched him until she could stand it no longer.

'Come on, Robert! I know thee well enough to know tha's have got something hidden up thi' sleeve. So come on, Robert let's be knowing an' stop beating about t' bush.'

'Well, I have a little surprise, but I didn't want to mar Pippikin's day – but now I have no option, and I can't contain myself any longer. This morning I'm going into Clay Cross to see George Kenning. You know, the pots, pans and paraffin man. He's started dealing in American cars. I want to buy one, and I hope you will both learn to drive it. It's quite simple, really. I could teach you. It was one of the good things I learnt in France.'

'What a lovely surprise, Robert,' declared Sara. 'But how can you afford all that money? They cost all of a hundred pounds.'

'Tha'd better check thi' books up, lad, afore tha' goes lashin' out like that,' uttered George in some doubt.

'Don't worry, Dad. It won't break the bank! Do you like the idea then, or do you think it's crazy? You know, to get on, one has to keep in step with the time, and owning a car is a step forward. Just think of all the advantages! You could do your shopping in town when you wanted and arrive home, not worn out and loaded with parcels. Apart from that, you would be able to make your deliveries of farm produce, attend your meetings and a hundred and one other things. What do you think then?'

'It's crazy,' was Sara's comment, 'but I like it.'

'What about you, Dad?'

'It's a great idea, but I have doubts about driving. I'm more at home with two in hand and a whip. My word, they'll think we're posh. It'll cost half a crown to speak to us.'

'The locals will soon see the wisdom of it, and clamour to follow suit,' declared Robert, 'you mark my word! Well, that's settled then,' he continued. I'll get Sammy to clean out that empty stable and take the door off. I think I can trust Sammy to do that! I'll see Harry Fletcher to do the brickwork and fit a bigger door, and that will be the garage.'

Robert stroked his chin and wrinkled his forehead in thought.

'Dad, I shall be out this morning and the vet is coming to do some artificial inseminations. Benny has separated the cows to be done. Do you think you can see to the vet when he comes?'

'Yes, of course I will.'

'Right then, I'll be off. I'll see you this evening for dinner,' he called out, as he disappeared in a flurry through the door.

'What's tha' reckon to that then, George?'

'Oh, I think folk'll think we've come into a fortune. Tha' knows what people are like at putting two and two together, especially one or two Nosy Parkers that I needn't mention.'

'Oh well, it'll give the locals something to gossip about, won't it?'

'It'll be news for a day,' replied George, knocking his pipe on the hob. 'I'd better go down t' yard and make sure everything is ready for t' vet.'

'I don't hold with this insemination idea, George. The very thought fills me with revulsion. I think the poor cows miss out on a natural pleasure.'

'Trust thee to think of that! Tha' didn't miss out, did tha'?'

'Well, there can't be any thrill in having a syringe stuck up your behind, no matter how big the syringe. They'll be wanting to use it on us women next! Just fancy if our Robert and Mary had been born in that way. Just look at all the fun and games we would have missed. Just think of all the frolics we had in the hayricks. Come to think of it, we women would be able to manage without men! Perhaps one or two specimen men would be caged up for us women to drool over and pick out the most suitable to supply the sperm. I don't know what we women would look for, George. Can you think of any outstanding feature?'

'No, I can't,' replied George, slightly worried and breaking out into a cold sweat, 'but I expect you could think of something! Anyway, stop thi' blitherin' and hand me mi' coat.'

George was pleased, as he noticed the vet crossing the yard, and was able to extricate himself from this disquieting conversation. With a relieved expression on his face, he hurried off in the wake of the vet.

'Saved by the bell!' said George. There was a puzzled expression on the vet's face. He didn't let on, but led the way to the cows. Sammy was waiting, and looked on with interest as the vet set to work.

It was early evening when Robert arrived back at Slippery Edge Farm with his new acquisition. He was bright and breezy, in sharp contrast to the dark forbidding sky which heralded further falls of snow. Robert parked the Morris, splendid in its newness, by the window so that his parents could have their first view of it. George and Sara went outside to share Robert's excitement for a few minutes, then Robert drove it under cover. The front of the stable had been knocked down and cleared, and now provided temporary cover for the car.

Winter had arrived with a vengeance. Day had suddenly turned to night. Snow was falling, with flakes as big as half-crowns, and the light covering of snow deepened by the minute. 'Come on, Sara,' said George, 'I'm as cold as Christmas. My teeth are chatterin'. It's enough to freeze your b—'

'That's enough, George! You don't need to go into details about your extremities. Get inside and stoke the fire, while I get the soup on.'

In no time at all, the three were sitting at the table behind three steaming-hot bowls of soup, which they mopped up with gusto to the millions of reflections of the dancing flames shimmering from the ornaments and trinkets which adorned every available space.

Now feeling warm and comfortable, Robert asked, 'Everything all right, Dad?'

'Yes. The vet came. I didn't reckon much to the insemination, though, an' I don't think the cows thought much of it either. I suppose it's all in t' course o' progress.'

'There you are, Robert. Get that lot down you! You must be starvin',' said Sara, as she placed a piled-up plate of dinner in front of him.

'That smells good! I feel as hungry as a hunter, and I've done nothing this morning,' commented George. 'Must be the weather. I'll see if I can lay my hands on a bottle of wine. Besides, it'll warm us up a bit.'

Glasses were filled and raised.

George offered a toast: 'Here's to Pippikins and the car,' and added, with a sideward glance at Sara, 'and all who dare drive her! Now that we have a car, what's goin' to happen to Clare and the trap?' he asked.

'We'll keep them,' replied Robert. 'It would break Sammy's heart, he's so attached to Clare. Besides, he makes good use of the manure. I see he's already digging over the vegetable plot and spreading muck. He's planning to have a bumper crop next year, and I shouldn't be surprised to see him enter something in the show. I think his cauliflowers and beans this year wouldn't have disgraced the show table. You know, Dad, he's not so daft as people make out. He's a hard worker, with his heart in farming. He's worth two of some I know.'

It just shows how unpredictable the English weather can be in early winter, for the next morning much of the snow had disappeared. It was still very cold, but much better than expected.

Sara, full of beans and anxious to get her parcel off, had

risen early. She was happily singing to herself in the kitchen as she prepared breakfast. George and Robert arrived on the scene to the appetizing aroma of a good old English breakfast: fried bacon, eggs and sausage, with a slice of fried bread for good measure. They were sitting at the table taking deep breaths and rubbing their hands in ravenous anticipation as Sara entered with hot mouth-watering plates.

'Morning, Mam!' greeted Robert. 'I see your parcel is almost ready. If you like, I'll run you down to the post office. I know you are anxious to get it off as soon as possible.'

'Thank you, Robert,' she replied. 'That's kind of you.'

Breakfast over, Sara busied herself putting the finishing touches to her parcel, which included letters and messages from George and Robert. By the time she had sealed it and put on her hat and coat, Robert was at the door, tooting his horn. 'Come on, Dad,' he urged. 'You may as well come along. I'll have you back in ten minutes.'

They set off with a feeling of elation.

'Oh, this is the life,' said Sara, puffing herself out like a peacock, with George doing his best to imitate her.

Ashover was quiet, as usual. Owd Jack Straw was blowing up his fire, ready to start his day's work.

'Owd Mrs Podmore's spotted us,' cried Sara. 'And she's better than the town crier!'

Robert, conscious of the many envious eyes, pulled up by the post office. Sara, a bit flushed, hurried in with her parcel.

The postmistress whispered discreetly, 'It's the happy day then, Sara?'

Sara mouthed a silent reply, 'Yes! It's a boy.' She handed over her parcel, and resumed her seat in the car.

Robert, proud as Punch, moved off to the wide-eyed amazement of a group of youngsters, perhaps seeing a car for the first time.

Back at Slippery Edge Farm, Robert drove the car under cover, just as a flurry of the expected snow feathered its way along the roof-tops.

'I didn't think we'd get away with it,' he commented.

A solitary robin fluttered about from branch to branch in

the holly bush by the back door. The ground had hardened during the night and the scene was set for a heavy fall.

'Isn't it amazing how dramatically the weather changes,' whispered Sara to herself.

Benny and Sammy were busy feeding silage to the cattle in the covered-in cattle yard. The heat from the cattle turned to steam as it mingled with the icy atmosphere, dispersing outwards and upwards, enveloping the building like an eerie spectre.

George and Sara shuddered as they scraped the snow off their shoes. George made for the fire, added a few logs and warmed his hands. Sara, shedding her gloves, made a beeline for the kitchen, where she quickly set about making tea. George had hardly got his hands warm before Sara arrived and set the tea tray on the table.

'Like to finish, and pour out, George,' said Sara.

George was halfway to the whisky bottle and called back over his shoulder, 'Righty-ho! Will do.'

They were soon joined by Robert, and the three warmed and sipped in pleasurable silence. Suddenly, Sara, thinking beyond their immediate comfort, disappeared again into the kitchen and quickly made three extra large mugs of tea for the farm hands. 'Must keep the lads happy,' she muttered, as she disappeared through the door. She was soon back to enjoy her tea.

'You're pleased now, Mother, that your parcel is on its way?' said Robert. 'I don't suppose Marseilles is worried about snow yet.'

'Marseilles will be still enjoying marvellous sunshine,' replied Sara. 'I don't suppose snow ever reaches there. Yes, I am glad the parcel is on its way. I hope Mary will be pleased with it.'

'I'm sure she'll be chuffed with it,' remarked George, having his little say. 'You'll be wanting to pop over to Marseilles to see her.'

'Yes, you're right. Perhaps in the spring.'

PART II

MARSEILLES

5

Charles Pipkin-Brodeau had relations scattered about in many countries, particularly in Switzerland and Italy, where as a child he had spent most of his holidays. He spoke all the continental languages, including English. This ability proved paramount in securing rapid promotion in the international firm in which he worked. He was now a sales director, which necessitated much travelling and frequent changes of location. He hoped to have a spell of duty in England at some time in the future.

Charles and Mary's marriage was truly a love match. They had a deep affection for one another, and the birth of Philip bound them irresistibly in an harmonious bond of togetherness. Even their names, as is the custom in latin countries, were now linked. They were known as Monsieur et Madame Pipkin-Brodeau. The Pipkin-Brodeaus were financially in a position to afford a nanny, but Mary wanted to have a perfect bonding with her baby and chose to tend to its needs personally.

It was November, cold and bright, as the Pipkin-Brodeaus awoke to a new day. Baby Philip was yelling his head off to get some attention to satisfy his hunger. Mary, with comforting words, picked him up, changed him and fed him. Her cuddles and baby talk were soon rewarded with chuckles and bubbles, and lots of jerky leg and arm movements. Charles, like a dutiful husband, roused himself and made coffee and croissants. He returned to the bedroom, preceded by the fragrant aroma of fresh-ground coffee. *'Le voilà!'* he said, placing the tray on the bedside table.

It was a happy time, sipping coffee and sampling nice tasty croissants and chatting about this and that to the contented baby noises coming from the cot. Sometimes the exuberance of such moments overflowed and ended in a passionate embrace, as happened that morning.

The Pipkin-Brodeaus lived in a prestigious company house in Marseilles, situated in an elevated position, surrounded by beautiful gardens overlooking the Mediterranean. Charles drew back the curtains to reveal the breathtaking panoramic view of the sea, whose waters sparkled in the cold November sunlight.

In the street below, Monsieur Dupont, their neighbour, was passing. As usual, he was reading his outstretched journal, a cigarette dangled from the corner of his mouth, and one arm was gripping a half-dozen baguettes. '*Regarde, chérie!* I don't know how he does it! *C'est formidable!* I wonder what happens if he is taken short?'

Marseilles is a large maritime port on the Mediterranean, and home of the French Navy. Out to sea there was the usual assortment of boats, from fishing smacks to large ocean-going liners and the occasional naval vessel.

Along the beach, small flocks of waders scurried up and down the shoreline in search of food. Overhead, seagulls dived and screeched, scavenging anything that looked edible.

Charles's interest in the panoramic view was abruptly ended by the sound of the doorbell. Looking down, Charles called over his shoulder, '*C'est le facteur à la porte, chérie!*' He hastened downstairs and signed for and received a large package from the postman, which he carried upstairs to Mary.

'It's from England! From your mother, *chérie!*'

Mary excitedly tore open the parcel. She half guessed its contents.

'Oh Charles, *regarde! Tous ces petits vêtements pour* Philip. How pretty, with *tout ce ruban*. What do you think, Charles?'

'They are beautiful, *n'est-ce pas, chérie?*' he replied, then to baby Philip he added, 'How lucky you are, Philip. *Ton premier paquet.*'

Mary eagerly opened the enclosed letter. 'Oh I say, Charles! Robert has bought a car, and hopes to meet us at Chesterfield station one day.'

'It can't come too soon. A change would do us both good.'

'We had better wait a while, though. According to Mam's letter, they are knee-deep in snow. The very thought makes me shudder! I know what it can be like in Ashover. It's not the place for a holiday in winter.'

'We could perhaps ski down the slopes at Chatsworth. The last time I was there as a boy, I slid down the hillside on a copper shovel. *C'était merveilleux!* But I wouldn't find it so thrilling today.'

Letters between England and France continued to flutter through the letter boxes. There were always plenty of things to write about. Sara kept Mary well informed about the local gossip and happenings in Ashover and the surrounding villages. There was always someone getting married or having a baby, and owd grave-looking De'ath was never out of work for very long. One wonders if he was at his happiest when putting someone under. On such occasions he never looked happy, yet this was the zenith of his occupation, for which he was paid.

Mary had the knack of ferreting out witty or amusing goings-on. She liked rummaging round the markets. There was always something happening, something to write about. Like the day Madame Renard, a no-nonsense little woman round the corner, chased her butcher around his stall and walloped him with a tough old joint he had declared would eat as tender as a chicken.

This little squabble turned into a battle royal as friends and relatives of both sides joined in. Nothing serious happened. All the participants seemed to enjoy it. Suddenly whistles sounded from many directions, followed by the sound of running feet crashing on the cobbled market square. Police arrived on the scene as if by magic. After lots of shouting and gesticulating, the battle simmered down. Finally the situation was calmed, as the embarrassed butcher handed over a prime cut to the irate Madame Renard. The pushing and poking ended amicably, and the hustle and bustle of the market continued as though nothing had happened.

Mary had a lot of time to herself as Charles's business took him as far away as Paris and Brussels, usually with several nights or even a week's overstay. Occasionally his travels would take him to Switzerland and Italy, when the overstay could be much longer. As Charles's workload increased, it became necessary for his secretary to accompany him. According to Charles, his secretary, Mademoiselle Colette Lenoir, was a puritanical, stumpy lady, very efficient in shorthand, typing and figures, and made a smashing cup of tea. 'I wouldn't be without her,' admitted Charles one day.

'*Eh bien*, Charles, you seem safe enough with her. She sounds like a motherly sort of person.'

'Oh *oui! certainement, chérie* – one could say that.'

Mary didn't mind Charles's frequent excursions and became accustomed to them. Over the next four years, Sara, sometimes accompanied by George, came over for a few weeks' holiday, which made a welcome change for Mary and helped to ease the monotony. They were a great help, and enjoyed taking Philip out for walks. Though as time went by, it was Philip, or Pippikins, as Sara called him, who used to take his grandparents for walks, which usually ended with ball games in the park.

It was when George and Sara left to go back home to Slippery Edge Farm that Mary felt at her loneliest. Her eyes clouded with tears. She would be comforted by Philip. Mary would give him a little hug and kiss. 'You're a little treasure, Philip. I don't know what I would do without you.' Sometimes Philip would shed a tear in sympathy.

After such partings Mary would suddenly cast away her sorrows and declare war on her housework and do all the little jobs she had been going to do, but never did. This soon banished her sadness and, not wanting to transfer any of it to Philip, she burst into song, to which Philip added his little contribution.

Philip was growing healthy and strong, and was hardly ever ill – the odd cold was soon shrugged off. After breakfast he would be quite contented to play with his toys, while Mary got on with her house-work. With baking bread or cakes, it was a different kettle of fish. He was always keen to have a go. Mary would sit him at the table with his board and rolling pin and a lump of dough. He'd be quite happy to sit there all day, rolling out and cutting out little cakes, all of which had to be baked.

Afternoons were usually reserved for taking Philip for a long walk, which always finished up in the park. He liked to watch the ducks and geese, and loved feeding them with household scraps. It was during one of these afternoon jaunts that they happened to meet their *laitier*. He was going their way and asked politely if he could join them. Mary raised no objections and rather enjoyed his company. He kept Philip amused with his lively chit-chat and the occasional piggyback. With a wave and a smile, he left them at the park gates. Philip waved until he was out of sight. 'That was a nice man, Philip, our milkman!'

Mary liked the milkman, whose name was Duprés. In other circumstances she could well have fallen for him. He was full of enthusiasm and so extrovert one could not help but like him. Thrusting all naughty ideas behind her, she made her way home.

6

It was mid-April when Charles arrived home from one of his official excursions. He was in high spirits. He grabbed hold of Mary and waltzed her round the room. Though she didn't know what had brought on this playful burst of energy, she was quite delighted to go along with it, and her heartbeat increased rapidly in anticipation of his next move. Usually he arrived home shattered, ready for a meal and his carpet slippers. Philip usually brought his slippers, as he did now. Charles lifted him up and gave him a little cuddle. 'Have you been good?' he asked.

'*Oui, Papa!* I have seen the ducks in the park.'

'I have some good news for you both,' said Charles, with a hint of mystère. 'We are going on holiday next week. I want to take you to Troyes. It is a beautiful city, with an historic cathedral and many interesting places to visit. Apart from that, the countryside is *magnifique. Qu'en penses tu, Mary?*'

'Oh Charles! It's a gift from heaven.' Mary put her arms around Charles in a warm embrace. '*Comme je t'aime, Charles,*' she whispered, snuggling close to him.

Mary had never been in the habit of meeting Charles off the train, but the next evening, still bubbling over with excitement about the holiday, Mary said to Philip, 'Shall we go and meet Papa's train and give him a big surprise?'

'Oui, *Maman*! Goody goody.' Philip got so excited he wet himself. This delayed things a little, but Mary, excited herself, didn't have the heart to scold him. By this time Philip was four years old, healthy and strong. He could walk well, and was a little chatterbox both in English and French.

They set off for the station. Mary took along the pushchair, just in case Philip became tired. At that moment he seemed far too excited to be tired, but from experience Mary knew that over-excitement could sap energy and bring on a bout of weariness.

On arrival, Mary bought a platform ticket. They strolled along the busy platform and found a seat. 'The train will come from that way,' said Mary, indicating the direction.

'Papa will be surprised, won't he, *Maman?*'

'I'm sure he will, Philip! This is the first time we have met his train.'

A loud voice suddenly blared out from a nearby tannoy, giving Philip a startling shock and causing him to hold on tightly to his mother.

'That's the loudspeaker, announcing Papa's train,' explained Mary. 'Did it make you jump, darling?'

'*Oui, Maman.* I didn't like it!' he replied, hopping on one foot and then the other.

'Do you want the toilet, Philip?' asked Mary.

'*Oui, Maman,*' he replied with some urgency.

'*Alors!* Come quickly,' she said, pulling him along in the right direction.

She got him there just in time. Another few seconds and he would have disgraced himself. As it was, they arrived back on the platform just as the train was pulling in.

The train thundered to a halt, with screeching brakes and a loud belch of steam, which frightened the life out of Philip.

'*Regarde là bas, Philip!*' she said pointing to the front end of the train. People poured out onto the platform. Then Mary's gaze was suddenly transfixed by a beautiful lady, fashionably dressed and exuding an aura of presence. She stepped off the train as though stepping off the catwalk. People made way for her, and stood back to admire her bewitching beauty. It was at that very moment that the unbelievable happened. Charles stepped forward, like the perfect gentleman he was, to guide her to the exit. Mary was flabbergasted. You could have knocked her down with a feather!

Charles, on seeing Mary and Philip, was equally astonished,

but took good care not to show it. He ran forward, kissed Mary and lifted Philip. Charles introduced his family, and then, to the amazement of Mary he said *'Je te présente Mademoiselle Colette Lenoir, ma sécretaire, chérie.'* They all handed in their tickets, then after a brief conversation, Colette bid the family au revoir, gave a little kiss to Philip, and made her way to her car.

Charles drove home along the scenic way. It was a delightful route, and gave Charles an opportunity to point out to Philip all the interesting beauty spots, and at the same time to cover up his embarrassment and prepare himself to answer the stream of questions which were surely to follow, and which at the very moment were gyrating heatedly in Mary's brain.

The unease built up in Mary until she was unable to restrain her shocked feelings any longer. She exploded and burst out resentfully. 'I like the way you describe your secretary, Charles,' she said, with a strong hint of sarcasm. 'Stumpy, but good at figures, and makes a good cup of coffee. I wonder what other qualifications she has which you haven't told me about! What else is she good at?'

'Don't be jealous, Mary darling, I don't pick them, you know. They come with the job, and they're thrust on me willy-nilly.'

'Weren't you lucky? And not a word of protest!'

Mary, not wanting a row, let the matter drop. She could not help feeling uneasy, however, and began to turn over in her mind little incidents which she had brushed aside as insignificant but now seemed to gain in importance. No wonder, she thought, that he frequently arrives home shattered, complaining of the pressure of work, and ready for a good meal and his slippers. No wonder that on such occasions I get scant attention.

Mary spent a restless night, tossing and turning. The niggling suspicions would not go away. Charles, on the other hand, in spite of Mary's sleeplessness, slept like a log. Whether justified or not, she looked at him and exploded. 'The self-satisfied bugger!' Mary was not given to swearing but she was so full of indignation that she could not help herself.

Sleep was out of the question. Mary got up and busied

herself around the house. Her troubles didn't feel so pressing, and in the light of day she began to have misgivings about her suspicions. Determined to get on with her daily chores, she prepared breakfast and attended to Philip's needs, then brought out the suitcases and sorted out clothes to be washed ready for the holiday. She was a very methodical housewife and by the time Charles arrived down for breakfast, Mary had the first batch of washing on the line.

It was so difficult to be at loggerheads with Charles. He was so extrovert! So entertaining! He was so enthusiastic over the coming holiday. He described many of the places around Troyes that he wanted her to see. 'You know, of course, that I was born near Troyes, in a little village named Maisons Blanches,' he said.

'*Oui, chéri,* you have told me often enough! I have a vivid picture in my mind of Maison Blanches, with the white cottages and the little church.'

'Oh, but wait until you see it! It's so charming,' replied Charles.

Breakfast over, Charles dashed off to catch his train and Mary settled Philip down in his nursery. He liked his nursery and would spend hours there playing with his toys. Mary hung more washing out and continued with her holiday preparations.

Now completely absorbed in her arrangements, she became suddenly aware of someone calling rather urgently. It was Pierre Duprés, the milkman.

'*Madame, votre blanchissage! La pluie!*'

'*Oh mon Dieu,*' said Mary, running down the garden with the clothes basket to rescue her washing, closely followed by Pierre.

'*Je vous aide, Madame.*'

'*Ça c'est très gentil*, Pierre.' It was raining cats and dogs. They might just have well left the washing on the line. They were both soaked to the skin. Mary had little option but to invite Pierre inside.

'*Ce n'est rien, Madame.*

Mary insisted, however. Pierre, in stepping into the kitchen, tripped and lurched forward, straight into Mary's arms. She was caught off balance, but managed to hold onto him. They were both drenched to the skin.

Mary held tight to prevent them both from falling. Pierre's face came close to hers, and as their eyes met there was a spontaneous irresistible attraction. A spark, like the magnetic force of the buddleia to the butterfly. Their dripping bodies clung together. Their lips met as though it was the natural thing to do. They held each other in a tender embrace until their wet clothes began to steam. They savoured the moments in silence, then Pierre's hand strayed to the soft warmth of Mary's breast. She was unable to resist. She trembled to his touch and pressed herself to him, until she could feel the warmth and strength of his manhood as it throbbed appealingly against her thighs. In a pang of passion, Pierre gently lowered her on to the deep-pile rug in front of the fire.

Consumed in passion, they eagerly helped one another to peel off their wet clothes. Mary locked the door leading to the nursery just in case Philip took the unusual step of coming down. Now as naked as new-born children they lay together in the warm glow of the fire. Pierre fondled Mary's breasts and she gently explored his body. Pierre slid his hand between her shapely legs. He lovingly parted her dark curly cushion of love and gently thrust himself inside her. They floated on a higher plane as they worked slowly together in harmony, in complete ecstasy of the moment. Their breath became hot and laboured as their energies fused in an explosion of joy and contentment. They lingered there for some time, entwined, spent, but deliriously happy. Reluctantly he withdrew and tore himself away from her.

'*C'était merveilleux, Mary,*' he said.

'*Oh oui, Pierre, c'était bien! Tu sais comment faire plaisir à une fille.*'

By this time their clothes were almost dry. Mary turned the damp sides towards the fire, then made coffee. They sat close together in the nude, sipping their drink, but after several minutes Mary became a little anxious about Philip. She noticed that Pierre was rigid again and about to seek another close encounter. Reluctantly Mary tossed Pierre his clothes and commenced dressing herself. Pierre made much of putting his trousers on. He danced around hitching his trousers up, his erection causing difficulties and embarrassment to Pierre, but great amusement to Mary.

They arranged to meet the following morning at seven o'clock, when Charles would be in Paris. Mary said she would put the outside light on and leave the door ajar, so he would know it was safe.

'*Alors! Demain matin, à sept heures.*'

They kissed, and Pierre made his exit.

Mary felt sure in her heart that Charles could not resist having an affair with his stunning secretary. Who could? But the thought did nothing to lighten the heavy burden of guilt of what she had allowed to happen, neither did the old saying, 'You never miss a slice off a cut loaf'. She had tasted the forbidden fruit, and nothing was going to stop her having another bite.

There was no question of a love match in Mary's affair. It was pure physical attraction, brought about by the sudden shock of finding Pierre in her arms. What had happened was a mutual impulsive urge to kindle the spark that was obviously there.

That afternoon Mary took Philip through the park, and as usual, he asked to see the ducks. As he trotted back and forth with bits of bread and shrieks of delight, Mary had time to ponder over her actions, and tomorrow's assignation with Pierre. Had she the will-power to resist his appeal? Or would she weaken under his seductive allure? She resolved to be strong and resolute, only to weaken with the very next thought. Oh, if only Charles was home tonight instead of tomorrow night. Then she thought, Tomorrow will be Charles's last day with Colette, his secretary, before the holiday. I wonder, perhaps we are both in the selfsame dilemma! Well, tomorrow will be the last time for both of us, then we shall both have time to readjust.

Philip was growing into a sturdy lad, with a mind of his own. He needed a watchful eye, and the occasional strong word to bring him to book. He was beginning to speak well in both

French and English, though sometimes in a mixture of both. Charles, who knew the advantages of being multilingual, was very pleased for him to succeed in this field, and gave him lots of encouragement and help.

7

Charles set off for the last day's work before the holiday. Mary tried hard not to show her mounting excitement.

'You seem excited about the holiday, Mary,' Charles remarked. 'I think the change will do us both good, and I am sure Philip will enjoy it too. It will be nice for the three of us to spend time together. We have never been able to do that, have we *chérie*?'

'No, Charles. I am looking forward to it! Now be off with you, before you miss your train.'

'*Tu as raison, ma chère.*'

Charles gave her a kiss and a big hug and hurried off to catch his train.

Philip was fast asleep in his room. Mary, still in her nightie, was clearing the breakfast table when Pierre the milkman arrived. She let Pierre in with the milk. '*Bon jour*, Mary! *Comment vas-tu?*'

'*Je vais bien! Et tu?*'

He told her he was completely happy now that he was with her, holding her at arms length, to feast his eyes on her dazzling beauty. All Mary's yesterday's thoughts of being strong and resolute faded away at a glance. She was putty in his presence. Pierre looked at her admiringly, in her long flowing nightdress. The sight was unbearable. His ardour quickly reached boiling point, he couldn't contain himself further. He swept her into his arms. They kissed in a passionate embrace, and his hands explored the graceful contours of her body. '*Comme tu es ravissante*, Mary!'

Mary, in feverish anticipation, pressed close to him, to feel the might and throb of his vigour. Her pent-up emotion surged up in a burning desire to be possessed by him. Their hands met in an intense scramble to undo his flies, to release the mighty monster within. Pierre kicked off his trousers and almost tore off Mary's nightdress in his eagerness. He lowered her on to the thick rug in front of the fire. There was little time for fondling.

Mary's 'little man in a boat' was as stiff and upright as a guardsman in a sentry box. They were both on the threshold of ecstasy.

'Oh Mary! *Comme je t'aime.*'

Their lovemaking was wild, passionate and exhausting. They lay locked together in an embrace they wished would never end.

It was very emotional to part, not knowing when or if they would meet again.

Mary promised to write to him if they moved away, though in her heart she realized it would be foolhardy and fraught with danger. Better to make a clean break! But she hadn't the courage to tell him. Perhaps it would be better all round if we moved far away, she thought, perhaps to some other country, then she wouldn't have the niggling doubts about Colette. Perhaps she was maligning Colette unjustly. It was just feminine instinct, intuition, call it what you like, that seemed to emanate persistently from within.

Finally, with a tremendous hug and a lingering kiss, they parted.

Thrusting aside the memories of the last hour, Mary busied herself with her mundane chores. She looked in on Philip. He was just stirring. 'Hello, Philip! Are you awake?'

'*Oui, Maman!* Can we go in the park to feed the ducks?'

'I don't see why not. I've some packing to do first, then we'll go.'

Philip's welfare was Mary's priority. She bathed and dressed him, then brought him down to breakfast. He was a chatty little boy who kept her amused with his funny little ways. He was anxious to stroll through the park, and keen to feed the ducks this morning. As soon as he had swallowed his last crumb, he said. 'Shall we go now, *Maman?*'

'Yes, all right then. Just go and wash your hands, and get your hat and coat, while I get ready.'

It was warm and sunny, and walking through the park was a delight. Mary sat on a bench by the lake side, while Philip wandered back and forth with scraps for the birds. Her mind drifted over the morning's assignation with Pierre. He was a marvellous lover whom she would never forget. She was pleased he had not come to the park that morning; it saved her having to tussle again with her conscience. She resolved to obliterate her infidelity of the past two days and concentrate on all the things that really mattered. Just looking at Philip and thinking of Charles seemed to fortify her resolve. She felt happier now, as if a cloud had lifted from her mind. She gathered up Philip, hugged and kissed him, twirled him round and chased him up and down, to his screeches of delight. They played around in this frolicsome fashion until they reached the park gates.

Mary gathered Philip up and calmed him down with an ice cream. '*Maman* has a lot of work to do. Lots of packing to do for the holiday. Are you excited?' she said.

'*Oui, Maman!*' he replied, between licks of his cornet. 'Can I help to pack?'

'Yes of course. I'll be glad of a little help.'

Back home, after a bite to eat, Mary brought out the suitcases and started to pack. Philip, full of enthusiasm, waded in with a will. 'Where does this go, *Maman*?' he'd say.

'Oh, just put it in there.'

'And this?' he would ask immediately.

In the end, Mary gave him a case to fill all by himself. Finally he got tired or bored and fell asleep in the clothes basket. Mary looked at him and smiled. She put him in a more comfortable position and placed a pillow under his head. Now she could really get on without interruption.

Charles had decided to take the car, which made it easier to pack as clothes, such as overcoats, pullovers etc. which might be needed during the journey could be left out.

Now left quietly to herself, Mary commenced folding and packing Charles's suits and shirts. She did not realize until this point just how many clothes Charles had accumulated or how many suitcases were needed. It looked as though Charles would have to forgo some of his suits or buy more cases.

He had laid out all his suits on the bed, together with a pile of shirts and underclothing. 'Good heavens!' sighed Mary. 'Charles has enough clothes to stock a shop.'

It was while Mary was folding and packing his clothes that she became aware of the overpowering smell of perfume that pervaded the bedroom. She examined his suits with a certain amount of curiosity, which grew by the moment. They all reeked of the same perfume, not her modest one, but an expensive Chanel number. Mary, bewildered, cast her mind back to the vision of a ravishing lady stepping gracefully from a train to a gaping crowd of onlookers. Breaking out into a cold sweat, and holding back an overwhelming impulse to take all his suits outside and put a match to them, Mary sat down to consider. With each solution, she was forced into a corner by her own recent misdemeanours with Pierre. She decided in all honesty she could never accuse Charles of something that at best was only a suspicion. Best let sleeping dogs lie! If she couldn't come to terms with her suspicions, she could at least try to remove the perfume from his suits. With a gust of vengeful feeling, she gave them all a real good fettling with a hard brush, then she shook them as though she had Colette's neck in her grasp.

It was whilst in this wild mood that something flew out of his pocket and hit the floor with a slap. She gazed at the object in horror. It was a packet of three French letters, or *cap Anglais*, as the French call them. Mary never quite knew whether these titles were complimentary remarks or the pot calling the kettle black, but the significance of this unexpected bombshell needed little explanation, and the fact that Charles was taking precautions did little to alleviate her anxiety. Mary's head was in a whirl as she picked up the packet. It was sealed! Should she challenge Charles? To do so would certainly put paid to the holiday and maybe her marriage. Could she take that risk? And what about Philip? He was so looking forward to his first real holiday. How could she disappoint him! There must be another way. She thoughtfully replaced the packet in his pocket, as her mind turned to her own infidelity. That at least was true, while Charles's unfaithfulness was only supposition. There was nothing she could do! Her wickedness and sinfulness was a fact, and her reflection was tinged with shame. She could only suffer in silence. There was little comfort in the thought that the French often accept a mistress in the family. She resolved to play fair in the future, and hoped that her suspicions were misplaced. Perhaps this holiday would cement their relationship and put a seal on family values.

By the time Charles arrived home, the packing was more or less completed, and Philip, aroused from his slumber, was poking around as lively as a cricket. Charles was in high spirits. He had booked a fashionable hotel in Troyes, near the cathedral and convenient for exploring all the interesting places. He had seen to the car, petrol etc, all that was necessary now was to load the baggage and hope that everything would fit in. It was the intention to make an early start. With this in mind, the car was loaded; then, satisfied that everything was done that could be done, they had a meal, followed by an early night.

8

The next morning, bright and early, Charles and Mary were roused by Philip meandering around the house. 'He's excited about the holiday,' whispered Charles. 'We had better get up and see what he's up to.' Charles leapt out of bed and entered Philip's bedroom, returning immediately. 'Just come and see what Philip is doing.'

Philip was as busy as a little bee, stuffing all his toys into his little bag. 'You'll never get all your toys in there, Philip,' Mary said. 'Pick out the best ones to take and leave the rest behind, there's a dear!'

After a quick breakfast, Mary collected Philip and settled him in the car. She called back to Charles, 'Don't forget to lock the doors.'

'Of course, *chérie*.'

They set off at last. Once Charles had left the busy thoroughfare, he speeded up to put as many miles on the clock before the roads became too busy with the holiday crowds. The journey took longer than expected. It was late at night before they arrived at the *grand hôtel*. They were travel weary, and after a nightcap and a glass of milk for Philip, they toddled off to bed.

The next morning, refreshed and happy, they sat down to a breakfast of croissants, marmalade and coffee. Mary would have enjoyed a good English breakfast of eggs and bacon, but that was a dream of yesterday, with the unforgettable aroma issuing from the kitchen.

The day was cloudless and bright. 'Just the day for exploring the town,' said Charles.

The cathedral, which was nearby, was naturally their first objective. Philip was overawed at the size and magnificence of it, and excitedly pointed out the figures and gargoyles which abounded in profusion.

The first week was spent touring all the interesting places, including parks and zoos, to Philip's delight. He particularly enjoyed boating on the lake among all the wild birds. He was never bored. He amazed Charles and Mary by the way he remembered most of the names of the birds. Philip even showed a keen interest in the museums and had comments to make on the pictures and objects which captured his imagination. It was really a delight to be with him, to watch his face light up with enthusiasm as he discovered something new and interesting.

The second week was spent travelling to outlying places. Walking through woods and country lanes, picnicking in scenic spots, where one could still lie back on the grassy slopes, close one's eyes and dream a little, to the chorus of the birds, the sweet intoxicating smell of brier and the exquisite drift of a pot-pourri of wild flowers.

One special day was given over to Charles. He was anxious to give Mary and Philip a conducted tour of the little village where he was born. About 8 miles from the cathedral was a little village called Maisons Blanches. It was there that Charles saw his first light of day and passed the early part of his life.

They travelled by car to the outskirts of the village, then decided to leave the car and walk the rest of the way to fully absorb the ambience and serenity of the picturesque approaches to the village.

The day was ideal. The road was dappled as the sunlight shone through the avenue of tall and majestic poplars. The semi-shaded pavement made walking pleasant and the gentle breeze rustling through the branches refreshed the senses.

'Charles, *cette petite promenade est magnifique.*'

'*Oui, chérie*! I thought you would like it. It's my little bit of heaven.'

They soon came to a bend in the road, and there, spread out in all its splendour, was the olde worlde village of Maisons

Blanches. It consisted of a spread of 50 or so cottages, all snowy-white, whose outlines were half-veiled by a scattering of trees and shrubs. To one side, and overlooking this all-embracing vista, was the church spire, whose pinnacle glinted like a star in the morning sunlight.

'There you are, Mary,' enthused Charles. 'Just as I always remember it.'

'It's beautiful, Charles! It really is! So quiet and peaceful.'

'*C'est* Papa's borning place, *Maman?*' questioned Philip.

'*Oui, ma chér,*' answered Mary, giving him a little hug.

Going through the gate leading to the burial ground, Charles pointed out the headstones of his family and relatives. A large number bore the name Brodeau.

'This looks like the family resting place, Charles,' commented Mary.

'*Oui,*' said Charles, showing a little emotion. 'There is the grave of my mother, and next to it is my father's. The place in between is for me.'

This announcement shocked Mary. 'Is that your wish, Charles?' asked Mary.

'Yes, my love,' he said, putting his arm around her. 'It's always been understood that I should lie between them.'

'So be it, *mon amour,* it's a lovely resting place!'

'I would like to think that you would lie there with me when your time comes. I have written a little poem about it. Would you like to read it?'

'Oh yes I would, dear,' said Mary, taking the offered sheet of paper.

Mary read his poem, which touched her heartstrings and brought a flood of tears.

> If life goes on above the ground,
> Tis here you'll feel me, all around,
> And when your time comes, and you are free,
> Come join me here, where I wait for thee.
> We'll glide above, just thee and me,
> To find our world, where peace there'll be.

Mary clung to Charles as never before. Tears unashamedly rolling down her cheeks. 'It's beautiful, Charles, simply beautiful.'

Philip, not to be left out, snuggled in between them. Thus they stood for several minutes, held in the emotion of the moment, the ambience of the place. Then the distant, compelling notes of the organ drew them irresistibly through the portals of the church.

Out of the bright sunlight, the church seemed at first gloomy, but as their eyes became accustomed to the dimness, they were drawn to the beauty of the stained-glass windows and the memories of the stories they depicted.

The church was empty, save for three old ladies sitting side by side in the pews, heads bowed in prayer. The three Pipkin-Brodeaus sat in a vacant row. Still full of emotion, they sat, heads bowed, in reverence and thought.

Philip copied his parents but, childlike, kept one eye open to cast around, determined not to miss anything.

Charles was deep in thought about his life here as a boy, interrupted only by a little flashback to Colette as he wondered what she was doing.

Mary, her feelings emotional and tinged with remorse, gave a passing thought to Pierre and took a solemn vow never to cheat again.

Dropping a few coins into the collection box, Charles, an arm around Mary opened the gate, and the three continued their tour of the village, Philip tagging on behind. It wasn't long before Charles was recognized and hailed. Curious eyes peeped out from behind trembling curtains. Soon the three were surrounded by aunts, uncles and cousins, all falling over one another to welcome a long-lost relative.

'My word,' said Mary to Charles. 'I never realized you had so many relatives! And all in one village! They must own Maisons Blanches.'

'You are right there, Mary. Most houses have a Brodeau connection.'

The men quickly encircled Charles, firing questions quicker than they could be answered. The women in turn introduced themselves to Mary and made a great fuss of Philip, and voiced their surprise when Philip answered them in good French. '*Il est veritable Français,*' they declared. They all wanted to cart him off into their homes, and Mary had little option but to tag along. It appeared that there were more Brodeaus in the village than houses.

The rest of the week proved to be one round of festivities. With so many invitations, they were passed from one family to another. Mary declared she had never drunk so many glasses of wine or cups of coffee in one day in her life before.

The Pipkin-Brodeaus were split up among the relatives. One minute Charles was playing boules and the next playing cards. He was obviously enjoying himself. On the last day the family was united, only to say farewell for the last time.

The next day they made an early start on their journey back to Marseilles. Returning home after an exciting holiday is never quite so thrilling as first setting out. It lacks the zip of anticipation of seeing new things, new sights and experiences for the first time. So it was with a feeling of bleakness that the Pipkin-Brodeaus set off for Marseilles. Give Charles his due, he livened up the journey by stopping at interesting places and pointing out features of note, and choosing fashionable cafés and restaurants for meals and snacks.

The Brodeaus were not finicky over food. They liked a good hearty meal. Philip was a growing lad and his parents marvelled at the way he tucked away his food, so much so that Charles wondered if he had worms or something.

'It's just a young healthy appetite,' replied Mary. 'I think he is going to grow into a strapping young man.'

'Yes! With all the young lasses drooling over him,' added Charles.

'He takes after you, *n'est ce pas*, Charles?'

'Oh, I was never so lucky,' responded Charles, 'Although I did catch the eye of one or two,' he added, casting a Come hither look at Mary.

About halfway to Marseilles, Charles decided to spend the night at a welcoming-looking inn. Charles was feeling travel-weary and Philip was trying hard to keep his eyes open. Mary put Philip to bed immediately.

'*Regard*, Charles,' said Mary, 'how peacefully he sleeps.'

'Oh *oui, chérie*, he has used a lot of energy.'

They awoke the next morning to a bright cloudless sky and a chorus of birds fluttering about in the treetops. The sleep had revitalized spirits and everything was set for a pleasant journey home. Philip was bright-eyed and amusing, with his eyes glued to the window, not to miss a thing. Then for something better to do, Mary and Philip played I spy with my little eye. This helped to pass away the time, and as soon, it seemed, as interest began to flag, they approached the outskirts of Marseilles.

Arriving home, the family made a concerted effort to unpack the car and get back to normal as quickly as possible. Finally Charles gathered up the mail. Some was for Mary but most was business mail for Charles. The next half-hour was an exchange of news as the pile of mail diminished. Charles opened the final letter with a sigh of relief. The contents brought the holiday spirit to a dramatic end.

'*Quel désastre! Quelle bienvenue!*' yelled Charles in profound exasperation. '*Regarde, chérie!*' Charles passed over the letter for Mary to read.

It was from his firm. A certain Monsieur Renard, a director of the Italian branch, had died suddenly and Charles was promoted to replace him. In spite of the financial gain, Charles showed no sign of enthusiasm. Perhaps it was the upheaval and hassle of moving. A more sinister explanation for his lack of enthusiasm immediately sprang to Mary's suspicious mind. Could she ever erase the spectre of that ravishing beauty stepping from a train? She tried, but perhaps this move would bring the final break to finish the affair.

'You don't seem very happy about the move, Charles,' said Mary.

'No! I thought I was a fixture! But there, this is one of the snags that goes with the job.'

'Where in Italy is the firm, Charles?'

'Oh, *nella provincia di Aquila*, in the town of Aquila. The province stretches from Pescara on the east coast along the Sulmona valley to Sulmona itself and beyond.'

'Isn't Sulmona the place where your cousins live?'

'Yes, that's right! It will be nice to see them all again, and the valley of Sulmona is beautiful, as is Sulmona. Sulmona goes back to Roman times. There is still an aqueduct, built by the Romans, which runs across the town over a series of archways. It still works. You will enjoy discovering the old building and churches.'

'It's a pity about Philip. He'll have to go to another school, and probably an Italian one at that, Charles.'

'Don't worry, he'll fit in fine. He'll be teaching you Italian after he's been there a fortnight.'

'What about your frumpy middle-aged wizard with a teapot secretary? Will she be tagging along too?'

'Oh Mary, don't let Colette blight your life! There's nothing between us, you know. Anyway, she won't be going. I shall probably get a fat, dumpy secretary addicted to wine and garlic.'

'Oh I'm sorry, dear, I shouldn't score points off you. I hope you get a lovely package.'

'I shall get all the details tomorrow. You can start thinking about the move, and I'll organize the packing cases, documentation et cetera.'

The roving commission was one of the accepted complications or advantages to the job, depending on which way one looked at it. Mary's first thought was for her mother, whom she always kept fully informed. She lost no time in putting pen to paper.

PART III

ASHOVER

9

Down on Slippery Edge Farm, life continued as usual, dictated by the needs of the animals and birds. Little had changed. Robert was running the farm. The staff were the same: Benny was head of staff, young Tommy was a cowman and Sammy Mottishaw was the jack of all trades. Sammy hadn't progressed very far up the promotion ladder, nevertheless he held an important position in the hierarchy of the farm. He was the person the farm would miss the most and could not do without. He was reliable, honest and a good worker who could turn his hand to anything. One could say he was the Jack Straw of Slippery Edge Farm.

The village of Ashover, with its scattering of farms, was really a very close community. This was never more highlighted than when there was a death in the parish.

The sudden death of Timmy Titmarsh from Squirrel's Dray Farm, from a heart attack, demonstrated the communal concern for anyone in distress.

Robert Pipkin, with his close friendship with Sally Titmarsh, Timmy's only child, was naturally the first person Sally turned to. She sent her cowman to let Robert know of the tragedy that had happened. Robert hastened to Squirrel's Dray Farm, closely followed by Sara. The cowman must have passed the information onto the grapevine, for on arrival, Prospero De'ath was already there with his tape-measure, processing the needs of his latest client.

Robert put his arms around Sally to comfort her and promised to help her with the funeral arrangements and the paperwork which would follow.

During that day a stream of sympathizers called at Squirrel's Dray Farm to express their condolences and offers of help. Even Jack Straw the blacksmith forsook his anvil for an hour to pay his respects, while Willy Blossom, his assistant, busied himself in his corner making wreaths and bouquets for the rush of orders.

Elisa Downs turned up to lay out the body and offered to order Teddy Collins's coaches and teams of blacks for the funeral. This Sally gratefully accepted.

Sara and a couple of ladies from the Women's Institute offered to do the catering and reception. Sara also offered accommodation to Sally to give her time and space to think what to do with the farm. In the meantime, Robert had sent Sammy to Squirrel's Dray Farm to take over the temporary running of it. Sammy deemed this a great honour and a fine show of confidence and trust in him.

Come the day of the funeral, Sammy and Benny, anxious not to miss anything, waited at the end of Slippery Edge Lane, by the main road, to see the cortège pass. Sammy and Benny doffed their caps in respect as the cavalcade approached. It was a very solemn procession. The coaches and the team of blacks looked regal. The black horse's headdress was crowned by a knot of black horsehair, which trailed over and enhanced the forelock. The black harness was highly polished, the steel rings and chains were burnished to a silver-like perfection and the brass buckles shone like pure gold. The drivers, dressed in black with top hat and driving whip, added to the aura of military dignity.

'What a grand sight,' murmured Benny, and added more to himself than to Sammy, 'Poor old Timmy. He'll be missed at the Crispin Inn.'

'He would have enjoyed all this,' said Sammy.

'I reckon he would, Sammy! Does tha' reckon he's looking down on us?'

'Nay, Benny. Mi dad allus said, when you're dead you're buggered up.'

'Happen tha' reight, but I reckon when t' body's dead the spirit detaches itself and hovers about a' watches what happens.

His spirit might be anywhere, Sammy. It could be resting on thi' shoulder at this very minute.'

Sammy jumped up with a sudden spasm. 'Ge'r off wi thee, Benny! Tha're havin' me on! Tha' trying to put wind up mi!'

The cortège passed slowly by, its passengers solemn-faced, some discreetly dabbing their eyes with white hankies.

'Well, that's that!' said Benny. 'Better get back tut grindstone, Sammy. Tha're managing Sally's farm all right then? If tha' wants anything, just pop down an' let me know.'

'Thanks, Benny, will do.'

After the funeral and reception, the guests began to depart. It was all a bit emotional and a little tearful, shaking hands and thanking everyone for their support, but Sally carried it off well without breaking down, though she was relieved when the last guest left.

Sara and the two ladies from the Women's Institute made short work of clearing everything away and tidying around. Sally thanked them as they left, then Sally, Sara, George and Robert returned to Slippery Edge Farm.

It took a week or two for Sally to come to terms with her loss. Robert left it to her to approach the subject of her future plans for the farm.

'Robert,' she said eventually, 'I've been thinking about the farm, whether I ought to sell up or not, but first I would like to hear your views on the subject.'

'Well, dear, I have asked you several times before, but you didn't want to leave your father. I could understand that, and I know he could not have managed without you. Now things are different. I'll ask you again. Will you marry me?'

'Yes, darling! There's nothing I want more,' she replied, with a blush.

'Now that's settled, I'll give you my opinion, but of course it is for you to decide. My advice is to sell the farm. It would give you a nice bit of capital, which you could invest. There is enough work here at Slippery Edge, if you want to work. I think it would be sufficient to help Mother in the home. She is getting on a bit now, you know. I'm sure Mother would like that. We could have more time together. I don't really want you working your guts out on the farm. In the meantime, stay here. I'll leave Sammy to look after your farm. I'll get him to get all the farm implements and machinery cleaned up and set out for auction. He can also clean the yard and standings and generally tidy round, ready for the farm sale, after the stock has been sold off. I could perhaps spare Benny for an hour or two each day if necessary. Well, what do you think, Sally?'

'Oh Robert! You make everything seem so easy and simple. We'll do it! And when it is all settled, we'll get married, and that's a promise.'

They held one another in a long, tender embrace.

'We have been together so long now, it will be nice to make our love legal and binding,' said Robert, giving Sally an extra little squeeze.

'We've always regarded our love and affection binding. It is only the legal bit that smooths out our relationship and makes everyone happy.'

'It's plain to see that you are as happy about it as me. You know, Mam and Dad have a great affection and admiration for you, and the way you looked after the farm and your dad. Mam and Dad are happy with the arrangements and Mam welcomes you into the kitchen whenever you feel like it. All that remains now is to give them the happy news about our wedding, and there's no time like the present.'

Sara and George were relaxing by the fire. Flash the dog, head resting on George's foot, with one watchful eye was keeping tabs on events, and Cuddles the cat was fast asleep on his usual cushion.

Robert and Sally, all smiles and bubbling over with happiness, entered the room, Robert flourishing a bottle of champagne and four glasses. Flash, on full alert, stood up. Cuddles opened one eye for an instant then fell back to sleep, exhausted.

'What's this in aid of?' asked George, clapping his eyes on the champers.

'Oh I say,' exclaimed Sara, pretending to be surprised. 'It looks like a celebration or something! I wonder what it can be?'

Robert, flushed-faced and trembling, filled the glasses and handed them round, then announced, 'Raise your glasses to the happy bride and groom.'

'We both hope you will be very happy,' said Sara and George together.

'We were only saying the other day that it was time you tied the knot,' enthused George.

'Well,' added Robert, 'Sally has decided to sell up, lock, stock and barrel. As soon as that is done, we shall announce the happy day. Now, Mam, don't start fussing around! There's plenty of time, and it will take a while to sell everything. We are not going to be stampeded into selling at knock-down prices to sell quickly. We are looking for a fair price. You can help, Dad, by alerting your Bakewell cronies as soon as we have fixed a date for the sale.'

'Don't worry about that. I'll pass the word round, and I hope they turn up with their pockets stuffed with notes and fat cheque books.'

'Let's drink to that then,' said Robert, and added, 'Bottoms up!'

Four glasses hit the table together. George and Sara shook hands and hugged the happy couple, and wished them a long and happy life together.

The day of the livestock sale was dry, bright and encouraging. It was not long before prospective buyers began to arrive, in ones and twos locally, then as time went on in horse-drawn carts and the odd lorry.

The auctioneer arrived and soon the bargaining started. Bidding was keen and soon everyone was at it. Business was fast and furious. The auctioneer's hammer crashed down in quick succession as bargains were clinched, 'To the gentleman over there,' he'd shout.

The livestock sale was a success, which brought a satisfied smile to Robert and Sally, and a comment from owd George. 'What's goin' to happen to that little pig that's left?'

'Oh, that little runt, nobody will shell out for him. It's more like paying out to take him off our hands,' said Robert.

'I think I'll give him to Sammy,' said Sally. 'He treats him like a pet. He follows Sammy everywhere, and Sammy talks to him all the time.'

'We'll ask him. He can bring him down to Slippery Edge if he likes,' said Robert, 'seeing as they get on so well together.'

The sale of machinery, equipment and tools drew a much bigger crowd than expected. The auctioneer did a good job. He took his time and squeezed out the last penny, and that was no mean feat. It is common knowledge that farmers are very canny and loath to part with money.

'Well, Dad, we've done pretty well so far. What do you think?' asked Robert, with a satisfied smile.

'I think you've done bloody well. Luckily the weather smiled on you and brought in the crowd. And a little help from me, rounding the buggers up,' he added, with a crafty smile.

'Thanks, Dad, you did a good job. We'll employ you again to sell the farm.'

Come the day of the farm sale, everything looked neat, tidy and well cared for. Sammy had excelled himself, having worn out three yard brooms on the outbuildings and yards and bribed owd Jack Straw to remove a heap of old iron, which no doubt owd Jack made good use of. Owd George reckoned owd Jack would make a fortune out of it. Anyway, Robert was pleased to see the back of it and Sammy was highly delighted with his wage packet.

Eventually the property was sold at a fair price, and Sammy brought the runt down to Slippery Edge Farm.

Sammy was glad to be back once more at Slippery Edge. He went about his work as happy as a sandboy, and now, with his new friend Runt to talk to, he almost forgot to have his 'snap' - his lunch. Runt was always at his heel, like a shadow. He seemed to like Sammy's chit-chat, so much so that one would swear that he understood. They certainly had something in common, but what it was, was difficult to pinpoint. Owd George reckoned that Sammy had had so much to do with pigs, that he had a pig-like aura which attracted Runt. Runt protested every night when Sammy left him in the sty to go home. Soft-hearted Sammy asked his mam if he could bring him home at night.

'Not bloody likely,' she exploded. 'The very idea,' she grimaced. 'I've enough on wi' thee! Tha' stinks like a pig! Go an' get thi' sen scrubbed down, an' put a bit of Jeyes Fluid int' water. Then come an' get thi' dinner, an' stop thi' blitherin' about pigs.'

Robert slept in a room upstairs, at the end of a corridor, and now Sally was firmly established in a room at the opposite end.

This situation seemed to suit everyone, but as time went on George, who was a light sleeper, grumbled to Sara.

'When are those two up there,' said George, pointing a finger to the ceiling, 'going to wed? I get wakened every night by the floorboards creaking as somebody tiptoes along the passage.'

'Oh well, George Pipkin, you of all people should know about creaky boards. Don't forget we occupied those two rooms before we were married. Your mother told me years later that your dad used to grumble to her about squeaky boards. She didn't grumble, though. She said the squeaky boards and creaky beds got your dad going. He used to say, if you can't stop 'em, join em. Your mam didn't mind at all. I can remember one day when your mam and dad were out, you went upstairs and tried to nail the boards down but you couldn't because the boards were warped. I think that must have pleased your mother no end.'

'I expect you're hoping that history will repeat itself,' said George.

'Oh, the chance would be a fine thing. It'll take more than squeaky boards to get thee goin'.'

'Happen tha' reight, lass! We've had our day, but we've lots of nice memories, haven't we?'

'Yes we have, George! Enough to last us to the end of our days.'

'Get kettle on, lass. Don't let's get morbid.'
'Like a splash of somethin' to get thi' goin'?'
'It'll take more than a splash, but tha' can try!'

PART IV

THE THREAT OF WAR

PART IV

THE THREAT OF WAR

10

It was now 1937. Mary and Charles had settled down in Italy in the province of Aquila, on the outskirts of its main town, Aquila, which was within easy reach of the Adriatic at Pescara, and not too far from Sulmona, where Charles had many relatives.

The Pipkin-Brodeaus spent many of their holidays around Sulmona, where Charles rediscovered his relations. It proved to be a succession of reunions, and Charles's family was welcomed with open arms, in good Italian fashion. It was during these visits that Mary was first initiated into the mysteries of Italian cuisine.

Philip had gained considerably from living in Italy. He enjoyed school there, where he excelled in most subjects. He had grown into a very robust young man, a good sportsman and very popular. He lapped up Italian and now spoke it fluently, which delighted his parents, his father in particular. Philip, being the extrovert that he was, got along well with his cousins and their friends, who clamoured for his company, all anxious to show off their country. Philip revelled in his popularity and was taken all over the place, even as far as Rome. Philip, with his thirst for knowledge, took full advantage of his excursions and became quite an authority on Rome and its history. He was now studying at the Universita de Roma.

Notwithstanding the horrors of the 1914–18 war, Europe seemed to be slipping step by step to the brink of war. Hitler, now in power, was flexing his muscles by flouting the Treaty of Versailles. He built warships and created the Luftwaffe, with no response from Britain or France. This lack of initiative and action only fuelled his ego to press on more ambitiously. In 1936 the German Army marched into the Rhineland, again with no response. There was a nationalist war against the Spanish government going on, supported by Italy and Germany. In 1935 Mussolini took advantage of the smouldering situation in Europe, and invaded Ethiopia.

With all the sabre-rattling and the uncertainties prevailing in Europe, Charles's company was running down its business activities in Italy and Charles was duly transferred back to Marseilles.

Philip had already applied for a place at the Sorbonne in Paris, and been accepted. Charles and Mary were very pleased. The duel relocation coincided, so the whole family were able to go to Marseilles together.

As luck would have it, the Pipkin-Brodeau family moved into their previous house in Marseilles. Shortly after Philip moved to Paris, Charles found him a self-contained apartment within easy reach of the university.

Mary, now mostly alone in a large house, was sitting sipping her coffee, reminiscing to herself, remembering Philip as a baby, and all the fun and games: the walks in the park, feeding the ducks, and Philip, face and hands festooned in ice-cream as he struggled with his cornet. They were happy days, whose memories made her feel old, and a little sad, with a feeling that life had flitted by much too quickly.

Thrusting away memories of yesterday for the present, she fiddled about with the radio until she found some lively music, which finally flushed away her fit of despondency. A knock on the door ultimately broke the spell and brought her back to reality.

It was the *laitier*, the sight of whom triggered off memories of Pierre. Mary could not help asking about him.

The *laitier* told her that Pierre was a legionnaire in Morocco – perhaps because he had had a dispute with his fiancée.

Mary thought it better not to pursue further this line of thought. Nevertheless, it gave concern. Suppose she was the cause? She dismissed the idea as inconceivable. After all, she had only met him three times, apart from fleeting glances as he delivered the milk. No, it was out of the question! She dismissed it out of hand and concentrated on putting the house to rights and making a start on the pile of washing that had accumulated during the process of moving house.

Charles arrived home a little later than his usual time. Meeting once again his old friends and colleagues warranted a few drinks after work. He was in a talkative mood and Mary listened with interest, and without interruption, to all that he had to say. One fact that stuck in her mind was that his 'dumpy middle-aged secretary' was reinstated. Charles's welfare at least was secure. She was a dab hand at making a good cup of tea or coffee. Mary thought it best to leave well alone, having gone over this ground before. Colette was an indisputable fact that she had to come to terms with.

Mary also had to readjust her thoughts about Philip. He was no longer a child. He was a tall, sturdy, intelligent young man at university, on the threshold of a career yet to be established. She had no qualms about Philip. He was talented and his mastery of languages would stand him in good stead.

Charles's excitement at meeting his old friends, coupled with the flow of after-work drinks, took its toll. He was soon stretched out in his chair, and sleeping like a baby.

Mary grabbed this opportune moment to write to her mother and bring the family up to date with events. She longed to visit Slippery Edge Farm again, but there seemed little prospect of that at the moment. The future appeared unclear and bewildering.

Philip, now settled in at the university, became totally absorbed in its activities. Being an all-round sportsman, and well sought after, he was soon co-opted into football and rugby. Apart from sport, he was keen to explore Paris, his father having fired his imagination. To accomplish this urge, he had to learn to say no to some of his sporting invitations. He bought himself a cycle and started by touring the city and exploring the many places of interest which abound in its centre. Later, his foray radiated outwards from the city to the more distant places like the Palais de Versailles. After such journeys, Philip sought the cool relaxation of the swimming pool.

It was during one of these relaxing moments that he bumped into Lucile – literally. They collided under water, and surfaced spluttering face to face. Philip, being the gentleman that he was, hastened to apologize profusely and ask if she was hurt. *'Pardon, mademoiselle! Est-ce que je vous ai fait mal?'*

'Pas de tout, Monsieur! C'était ma faute.'

That was the start of their friendship. They swam to the side, and after a bit of chat Philip, anxious to heal any misgivings, invited her to coffee and cakes in the adjoining café.

Philip had had little to do with girls. He was a little shy and naïve in their company, and his invitation to Lucile was, for him, a leap forward into unknown territory. They dressed and met in the foyer. Both felt a little strange, seeing each other for the first time, as it was, dressed, and hardly knowing what to expect. Neither was disappointed, and Philip found a table for two and ordered coffee and cakes.

Philip broke the silence and asked her if she was sure she wasn't hurt.

She teased him that she had a broken nose and several loose teeth. Philip looked aghast, and hastened to voice his concern, but she told him not to worry, she was only joking.

The coffee and cakes arrived, and Philip offered the plate of cakes to Lucile. Lucile said that swimming always made her feel hungry, and chose a delicious-looking cake.

And so the conversation started. They found each other's company enjoyable and stimulating, and discovered a common interest in cycling.

Lucile was 16, a little young for Philip, but she looked older. Both were naïve and inexperienced in a sexual sense, which sort of evened things out.

Lucile Renoir, and Fleur Renoir, Lucile's elder sister, lived in Paris. The sisters had lost their parents in a terrible train accident. Fleur had taken over the running of the family home. Fortunately their parents had been well-to-do and left the two girls well provided for. Fleur devoted her life to bringing up Lucile as her mother would have wished. She taught her all the things she ought to know, introduced her to the better side of Paris life and took her to all the museums, art galleries and places of historical and cultural interest.

Philip and Lucile arranged to cycle out to the Palais de Versailles. Lucile, more at home in Paris, arranged to meet him by the gates of the university.

Luckily, it was a bright day with a gentle breeze and ideal for cycling. Nevertheless, the journey proved to be a little more arduous than at first thought. Eventually, feeling somewhat jaded, they arrived by the massive gates of the Palais de Versailles. Philip was a bit overawed by the sheer size of the building, and the large crowd waiting their turn to go in was off-putting.

The journey had made them hungry. Their first priority was to seek refreshment. Fortunately there was a variety of cafés and restaurants close by. They entered one, found a corner table for two, and sank with a sigh into the two comfortable seats.

'*Ca c'est mieux, n'est ce pas, Philip?*' said Lucile wriggling herself into her seat for better comfort.

'*Oui!*' replied Philip, adding that he would change this for his saddle any day.

Philip ordered two fruit drinks and two meals of meat and vegetables. They lingered over the food, then ordered coffee and chocolate sticks.

Now fortified, they decided to join the queue which stretched to the gate. It was a tiresome business but once inside they soon realized that the trouble had been worthwhile. They wandered about and marvelled in a world of beauty. The palace overflowed with beautiful paintings, exquisite tapestries, furniture, delicate porcelain, figurines and a hundred and one objets d'art of a bygone age. Their tiredness was soon dispelled by the ambience and magic of the captivating vista.

Philip and Lucile arrived back at the university late, stiff and tired. They lingered for a few minutes, then Philip, in saying goodbye, ventured a kiss. Lucile responded rather shyly and asked him if he would like to call round to her home the next night.

She slipped her address card into his hand, then with a little wave she was gone. Wandering through the grounds to his apartment, Philip wondered if he had been a bit presumptuous. Was he ready to commit himself? He decided not to let the relationship get out of hand.

11

Philip presented himself at Lucile's home the following evening, to find the table set for tea. Lucile introduced Philip to Fleur. They shook hands, and Fleur kissed him on both cheeks *à la français*. Her lips were soft and warm, and lingered a little longer than was the custom. Philip didn't mind, he thrilled to the touch and blushed a little. He was secretly captivated by her beauty. She was very like Lucile in some ways, but four years older, more mature and in full bloom, with all the curves tantalizingly in the right places.

Fleur said, '*A table*' with an indication to be seated. She went into the kitchen and returned with the coffee pot. In spite of Philip's initial shyness, the meal was delightful and the conversation warmed and became less and less an effort as time slipped by. Fleur was an accomplished conversationalist who kept up a lively and stimulating chat. Her exuberance was infectious and soon all three were contributing to an interesting chit-chat about life in university as if they had known each other for years.

After tea, Philip offered to give a hand with the washing-up but the girls wouldn't hear of it. So Philip, left on his own for a while, was able to survey his surroundings.

The house was rather posh, and elegantly furnished, with thick-piled, expensive-looking carpets everywhere. The windows were velvet draped, complemented with expensive tassels. The walls, covered in cream paper, sported a few strategically placed watercolours enhanced by inconspicuous spot lighting. A fire dancing in the grate completed the welcoming ambience of the room.

Philip made himself at home. He matched the outgoing nature of the girls. Fleur must have been favourably impressed with Philip for, as he bid them goodnight, she went to great pains to invite Philip to pop in any time, stressing the pleasure it would give them.

From that moment Philip spent much of his leisure time with the girls. Much to the envy of his colleagues, he could often be seen with a girl on each arm as he escorted them to a cinema or concert. As time went on, Philip became a bit bewildered. He was forever with both girls. He never seemed to have Lucile to himself. He tried to puzzle out why. Was it a ploy? A ruse to protect Lucile from what? Was Fleur afraid that Lucile might get pregnant? At the moment there was little fear of that. The nearest Philip had got to her was helping her off with her coat. All these questions revolved around in Philip's mind. Finally he came up with another idea. Was Fleur jealous? She was certainly a bit clingy when she greeted him. Then he had to admit to himself the pleasure was not altogether one-sided. He also had to admit to a sneaking passion for her. He tried to obliterate such thoughts from his mind. He could not have both, nor would he want to – or would he? Was there a teeny-weeny doubt? Time would tell. For the time being Philip was quite contented to go on as he was. He was happy.

It was one weekend sometime later that Philip had a weekend free. Perhaps he could take Lucile to the seaside or something? With this in mind Philip called round to Lucile's house, rehearsing on the way how he should approach the subject. He need not have bothered because Fleur answered the door and greeted him profusely. She waved him to a seat and offered him a drink, then came and joined him. 'Lucile has gone to see an old friend who has just arrived home,' she told him in French. 'She asked me to apologize. It happened suddenly. I am very sorry. Not to worry, I am still here to entertain you, if you don't mind?'

'Not at all! It's very kind of you,' he replied.

Fleur bustled around putting the finishing touches to the tea table. Philip had brought a bottle of wine to round off the evening. It seemed a little strange at first, just the two of them sitting opposite each other, and the conversation a wee bit constrained.

As the evening wore on, with another bottle of wine freely flowing, tongues began to loosen up. The conversation ranged from events in the city to the gloomy situation unfolding in Europe. They decided to leave the gloom and doom for another time and live for the present. Fleur spoke of her parents; both were talented.

'My mother enjoyed embroidery, and helped with the church tapestry. My father, on retiring from the Paris Bourse, took up a long-felt desire to paint,' she said, with a sweeping gesture to the many paintings that adorned the walls.

Philip being interested in art himself, spent some time admiring them.

'We must take you out, Philip, to see some of these beauty spots where Dad spent so much of his time,' she added. 'There are many more pictures along the stairway, and upstairs. Would you like to see them?'

'I would be very interested, if you don't mind.'

With that, Fleur made for the stairs. Philip followed the trail of her intoxicating perfume. Philip glanced upwards, the pictures momentarily forgotten; he was intrigued – no, fascinated – by the tantalizingly seductive movement of her shapely form.

'Hell's bells and bubbly gum,' he muttered to himself, as he entered into unknown territory.

'I forgot, Philip, you haven't seen over the house, have you? It was my mother's pride and joy. I have kept it as it was when my parents died. I wouldn't have it any other way.'

'It's beautiful, Fleur, I shall always remember it.'

Philip and Fleur did a tour of the upstairs. 'This is Lucile's bedroom, and this is the bathroom,' Fleur pointed out. 'And this was my parents' room, the biggest room of all. Last of all, this is my room.'

Philip could only repeat as before, 'It's beautiful, Fleur, simply beautiful. If I had a room like this, I would never get up.'

Fleur giggled and said with a little push, 'Try the bed! It's the latest design.'

Philip sat down, moving his weight up and down, trying out the springs. 'Very comfortable,' confirmed Philip.

Fleur, with a little mischievous glint in her eyes, gave him another little push. He lay back with an audible sigh. 'Oh *mamma mia*! It's heavenly, Fleur! Wake me up later.'

She tried to pull him up, bubbling with laughter, but Philip playfully pulled her on top of him. Their eyes met. They studied each other for several minutes, neither anxious to break the spell.

Then Fleur said, 'You haven't been with many girls, have you, Philip?'

'No,' he replied. 'But how did you guess?'

'Ho! Put it down to intuition, rather than experience. Most of my time has been taken up with Lucile's welfare, so I have to judge what is best for her. I don't want her to make any mistakes. I want her to gain her experience from an experienced man who knows what's what, and what life is all about.'

'I am sure you will do what is best for her, Fleur.'

Fleur lay motionless on Philip, who relished the moment and the smell of her hair. Then, rather startled, he felt her hand slide down his thigh. He recoiled in a kind of panic. She whispered encouragement and sweet nothings in his ear and nibbled his lobe. He could feel her hand undoing his flies. She grasped his manhood and did wonderful things. This was a new and shocking experience at first. Then, warming to her caresses, he felt himself harden. He was almost ready to surrender to her touch when she stood erect and gazed down upon him. Philip was well endowed, with a fair share of everything.

'Oh! What a whopper, Philip!' remarked Fleur, flushed with excitement. She undid a few straps and there she was, as if by magic, in front of Philip as naked as a new-born baby, in full bloom, nothing missing, and nothing out of place. The suddenness of it made Philip recoil a little, but only momentarily. He stiffened to the point of pain. Fleur's excitement bubbled over. Fleur could no longer resist. She straddled him in haste and made the connection, smothering him with kisses as she worked away smoothly and expertly. The poor bed creaked, groaned and twanged in protest, but Fleur and Philip were oblivious of any distractions. They reached their climax simultaneously, with a mingling of affection and perspiration. Philip, in the sudden anticlimax of his ardour, accidently let off a loud fart with musical intonations. Philip was embarrassed, but what could they do? Fleur set the tone, and said, 'Oh! Philip,' and burst into unrestrained laughter, quickly joined by Philip. Fleur was in stitches for ages.

'That was an accident, Philip,' she giggled, 'think nothing of it.'

They fell into an exhausted sleep for some time. It was not until Philip's thingy beat a tattoo on Fleur's thigh that she woke. Fleur still had a little sparkle, which needed little reviving. She kissed him from head to toe in a wild hungry passion. After this sensual display, Fleur lay on her back and pulled Philip on top of her with a fit of giggling. 'Now it's your turn, Philip,' she said moulding her body to his.

She soon realized how gauche and inexperienced he was. He fumbled about, this way and that, but to no avail. They both giggled, Philip in desperation, Fleur in anticipation. In the end, it was Fleur in a frenzy who grabbed his thingy and pointed it in the right direction, and Philip did the rest.

Their joy was rapturous. They lay quietly together in serene exhaustion, which soon lulled them into peaceful slumber. They did not stir until the next morning. Fleur slid out of bed. Philip turned over and continued to sleep until the clatter of cups and saucers announced the return of Fleur with the morning coffee.

'Good morning, my love. Are you awake?'

'Yes, my dear! I have just woken up. Have you slept well?'

'Oh yes! Like the dead.'

Fleur crept back into bed, poured the coffee and passed over a croissant. Neither seemed inclined to get up, in spite of the fact that Philip had to attend a lecture that morning. They snuggled down together, and the lecture was blotted out by the intensity of their sexual urge.

It was late evening when Philip staggered over the threshold of his apartment. There was a letter on the mat. Philip picked it up. His head ached fit to burst, and his mind seemed incapable of stable thought. He sat down with a sigh, and with a great effort focused his mind and bleary eyes on the letter. It was from his father in Marseilles, warning Philip of the escalating deterioration of the European situation. His factory had now turned over from tractors to tanks. He stressed the gravity and portent of events taking place in Germany, Italy and Russia. The voices of Hitler and Benito Mussolini were backed up by massive army, navy and air forces, all of which were growing at an alarming rate and seemingly invincible to challenge.

Charles Pipkin-Brodeau, Philip's father, a very practical man, had everything planned for a quick move for his family should war become inevitable. He urged Philip to be ready at a minute's notice to leave Paris. If the worst happened, he would get in touch with him in good time. He would bring his mother to Paris, pick up Philip and drive to the Channel port. He wanted Philip to take his mother to England, to Slippery Edge Farm, and then Philip could apply to enter an English university or college.

Mary and Philip both had dual passports. Charles was French, and could not go. In any case, he preferred to stay in Marseilles, where he could be more useful turning out tanks for the army.

Philip replied to his father's letter, saying he would be ready. He then saw the Principal, who said he would be very sorry to see him go.

'You have made a great impression,' he said, 'and have shown excellent progress in your studies. You have shown good team spirit on the field of sport, and I know you will be sorely missed. You mention applying for a place in an English university or college?'

'Yes sir, that is my intention.'

'Well, Philip, perhaps I can help you there. I'll write you a reference and introduction to the Principal. That should smooth the way for you, and if there is any other way in which I may be able to help, just let me know.'

'Thank you, sir, it's very kind of you.'

'Not at all, Philip, and good luck.'

* * *

George and Sara at Slippery Edge Farm were delighted to receive a letter from Mary telling them of Charles's plan to get Mary and Philip back to England should war look imminent. Sara, forgetting the reason for their proposed flight to England, was thrilled. It had been such a long time since their last visit. This time their stay could be for longer.

'What a grand surprise, George,' exclaimed Sara. 'I shall have to make a start on their bedroom. It wants painting and decorating, and perhaps a new rug or two.'

'Hold thi' horses, Sara! Tha're already getting thi' sen in a tizzwas, it might be weeks afore they come.'

'Yes, an' I want to be ready for them. I don't want to greet them with a paintbrush in m' hand.'

'Ah! Tha're reight, lass. I'll get Sammy to give a hand. He's not bad at whitewashin' and a dab hand wi' t' paint brush, but I don't know about hangin' t' paper. Why not have a word wi' our Robert's wife Sally? She's a wizard at slappin' paper on! I'm sure she'd be only too pleased to give a hand.'

'Oh, reight, I'll do that,' said Sara. 'I knew tha'd wheedle out of it!'

'Look, Sara, I don't want thi' tryin' to do it thi' sen, an' buggerin' thi' sen up. I know thee! Tha' still thinks tha're a spring chicken.'

'I know, George. Don't go on about it. I'm too old to alter my ways.'

12

In Paris, Philip, after a few days' recuperation, ventured along to see the girls. He was a little apprehensive; although he had never made a pass at Lucile, he really didn't know how she felt about him. Apart from giving her a little peck on the cheek, there had only been friendship, held together by their common interest in cycling and swimming. They enjoyed each other's company, and that was the extent of their friendship. Lucile hadn't given Philip the Come-on sign or any indication of wanting a closer relationship. He was naturally a little concerned about his reception as he pressed the doorbell.

He needn't have worried, they were both pleased to see him. They shook hands and exchanged kisses on both cheeks *à la français*. Lucile had some homework to finish, and after a short time she excused herself and disappeared to her room upstairs. Fleur immediately came and cuddled up to Philip on the settee. She couldn't resist him, even for one moment. She showered him with kisses.

'Oh Philip!' she said. 'I have missed you so much.'

They fell into a passionate embrace and then Fleur told him that Lucile had met an old friend during her weekend with her friend Annette, and was very much in love.

'I am pleased,' said Philip. 'I don't feel so guilty now about loving you, Fleur.'

'Don't worry, Philip! I have told her about us, and she is very pleased. Perhaps we can go out as a foursome occasionally. He is very nice. His name is Claude, and he is coming round tomorrow evening so you will be able to meet him. I am sure you will like him. He is two years older than Lucile, and still at college.'

Fleur put her arms around Philip, tickled his ears and put her nose close to his, as do the Eskimos. Then, hardly above a whisper, she asked in a voice filled with a longing, 'Will you be staying tonight, Philip?'

'I would love to, but what about Lucile?'

'Lucile and I have always been straight and truthful with one another. She will be happy for us.'

'That's settled, then. I was hoping you would ask. I'll stay, but I must leave early, to reach the university by nine o'clock.'

She nibbled his ears in loving appreciation. 'I'll bring breakfast up at seven o'clock. That should give you plenty of time, shouldn't it?'

Philip was in a quandary. Should he tell Fleur about his father's letter, and his proposal, or should he leave it until it really happened? He cogitated his dilemma at length. Fleur was a truthful person and he wanted desperately to be truthful with her. Then he thought, would it be fair to spoil her night with me?

He decided in the end to leave it a day or so, and then think out the best way of breaking it to her. Philip was hopelessly in love with Fleur and the last thing he wanted was to leave her.

The evening went well. A sumptuous meal, preceded by aperitifs and washed down by a couple of bottles of Chablis, put them in a festive mood. They sang lots of songs to the beat and rhythm of Fleur on the piano. Both Fleur and Lucile had a flair for music, which was more than could be said for poor Philip; however, he did his best. What he lacked in tone, he made up in volume. He whispered apologetically to Fleur that he could only reach top C in bed. Fleur giggled and pinched his bottom and said, 'Never mind, darling, you have a nice bottom C. I bet if I squeezed your what's it you'd reach top C.'

Claude turned up the next evening nursing a bottle of bubbly. Lucile welcomed him profusely and introduced him to Philip. Claude and Philip hit it off immediately. They were both sports fanatics; it was nice to have a common interest which they could discuss. The girls, however, bored to tears with football, had no intentions of listening to a one-sided conversation to their exclusion. They needed something a little more exciting and stimulating. Fleur quickly intervened and steered the conversation to a more general topic.

'Suppose we go into town,' she suggested.

'Perhaps the Eiffel Tower or a trip on the Seine on *La Parisienne*, where we could have a meal and view some of the sights of Paris in floodlight.'

The idea was instantly seized upon. A taxi was ordered, and the four were soon speeding along to the Eiffel Tower.

'This is great!' said Philip. 'I've been wanting to go on river boats for ages. It will be a treat!'

Going out as a foursome was a great success, to be repeated often.

Days, weeks and months passed by with lightning speed, and with it advanced the threat of war. In the spring of 1939 Hitler's troops marched into Czechoslovakia. Again, nothing was done to stop him. All Europe now seemed to be on the brink of conflict. General Franco's nationalist forces, had unseated the republican government of Spain supported by Germany and Italy.

Germany, flushed with success, was now planning to invade Poland, in spite of the fact that Britain had a treaty with Poland against aggression. Hitler was convinced that Britain would not go to war over Poland.

The whole continent of Europe was kindled. Who would strike the match?

Amidst the gloom and despondency, Britain and France, now awakening to the almost-inevitability of war, started to expand their forces and modernize their armies.

The threat of war and the added anxiety caused by his father's letter weighed heavily on Philip. What would be the effect on Fleur and their relationship? He thought hard and long about it, and decided he could not delay further. He must tell Fleur immediately. It was only fair, she had a right to know.

Philip arrived at Fleur's that evening with mixed feelings. How would she take it? Should he leave it until the end of the evening? He could not hold it back any longer. It was like a cancer burning in his guts which he had to rid himself of.

They exchanged greetings, then, taking his courage in both hands, he said, 'Fleur, I have something to tell you. Do you think we could be alone for a while?'

'Yes of course, Philip. You sound serious.'

'It is serious, darling. I wish it wasn't!'

Philip and Fleur sat quietly alone in the lounge. Philip told her about his father's letter and explained his plans. Fleur was devastated and burst into tears, and said, 'Oh Philip, what shall we do? I don't want you to leave me.'

He tried to console her. 'It won't be for long, dear. I'll take mother home to England, then I'll come back. It's only a precaution in case war breaks out. It may never happen. Pray God it never does.'

Philip tried to reassure her, but deep down he realized it was futile. Fleur clung to him, sobbing her heart out.

'Don't worry, Fleur,' he said. 'We'll work something out.'

From then on, Fleur and Philip stayed together. Although the uncertainty kept them on edge, their love became more intense. Their lovemaking was a respite from the horror of the fateful dark cloud which threatened to engulf them.

Daily news became paramount. The British Prime Minister, Neville Chamberlain, warned Hitler that an attack on Poland would mean an immediate declaration of war by Britain. The next day Philip received the dreaded letter from his father. He would arrive in two days' time to pick up Philip. He emphasized the urgency and told him to have everything packed ready for loading onto the car, and stressed the limitation of space.

Philip had already given his father Fleur's address, with instructions on how to get there. Now he went back to the university for the last time, to collect his belongings and bid farewell to the Principal and friends. The Principal shook hands with Philip and slipped him an envelope with his reference. He wished him good luck and *bon voyage*.

Charles and Mary Pipkin-Brodeau arrived as promised.

There was lots of hugging and kissing as Philip introduced his parents to Fleur and Lucile.

The girls insisted on Charles and Mary having a meal before continuing their journey. In the meantime, Charles and Philip packed Philip's things in the car.

Philip told his father about his relationship with Fleur, and informed him that as soon as his mother was settled in England, he would be coming back to Fleur.

'But you will have to join the French Army.'

'But if I stay in England, I shall have to join the British Army. It is either one or the other. It's all the same to me. What are you going to do, Papa?'

'Oh! I'm staying with the firm in Marseilles. We are already turning out tanks for the army. I think I shall be more useful there, if the worst happens.'

'Well then, Papa, I shall come and stay with you when I get my leave,' said Philip, to jolly things along.

'That will be nice, Philip. But what about Fleur?'

'Oh, we shall probably be married by then. Do you think you could squeeze another one in?'

'No problem. She's a very nice girl. You'll both be very welcome, Lucile also,' he added.

Mary called them in for the meal. 'What a spread!' said Charles, and added, 'What a shame we have to leave so soon.'

The meal was fantastic. It gave Charles, Mary and the girls a little time to get to know one another. It was plain to see, as the meal progressed, that there was a common bond of friendship in the making, which pleased Philip no end.

The decision about time was left to Charles. They lingered a while over coffee then, after a short interval, Charles glanced at his watch and rose to his feet, announcing that it was time to leave.

In spite of the short meeting, parting was a bit emotional, with a few trembling lips and wet eyes. The future was so uncertain and no one could guess what it held in store for them.

Fleur could never hide her feelings; she wept unashamedly as she kissed and hugged Philip. Mary put her arms around her and whispered words of encouragement. Lucile too hated goodbyes and shed a few tears. As the car pulled away, the two girls faded into the distance, waving with one hand and dabbing their eyes with the other.

Mary, Charles and Philip settled down quickly to the long journey ahead. There were lots of interesting things to talk about. Naturally, Philip's parents wished to know all about the two girls. Philip explained that their parents had both been killed in a terrible train accident, since when Fleur had run the house and brought up Lucile.

'She seems to have made a good job of it,' said Mary. 'They are lovely girls, so polite and welcoming. They must work hard to keep such a nice house though.'

'Oh, their parents left them well-heeled. They don't need to work, but Lucile is a secretary and Fleur runs the house, cleans and cooks and everything else concerning it.'

Philip told his parents how he had met the girls. His mother was delighted to learn that he was serious about Fleur, and wanted to marry her.

'Our only worry is this damn war, which seems inevitable now. Hitler is going to demand and demand until we say enough is enough. I think the longer we wait, the worse it will be.'

'I think you are right, Philip,' said Charles. 'Fortunately we have started to wake up and do something about it. When you get to England you will probably find English soldiers everywhere.'

'I have written to Mother and Father to let them know our plans,' said Mary. 'It's such a long time since we saw them, I have almost forgotten what Ashover is like! Anyway, they are delighted, and looking forward to our visit.'

'I wonder if the little railway is still running,' remarked Philip. 'I used to enjoy little trips out to Clay Cross. I remember going to a tanner hop there, to that little wooden building on Broadleys called the Brotherhood. Unfortunately I missed the last bus and had to walk over the hill and down into

Ashover. I didn't mind really, it was a bright starry night and I had one of the Marriot girls for company.'

'Trust you to find a nice girl, Philip,' added Charles. 'A chip off the old block, *n'est-ce pas*, Mary?'

'Yes, Charles! You said it, not me!' replied Mary, harking back to Colette Lenoir.

The journey continued smoothly. Both Mary and Philip could now drive, so, after meals or snacks, it proved to be a convenient time to change drivers. Eventually the party arrived at the cross-Channel terminal at Calais. The luggage was unloaded and Charles found a porter to carry it on board. Hating long lingering partings, Charles shook hands with Philip and gave him a big hug.

'Remember me to your grandparents, Philip,' he said. 'I'll be over as soon as I get a leave, and look after your mother!'

Charles swept Mary into his arms with a bear-like hug and a long passionate kiss.

'Goodbye, my love,' he sighed as Mary, overcome with tears and emotion, hurried off with Philip. They turned, and with a little farewell wave to Charles, they disappeared into the yawning bowels of the ship.

13

Slippery Edge Farm became a hive of excitement as the day for the Pipkin-Brodeaus' visit approached. The house had been redecorated by Sally – Robert's wife – aided by Sammy Mottishaw and Sara. George kept the workers' thirst at bay with lashings of tea and the odd cake or biscuit. George was a real slave-driver and chivvied them up no end.

They had just finished, and all the brushes and rollers were cleaned and put away. George came in with a tray of steaming mugs of tea, and as a reward, had added a splash of brandy.

'Tha're a good foreman, I'll give thi' that, George Pipkin,' congratulated Sara with a smile as she sipped her drink with relish. 'And I hope,' she added, 'tha's not slipped too much plonk in owd Sammy's tea. I don't want him fallin' in t' dung heap again.'

'Oh, stop thi' blatherin', Sara. It'll take more than that t' make Sammy dive in t' shit heap.'

'George! Shame on thi! I thought I'd got thi' trained to say manure, tha' let's mi' down good an' proper.'

'Oh sorry, duck, it just slipped out,' pleaded George. 'I think I must have tippled a bit t' much in mi' mug.'

'Never mind, everything is clean and ready for our visitors. By the way, George, would you mind running me into Bakewell tomorrow? There are several things I want t' get for t' weekend. I must get a nice big joint of meat. You're good at judgin' meat. Perhaps you can pop into your old pal's shop, Butcher Lamb, an' work thi' charm on him. Then tha' can go for thi' pint, an' look up some of thi' owd cronies while I look round t' market.'

'Reight then! What time does tha' want t' set out?'

'We'd better go early. I want to be back afore Mary and Pippikins arrive.'

'Will eight o'clock do thi?'

'Yes, that's fine! I'll be ready on the dot.'

'I've heard that before,' mumbled George under his breath. 'And don't be callin' him Pippikins. He's a man now, an' he might not like bein' called Pippikins.'

'Oh, I'll try an' remember. Philip Pipkin-Brodeau seems such a mouthful. Pippikins rolls off the tongue much easier.'

George, a stickler for time, sat in the car impatiently drumming his fingers on the steering wheel, with an occasional blast on the horn. Eventually the message got through and Sara came bustling along to the car, festooned with handbag, shopping bags and raincoat.

'Good heavens,' sighed George, holding back a blast of stronger language. 'You said eight o'clock. It's nearer nine. And you've forgotten your umbrella,' he added, with a touch of sarcasm.

'Anyway, stop thi' gruntin.' Tha'll still be there afore they take t' towels off t' pumps!'

'Reight then. Are tha' sure tha's got everything, Sara?'

'Yes! Get goin' an' stop thi' chuntin'!'

After a long-winded start, the journey to Bakewell was fine and enjoyable. George could be quite a chatterbox and amusing when in the mood. He kept Sara entertained with his jocular accounts of incidents which happened years ago.

'It's marvellous, George,' she said. 'Tha' can remember things that happened years ago, but tha' can't remember what date it is today or what tha' did yesterday.'

'Tha're reight there, lass! It's a bugger when you're gettin' old an' past it.'

'Never mind! We've had some grand times together, an' lots of happy memories. We've brought up two nice children, both nicely settled in life. We've done our little bit of procreation.'

'Tha're reight there. Now we're just sitting around waiting for the ultimate experience in life.'

'Don't be morbid, George! While we're waitin', let's enjoy ourselves.'

'I'll drink my first pint to that as soon as we reach Bakewell.'

They parked the car in the market car park. Sara made her way to the market, and George to his old friend Butcher Lamb. After a long chinwag, George returned to the car to deposit a large leg of lamb in the boot. Sara would be enjoying herself in the market for a couple of hours or so. George made a beeline for his usual pub in the market square. He was hailed from the four corners as usual, and settled for a pint with Charley Bradley and owd Harry Winterbottom.

'I see thi' team lost agin', George,' said owd Harry.

'I reckon school team could've done better! I've never seen such a bloody display in all mi' life,' replied George, and added, 'I think tha'd better get thi' boots down off t' wall, Harry, an' show 'em a trick or two.'

'Where's Sammy today?' asked Charley.

'Oh, he's bin doin' some decoratin' for Sara. I think it's buggered him up! Robert's given him a day off. He's a damn good worker, tha' knows. He's like one o' t' family.'

Come twelve o'clock on the dot, owd Harry said, 'Now tha's for it George. Thi' owd lady's lookin' for thi'.'

'Oh, she'll be wanting her dinner, I expect,' replied George. 'And come to think of it, so do I.'

George left his place with a farewell wave, and joined Sara in the dining room.

'You're on the mark today, Sara. Has tha' got everything then?'

'Yes, I've put it all in t' boot. I'm ready for mi' dinner – I don't know about the thee.'

'Oh, I'm ready. I could eat a horse!'

With that the two sat down to a hearty meal of steak and kidney pie with three veg, and a glass of beer followed by a bowl of bread and butter pudding.

They lingered awhile to savour the meal, then George

knocked his pipe out and said, 'Reight, lass, best get goin' now.'

Well satisfied with the meal, they trundled off to the car, but not before scattering a few scraps for the ducks along the riverside, as was their custom.

Mary and Philip would be arriving today after such a long time abroad. It was little wonder therefore that they were in high spirits and keen to be on their way. Leaving the car park, they took the road to Matlock, then turned left, up the hill to reach the Matlock–Chesterfield road. George drove along steadily towards Chesterfield, they chatted light-heartedly, mostly about Mary and Philip, and wondered if they had done everything to ensure their comfort.

'Oh, I'm sure tha's done everything. Tha's been scratchin' and cluckin' like an owd hen ever since tha' knew they were comin', so stop thi' whittlin'! Everything has been arranged with our Robert to meet their train at Chesterfield station, and Sally has promised to lay the table an' have a meal ready for eight o'clock,' George reassured Sara.

They approached the mile-long Slack Hill, notorious for its steepness and the several treacherous hairpin bends.

'Are you all right, Sara?' enquired George, knowing how squeamish Sara was about driving down Slack Hill.

'Yes, I'm fine,' she lied, 'But I'll feel better when we reach the bottom.'

George negotiated the first hairpin bend safely. The second bend was much more dangerous, and the scene of numerous accidents. On the left-hand side the ground had been levelled, so that anyone overshooting the bend might be able to pull up before hitting the wall and disappearing down the steep bank side.

He had probably approached the bend in too high a gear and maybe fumbled his gears on double declutching. His reaction was perhaps slow, or perhaps he became confused. One could only surmise what really happened.

People living in the few nearby cottages were alerted by the loud explosion as the petrol tank ignited. There were no actual witnesses and there was nothing that could be done to save them. They were probably dead before the tank exploded. The police, the fire service and ambulance were called. Police took statements and the ambulance took away the charred remains of poor George and Sara.

Bobby Prindle was the tall, rotund figure of the law in Ashover. His round smiling face might be seen in any part of the district. He was very popular with the younger generation, and always had a cheery word for them. It is in this light that most remember him. It was just the odd tearaway who had cause to remember him for his skill at administering a quick flick on the legs with his cape to any miscreant who crossed his path.

Owd Sammy Mottishaw ran foul of him one day when Sammy's little runt of a pig escaped and ran out suddenly in front of him. He was so startled that he fell off his bike and his helmet flew over the hedge. Poor owd Sammy was reprimanded in a friendly sort of way, especially as bobby Prindle saw the funny side of it.

Today bobby Prindle had a rather more serious duty to perform, which weighed heavily on his mind as he cycled down the lane to Slippery Edge Farm.

Colonel Robert Pipkin had just arrived from The Gables, where he now lived with his wife Sally, to oversee his farmhands.

Bobby Prindle knocked on the door, to be answered immediately by Colonel Robert. Robert often had a little joke with Constable Prindle, so on seeing him, it seemed appropriate when Robert held out his wrists.

'What have I done this time, Harry?' he said, 'I'm just making a cup of tea. Care for one?'

'It's very kind of you, Robert. I would please, but not too much brandy this time,' he added, with a knowing wink.

Robert remembered that Harry enjoyed his little tipple, and he was not to be denied this time.

They both sat down with large mugs of hot tea, tempered by a liberal splash of brandy.

'Now, Harry! What's it all about?'

'Robert,' replied Harry, 'this is something I wish I hadn't to do.'

'It sounds serious, Harry.'

'It is, and I am terribly sorry. I wish it wasn't! It's about George and Sara. They've been involved in an accident on Slack Hill.'

'Oh my God!' exclaimed Robert in alarm. 'Are they hurt?'

'It's worse, Robert, and I am very, very sorry. They plunged over the second hairpin bend on Slack Hill. They were both killed instantly. The car burst into flames. There was nothing anyone could do. I am terribly sorry. There's no nice way of passing on such terrible news. Is there anything I can do?'

'No thanks, Harry – and don't take it so hard, someone had to tell me. I'll just sit here awhile, until it has sunk in and I have come to terms with it. Then I'll go and break the news to Sally.

'I'll leave you to sit quietly now. I'll see myself out.'

Poor bobby Prindle was grief-stricken and overcome by emotion. Once in the deep lane and secluded from prying eyes, he burst into tears in deep sympathy and cursed his luck at having to pass on such terrible news.

14

Robert was devastated at such horrendous news. He sat at the table as if in a trance. He could hardly believe what he had heard. The shock of it numbed his senses. It seemed hours before his mind began to unravel itself. Gradually the terrible facts began to sink in, and bit by bit his mind began to grapple with the facts in some semblance of order. I must go and break the news to Sally, was his first thought, but first of all, I must have a word with Benny.

He found Benny in the cowshed and called him over.

'I have some terrible news, Benny,' he said. 'Mam and Dad have had a bad accident on Slack Hill. They smashed through the safety wall and plunged down the hillside and burst into flames. They were both killed.'

'I don't know what to say, Colonel,' said Benny, visibly shaken. 'I am very sorry, sir, I shall miss them terribly. Is there anything I can do?'

'Yes, Benny. I shall be up to my eyes for several days or more dealing with funeral arrangements and settling up the estate. What is more, Mary and young Philip are arriving today. I am meeting them at Chesterfield station. I am dreading having to tell them. Do you think you can run things, while I get everything sorted out?'

'Of course, Colonel, just leave everything to me. Don't rush back until you feel well enough and have got over the shock, and don't worry about the farm.'

'Thanks a lot, Benny. I'll make it up to you in your wage packet.'

'Oh don't worry about that, Colonel! Just do the things you

have to do. You've always helped me out in a crisis. It's a pleasure to help out. Though I wish it was for something happy.'

Robert drove the car up to The Gables to break the sad news to Sally.

'You're back early, Robert! Like a coffee, I'm just making one?'

'Yes, I think I would, darling,' he replied, sitting himself down in the lounge.

Sally came in with the coffee, and sat down beside him. 'Mam and Dad not back yet?' she questioned.

'No dear,' he said. 'It's Mam and Dad I want to talk about, and there's no easy way around it.'

Robert was so overwrought after he told Sally the details he collapsed in her arms. Sally was speechless with shock. She held him in a tight, comforting embrace for a considerable time; neither was able to speak. They were numb with sorrow and grief.

Sally, very sad but more able to hide her emotions, was the first to break the silence. She was very practical and quick at weighing up a situation, and despite her involvement, proved a pillar of support to Robert.

'There's nothing to be done today,' she said. 'The hospital is taking care of what is left of Mam and Dad. I'm sorry, Robert, but we have to face the facts.'

'I know, dear. But all this has knocked me for six. I'll get over it, but I don't know what I'd do without you.'

'Well, you're not without me! The first thing we have to do is to meet Mary and Philip. I'll go with you to the station. I suggest we take them out for dinner at the Station Hotel, which is only a stone's throw from the station. We can hurry there before they have time to mention Mam and Dad. I don't think we could drive all the way to Ashover without Mary asking awkward questions. We would be on edge all the time. It would be awful! Once at the hotel we could order drinks and then break the news to them. They will be shocked. We shall all have to comfort one another. There's no easy way out, Robert.'

And so it was arranged. Sally rang up the hotel and, after a little explanation, managed to book a table for four in a very discreet corner away from the main clientele, and ordered drinks.

They met Mary and Philip at the station. After the usual greetings, Sally took charge, and while Robert drove the few yards to the hotel, kept up a general conversation without mentioning the accident. On arrival at the hotel they were ushered to their table, and immediately drinks appeared as though by magic.

It was useless trying to make light or brush over what had happened. The stark truth had to be told. Sally took it upon herself to impart the shocking news.

'Mary,' she started, 'I expect you are wondering why we have brought you here for a meal instead of going straight home.'

'Yes, Sally, I was wondering. Come on, out with it!'

'We have some dreadful news to tell you, and there's no easy way around it. Mam and Dad had a terrible accident on Slack Hill.'

'Oh my God!' exclaimed Mary, immediate plunged into the depths of shock and despair. 'Are they badly hurt?'

'I'm very sorry,' Sally said, putting comforting arms around her. 'How I wish there was better news. They were both killed instantly. The car went over the precipice and burst into flames. There was nothing anyone could have done, it happened so quickly. The car rolled down the hill, before the explosion alerted the few people living in the cottages.'

Robert was too emotional to speak. He put his arms around Mary in a comforting embrace and Sally held Philip close and tried to comfort him.

The meal was hardly a success. The four had little appetite for food, although the drink helped to bolster their spirits a little. It took some time for the news to sink in, and for them to brace themselves for the heartache of what had to be endured during the next few days.

'We must help one another along,' said Robert, with the feeling that he must be strong for everyone's sake. 'We must think of it from Mam and Dad's point of view too. They wouldn't want us to be unhappy and miserable, so let's do our best for their sakes.'

On the way home to Slippery Edge Farm, which would always be home, they began to talk about what had happened. Robert said it was Sara's idea to drive into Bakewell to do some shopping in order to make the weekend special. They found talking about it somehow helped to get used to the idea that Sara and George were now part of the past, and no longer with them.

The four arrived home in better shape mentally, outwardly determined to keep their individual grief under control. Sally and Mary bustled about preparing a light meal. They felt better keeping busy. Robert and Philip found plenty to talk about, from the farm to the dangerous military situation. Robert said he would probably be found some sort of military post, if it came to war, probably an office job. He asked Philip what his intentions were.

'I shall be going back to France in a few days' time, depending on how Mother is feeling,' he said. 'I have a young lady in Paris whom I wish to marry, and I am thinking of applying for a place in L'Académie Militaire Française.'

'That's great, Philip! If war should break out, you may as well be an officer as a private. I am sure with your background, and your knowledge and flair for languages, you are bound for a job as interpreter or liaison officer, or even a language teacher or something equally important. The world is your oyster, Philip. Choose well!'

'By the way, Uncle Robert, I must write to Fleur – my girlfriend. Could you please let me have writing materials?'

'Certainly. You'll find everything you want in this drawer,' he said, pointing out the particular one. 'There are stamps too. Just help yourself.'

'Thanks, Uncle. I'll get on with it right away.'

Philip wrote, My dearest Fleur ... and told her of the terrible accident, and explained that he would have to stay a few days longer than expected to support his mother, who had taken the tragedy very badly. He promised to write and let her know when to expect him. He ended his letter by telling her how much he loved her and how much he missed her.

The next morning, Sally and Mary were up early, after a restless night. Getting breakfast ready brought a little rehabilitation to life, and helped them to readjust to the daunting situation.

The rattle of pots and the smell of bacon soon brought Robert and Philip down. Looking round the table as everyone was seated, it was plain to see that little sleep had been had.

Conversation was difficult. The two vacant armchairs drew the eyes of the family like pins to a magnet, until Robert could stand it no longer. With the help of Philip, the chairs were placed in the spare room, which brought a flood of tears to Mary.

'It looks as though we are even shutting out the memory of them,' she said.

Robert put his arms round Mary to console her. 'It's only temporary,' he said. 'We will be better able to concentrate on what has to be done.'

Flash and Cuddles, George and Sara's devoted pets, sensed that something was wrong. They couldn't seem to settle, and continually got up and down from their usual places, as though they had itchy bottoms. The poor creatures could not understand. Mary fed them, but they had little interest in food. Mary made a fuss of them, but they were inconsolable. Only time would heal their distress.

'Let's eat now. We'll all feel better for it,' suggested Sally, and continued, 'no doubt people will be calling today to pay their respects, and we want to be able to meet them with composure.'

The four found relief in eating and felt better for it. Soon they found their tongues and conversation developed.

It was agreed that Mary and Sally would remain at the house to receive the coffins and any sympathizers who might call. Robert and Philip would call on Jack Straw, to see if Willy Blossom – Jack's assistant – could make up some wreaths for the family, and find a few flowers for the house.

While Robert dealt with Jack Straw, Philip crossed over the road to the post office to post his letter to Fleur. He kissed the letter and dropped it in the box, to the amusement of a few lookers-on.

The next port of call was to Prospero De'ath, the undertaker. Entering the funeral parlour felt eerie, and the soft, almost whispering voice of Prospero De'ath only added to the unease. Prospero, however, did everything that was expected of him, even to ordering Teddy Collins's blacks and coaches.

'Now,' said Robert, 'we'd better pay the vicar a call so that he can co-ordinate the arrangements.'

The vicar was very sympathetic. 'I shall miss them at evening service, Robert,' he said. 'You and Sally will still come to the choir though?' he added, raising his eyebrows.

'You can bet your life on that, Vicar.' He quickly added, 'Sorry, Vicar, a slip of the tongue! You may be sure we shall be there to keep up the family tradition.'

'Good,' replied the vicar with a wisp of a smile. 'I'll see you then.'

The day was bright and cloudless, and the funeral had been arranged for two o'clock. A larger crowd than expected had turned up to bid farewell to two old friends. Promptly at two owd Teddy Collins and his cortège of blacks clattered to a halt on the cobbled drive of Slippery Edge Farm. The black horses with their black head plumes, the shiny black harness, and the drivers dressed in black with top hats and long driving whips completed the regal scene.

Sammy and Benny, standing at the bottom of the yard cap in hand, looked on with sad interest.

'Oh Benny,' said Sammy, wide-eyed with wonder, 'owd

George an' Sara would have loved to see all this. It's grand!'

'Tha're reight there, Sammy! Perhaps they are up there,' he said, pointing upwards, 'lookin' down on us.'

'Go on wi' thi', Benny! Tha're havin' me on agin'.'

'But we shall miss them, an' no mistake. Sara always brought us a mug of tea when she brewed up, an' somethin' special at Christmas.'

The two coffins were carried out with due ceremony and placed in the hearse. Relatives and friends, with a helping hand from Prospero De'ath, clambered up on the coaches, and the remaining friends walked behind in twos and threes, clutching their wreaths and bunches of flowers. The dignified procession proceeded slowly towards the church, where the service was held.

The vicar conducted his service with great reverence, and paid homage to George and Sara for all the support and help given to the church and the community. The choir and congregation sang owd George's favourite hymn 'The Old Wooden Cross', which brought a lump to many a throat and a flush of hankies to weepy eyes. The pall-bearers trod the narrow path through the graveyard to the allotted resting place. The vicar stood in his accustomed place by the graveside, the mourners gathered round in silence. The vicar performed his usual graveside ceremony. Ashes to ashes, dust to dust, a scattering of soil on the coffins. The family lingered awhile at the graveside and Mary scattered a few roses on the coffins.

Thinking back to the happy start of the journey and the anticipation of a fond and exciting reunion with her family was more than Mary could stand. She collapsed in a heart-rending flood of tears. She was beside herself with grief, only the steadying arms of Philip and Robert prevented her from collapsing on top of the coffins.

Robert and Mary thanked the vicar, then the relatives and a few close friends returned to Slippery Edge Farm for a sit-down meal, with ham to it, as Derbyshire folk would say.

Robert made a short welcoming speech, and bid everyone to be seated, and added, 'I would like everyone to enjoy the meal prepared by Mary and Sally, just like my parents would have wished. There's plenty of food and drink so tuck in, we want to see a clean table when the meal is over.'

Everybody did justice to the meal, as George and Sara would have wished. A meal and drink had been put aside for Benny, Sammy and Tommy, the latest addition to the farming staff. Robert went and called them into the kitchen, where a table had been laid for them. It had been a very emotional, sad and tiring day for the Pipkin family, and as the four settled down for the evening, the house felt cold and empty, and it was unanimously agreed to call it a day. After a nightcap the four toddled off to bed.

It took the family a fortnight to come to terms with the tragic loss, but it would take much longer to get used to it.

Life goes on, and the Pipkins carried on, though with adjustments. Robert and Sally were settled in The Gables, though Robert since leaving the army had always taken an active part in running the farm for his parents. He didn't need the money. He and Sally, with the sale of her farm, were quite well off. Robert, however, promised to come down each day until Mary had rehabilitated herself into running the farm herself.

Philip had written twice a week to Fleur, keeping her abreast with actualities. Mary was feeling much more settled now, with the farm to occupy her mind, and having regular correspondence from Charles, who was still in Marseilles making tanks for the army.

It was at this point that Philip decided to approach his mother to warn her of his intention to return to Fleur and Lucile in Paris. Mary was sad to see him go, especially with Europe coming to the boil. She made no fuss, having got used to him being away at the Sorbonne. He promised to keep in touch with his father and to write regularly.

Robert drove Philip and Mary to the station. Philip would rather have said his goodbyes there and then – he hated long-drawn-out farewells – but his mother insisted seeing him off properly at the station. As luck would have it, the train thundered into the station just as they arrived. There was a mad scramble to cross the line through the tunnel. They just managed it.

With hardly any time to say goodbye, Philip gave a handshake to Uncle Robert and a big hug and kiss to his mother, and jumped aboard just as the door clanged shut, followed by the ear-piercing sound of the station-master's whistle. The train pulled out and quickly gathered speed. Philip's last view of his mother was of her dabbing a few tears away as Uncle Robert, with a strong supporting arm around his sister, guided her to the exit.

Philip settled down with his paper to the long tedious journey ahead. Although not cut out to be a sailor, he survived a rough crossing and was pleased to have his feet once again firmly planted on terra firma. He was happy to be in France again, and the excitement of seeing Fleur and Lucile mounted the nearer he came to Paris.

PART V

WAR

15

Germany agreed a non-aggression pact with Russia in August 1939. As a precaution Britain and France had introduced conscription in April 1939 and the armed services started to expand. NCOs and officers were drafted from regular regiments to form the nuclei of new regiments. War now seemed inevitable.

And so it was in this climate that Philip found himself. Everywhere he found crowds with a noticeable sprinkling of uniformed personnel.

Arriving in Paris, he hailed a cab. 'Rue de la Paix,' he instructed.

'*Et quel numéro, Monsieur?*' said the driver.

'*Oh! Dix, Monsieur.*'

Arriving there with a sigh of relief, Philip paid the cab driver and pressed the doorbell. He was expected! There was a scurry of feet on the tiled passage as Fleur and Lucile raced for the door. Philip was besieged by both girls with a flurry of kisses on both cheeks at once. For a moment the three were too breathless to speak. Then Fleur broke the silence. 'Oh Philip, how happy I am to see you again, my dear,' she said.

'And me also,' added Lucile.

'Come, take a seat,' said Fleur guiding Philip to an easy chair, while Lucile brought in Philip's bits and pieces. Then Lucile tactfully excused herself saying, 'I'll go and prepare dinner.'

Fleur and Philip kissed and cuddled with expressions of love and devotion. Then back to reality; Fleur expressed her sorrow about his grandparents. She didn't pursue the subject further at that point for fear of upsetting him. However, Philip told her the bare facts, and the arrangements regarding his mother and Uncle Robert, also that the farm had been left to his mother and she was now running it.

'Your mother must be a remarkable lady, Philip,' said Fleur, 'to be able to run a farm.'

'It's not new to mother,' replied Philip. 'She ran the farm during the fourteen-eighteen war quite successfully, and even found time to study French. It will feel a bit like old times, but I imagine she will find it a little lonely without her parents. I know she will overcome her loss.'

'By the way,' she said, 'here's a letter for you.' Handing it over, she added, 'I don't like the look of it! It looks official.'

'You are right, Fleur,' agreed Philip. 'It's my calling-up papers. As a matter of fact I intended to present myself at L'Académie Militaire Française. Perhaps I had better do that tomorrow, before the Police Militaire come looking for me.'

'I hope they won't send you away. I couldn't bear being parted again. Enough of the bad news. I've got a bit of good news for you.'

'And what is the good news, darling? I can't wait!'

'I'll give you three guesses.'

'Someone has left you a fortune?'

'Better than that,' she replied.

'You have won the lottery?'

'No.'

'Then I give up.'

'I'll give you a clue. We had better start looking for a cradle.'

'Marvellous! You're pregnant.'

'That's it. Are you happy, Philip?'

'Oh darling, of course I am.'

They waltzed round the room with such peels of laughter that Lucile burst in on the merriment, wondering what had happened.

'Fleur is pregnant!' called out Philip. 'We're so happy, Lucile.'

This was news to Lucile, who hadn't even suspected, but she happily joined in the celebration. Fleur apologized to Lucile for not telling her sooner, but she wanted to be sure, and felt that Philip should be the first to know.

'We had better have a celebratory drink,' announced Lucile as she disappeared for a moment, to re-emerge bearing a tray of glasses and bottles.

A little out of breath with the exciting news, the three sat down. Lucile passed round the drinks and the three raised their glasses.

'To the baby,' they pronounced together.

'What would you like, Fleur, a boy or a girl?' asked Lucile.

'A girl just like you, Lucile,' replied Fleur.

'And I can't wish for anything better,' added Philip.

Then Philip, with a great flourish, knelt in front of Fleur, her hands in his. 'Fleur darling, will you marry me?'

'Yes dear,' she replied, her eyes sparkling with tears of happiness. 'With all my heart.'

It was the first of September 1939. The world woke up to the shattering news that Germany had attacked Poland in the belief that Britain would not honour her pact with Poland.

On the morning of the third of September, Neville Chamberlain, the Prime Minister, delivered an ultimatum to Hitler that unless the attack on Poland was halted by 11 o'clock that morning, England would be at war with Germany. 11 o'clock arrived, Neville Chamberlain announced to the world that Germany and England were now at war.

'Britain At War With Germany', said the headlines of every newspaper in the land. The world was stunned. Memories of 1914–18 with all its horrors, the inhuman slaughter and mutilation of millions on both sides, were still fresh in the minds of many and the horrendous use of gas, which killed, blinded and burned, and left thousands to struggle through a life devoid of its many pleasures. This then, was the mind-shattering future prospect which sent shivers down the spine.

Philip could not tear himself immediately away from Fleur.

They spent two rapturous nights together, before his national pride pricked his conscience and compelled him to answer the call of duty.

The population appeared to be on the move. Young men were everywhere queuing at the recruiting offices, all fired up to do their bit. The mood was infectious, and the queues grew.

Philip presented himself at L'Académie Militaire Française and handed over the Principal's reference from the Sorbonne.

'I see you did very well at school, and you have an excellent report from the Sorbonne. It describes you as popular and outgoing, with a keen and active interest in sport and most activities, with fluency in four languages. Well, Philip! What can I say? I am certain we can make good use of you, but first of all you will have to undergo officer's basic training of three to six months. With your record, you shouldn't have any problems – in fact, I'm sure you will enjoy the course. After your course, I fancy you could be posted anywhere in several capacities. With your background and languages the choice is endless. Now for practicalities. Come back here in a fortnight and I will have something sorted out for you,' he said. 'Meanwhile, go and enjoy yourself!'

Philip, feeling chuffed, puffed his chest out and swung his arms, and stepped out in military fashion. 'I'm in the army now,' he said to himself, as he marched back to Rue de la Paix and Fleur.

Fleur was a little surprised, but delighted to see him back again so soon. 'Oh Philip,' she cried hopefully, 'you haven't been accepted?'

'Not at all, dear. 'I have a fortnight's holiday before I report back for training. Then I shall be posted to wherever I am most needed.'

'I hope that won't be too far away,' she replied, crossing her fingers.

'Let's put all conjecture to one side for a fortnight. How would you like a trip to Marseilles to see Papa? It may be some time before I get another opportunity.'

'I'd like that very much, Philip,' she affirmed. 'You will be able to pass on your news first hand. Does he know about your grandparents?'

'Yes, Mother wrote and told him,' he disclosed. 'That's agreed then?'

'Yes, darling,' she confirmed. 'Your father invited Lucile too, don't forget. Perhaps I had better ask her. She may have arrangements for the weekend.'

'By all means, Fleur. It will make a nice change for her. I'll ring Papa immediately.'

Philip got through and gave Fleur the thumbs-up to confirm his father's agreement. 'He sounded a little down in the dumps,' announced Philip, 'but he perked up a little on hearing my suggestion. He will be delighted for Lucile to join us too.'

Fleur told Lucile, and the two of them, full of excitement, bounded off up the stairs. Philip smiled to himself at the rumpus as suitcases were pulled across the floor and drawers opened and shut.

Philip rang the station and booked three first-class seats and a taxi. The following morning the taxi arrived promptly at 10 o'clock and whisked them off to the station in time to catch their train.

The journey to Marseilles was pleasant but uneventful. The three settled down with their papers and magazines. Eventually, tired eyes lulled the three into intermittent slumber; so it was with the sudden and rather erratic deceleration of the train as it approached Marseilles station that they were startled into action. Needless to say, they were the last to alight. They stepped onto the platform to the stimulating sea air, with its hint of fish and oil from the thriving maritime commerce.

An agitating handkerchief well down the platform caught their attention. It was Charles. He was delighted to see them, and determined that, in spite of the gloom and despondency which pervaded the country, he would give them as memorable a time as possible.

Arriving home, Charles quickly made the girls feel at home,

then he gave them a tour of the house, and finally showed them to their rooms.

Charles had provisionally booked a table at one of the most fashionable restaurants, which provided dancing and live entertainment. They were thrilled and enthusiastic when told about the arrangements, and after a glass of wine and a sandwich the girls disappeared to put on their evening dresses and titivated themselves appropriately for the occasion.

Charles drove them out to the palatial-looking restaurant. They were treated like royalty. They were ushered to their table, discreetly placed in an alcove with a clear view of the orchestra and with easy access to the dance floor.

It was a good start to their holiday. The food was excellent and the crowd jolly, bent on having a marvellous time.

The dark shadows of war spreading over Europe were pushed to one side for the time being, as the crowd, living for the moment, took the floor in a waltz to the slow lilting strains of 'Let Me Call You Sweetheart'.

'*C'est une soirée merveilleuse,*' declared the girls, confirmed by Charles and Philip.

The rest of their stay was just as entertaining. Unfortunately, Charles had to work, but what he missed, he made up for in the evenings.

The girls were very communicative, never at a loss for words, and chatted together contentedly. On such occasions Philip and his father took the opportunity to discuss the world situation and the war in particular. Charles seemed uncertain as to his future. He hinted that he would like to take a more active part than overseeing people making tanks. He wanted to be nearer the action. Philip told him of his plans, and of his interview and acceptance into the Académie Militaire. Naturally they talked about England, about his mother and the devastating accident.

Since Neville Chamberlain's declaration of war on Germany, little more had happened apart from the sporadic artillery exchanges between the Maginot Line and the Siegfried Line.

This period of inactivity became known as the 'Phoney War'. It was '*la bonace*' – 'the Calm before the storm' – as Philip called it.

The weakness in the French defences was on the left of the Maginot Line, namely the low countries, Belgium and Holland. It was in support of these countries that the British Expeditionary Force was deployed. The situation stagnated and the troops relied on the songs of Vera Lynn to keep them interested.

Charles, having to work each day, left Philip to entertain Fleur and Lucile. Fortunately Philip remembered his childhood walks through the parks, the countryside and the shopping forays. Philip managed to hire three bicycles, and on suitable days, after getting over the initial stiffness, their jaunts ranged ever wider. Each night Charles pointed out and suggested places of interest worth visiting. They noticed that each expedition was a little further afield. They found it enjoyable but tiring. Arriving back rather later than usual, Fleur remarked, 'If we haven't explored the whole of Marseilles, and my body says we have, at least we shall return to Paris a little fitter.' To which they all agreed.

The holiday passed all too quickly. After sampling many sights and delights Marseilles had to offer, it was with sadness and regret that the girls and Philip returned to Paris. Charles had driven them to the station before going off to work. He had been very impressed by the girls and invited them to come again. During one of his quiet chats with Philip, Charles went to lengths to congratulate him on his choice of girls. 'You have my eye for beauty, Philip,' he said. And when Philip told him that Fleur was pregnant and that they intended to be married soon, he was overjoyed.

'Do let me know when the wedding is to take place. I'd be honoured to come, but I fear it may be difficult for your mother, now that the war has started. I can appreciate your anxiety to marry immediately. It happened to me! It's history repeating itself, and I wish you all the happiness in the world, Philip.'

16

Back in Paris, Philip had a couple of days to spare before his appointment at the Académie. However, thinking of his plight, Philip deemed it only fair and proper to let them know his position. The next morning, Philip presented himself to the recruiting officer. It was the same officer who had interviewed him previously. Philip explained his predicament. The officer listened to Philip's story. He showed patience and understanding. He was sympathetic, and after a brief consideration said, 'Suppose I extend your leave by a fortnight, do you think you could get yourself sorted out?'

'I am sure I can, sir.'

The officer signed his pass and handed it to him, and wished him luck and happiness.

Cock-a-hoop, Philip could not return quickly enough to Fleur to tell her the good news. Fleur was so elated she fairly flew into his arms.

'Oh Philip!' she exploded in wonderment, smothering him with kisses. 'How I love you, Philip. I must let Lucile know.'

It was unnecessary. The outburst and commotion made by Fleur had brought Lucile, hotfoot, downstairs. They almost collided in the passage. Fleur grabbed hold of her, twirled her around, imparting her news in a gush of words.

In France it is the law to get married at *le Mairie*, or as the French would say, *'passer devant Monsieur le Maire'*, after which one can get married in church.

Philip and Fleur, because of limited time, decided to *passer devant Monsieur le Maire*, then later, when time was less pressing, to get married in church.

With no time to waste, Philip and Fleur set in motion the course of action. They notified the *Mairie* and Philip wrote to his parents, while Fleur sent out invitations to her closest relatives and friends. They were not planning a grand affair – that would come later with the church wedding. Lucile offered to take on the reception arrangements.

The wedding proved to be a bigger affair than anticipated. Everything went off well, and everyone enjoyed themselves. After the reception, the toasting, the wishes and the hilarious jubilance, the happy couple drove away to their *lune de miel*.

Philip was pleased that his father was able to come to his wedding, but a little sad not to see his mother. She sent a nice letter wishing both every happiness and a long life together. Philip was not surprised, considering his mother's situation and the war.

Philip and Fleur were lucky. They were resigned to forgoing their honeymoon through the pressure of time, then out of the blue came an offer from one of the girls' friends, who kindly offered them her cottage in which to spend their honeymoon. It was a very welcome gift.

The cottage was situated some 20 miles from Calais, in a pretty little village called Tourne Hemme. The countryside was undulating, broken by hedges and woodland.

The cottage itself rested above the River Hemme, with a halo of trees and a garden which stretched down to the river. There was a beautiful panoramic view along the valley, where the peaceful silence was only broken by the musical sound of rippling water and the song of birds which lay claim to the riverside.

This, then, was the little bit of paradise that welcomed the happy couple. The car that brought them here was loaned by Philip's father for the duration of their honeymoon.

'Oh Philip, aren't we lucky,' proclaimed Fleur with a flourishing sweep of her hands. 'It's like a little bit of heaven! We must take some photos to send to your mother. I wish she could have been here.'

'She would have loved it. Perhaps we could have a church wedding in England when all the troubles are over and sanity reigns once more.'

'That will be something to look forward to, darling,' replied Fleur. 'It's a lovely thought. But I dare not look too far ahead. Let's live and enjoy each day that comes, as if it was our last.'

'Oh darling Fleur! Let's look on the bright side. We have such a lot of happiness to look forward to. I am sure God will be kind to us. Let's think about all the nice things – our family, our church wedding, our baby, our baby's name. Now that's something we can think about. Have you any ideas?'

'Well, I've thought of one or two – Jean, Mark, Joseph, Marie, Clare. Oh Philip, I'm too excited to think straight at the moment. How about you?'

'I think it will be a girl! I feel it in my bones, so I am thinking girls just now, like Avril, Marguerite. I have a strong feeling she will be just like you – a pretty flower – and she will be a pretty little flower, so I fancy calling her Fleurette – a pretty little you, dear. What do you think?'

'That suits me fine, dear. Let's settle for that. I like it, *petite* Fleurette! It rolls off the tongue nicely. How good you are Philip!'

The cottage was stocked with food, and the next morning milk turned up on the doorstep as if by magic. The village had three shops which supplied the essentials of life, the butcher, baker and a general store. There was a bus and train service into Calais, where people shopped for clothing et cetera.

That first night, Fleur prepared a meal, after which they set out in the cool evening dusk to explore the village and get their bearings. The village seemed deserted. The only sign of life was the odd chink of light filtering through the slatted shutters. It was very pleasant walking slowly through the village. Philip put his arm around Fleur's waist, pulling her leg saying, 'I won't be able to put my arm around you for much longer.' Her reply was a little giggle and a little dig in the ribs.

Their honeymoon went with a swing. They caught a train and spent a nice day in Calais. Walking along the main street, they soon found what they were looking for; a nice restaurant offering a good meal at a reasonable price. Feeling refreshed and well pleased, they left the restaurant to mingle with the crowd. One became aware of the military aspect of the throng. There was a mixture of French and British forces and the movement of lorries and equipment.

Fleur and Philip were contented walking along the promenade chatting about this and that enjoying each other's company. They made a lovely couple, obviously very much in love, and passing troops cast an envious eye and gave the odd wolf-whistle. The happy couple were so wrapped up in one another that they hardly noticed the lively interest shown by the passing crowd, or the activity going on along the beaches as military engineers sweated away erecting coastal defences. Much of the joy and glamour of Calais was missing. People walked along in rather a serious, though purposeful way. The day passed swiftly for Philip and Fleur. It gave them time to learn about each other and their families.

It was dusk as they made their way to the station, and only then did their legs tell them of the miles they had walked. It was only then, too, as their eyes caught the lit-up crêpe stall, that the smell of frying and the vision of pancakes awoke their hunger pangs. Their approach brought a smile to the face of the vendor.

They sat close together on a bench, relishing their pancakes.

'I didn't realize how hungry I was,' announced Fleur.

'Don't forget, Fleur darling, you are eating for two now.'

'How can I forget?' replied Fleur, tapping her tummy.

Philip fetched two coffees to wash the pancakes down.

'Oh, that feels better,' said Fleur, sipping her coffee.

Energies revived, the two lovers set off for the station at a brisk walk. They had little time to spare and scrambled on the train by the skin of their teeth.

The next morning, they were aroused from their slumbers a little earlier than expected. It was Madame Benôit, a neighbour, who apparently popped in once a week to clean and tidy round the cottage. She was a very jolly person, very chatty. The Pipkin-Brodeaus, unaware of the arrangements, were very surprised, but Madame Benôit soon put their minds to rest. She was very easy to get along with and flitted about doing her job without too much intrusion.

Fleur and Philip were soon sitting down to coffee and croissants. Fleur called out to Madame Benôit and offered her a cup of coffee. She thanked her, but declined the offer; instead she kindly offered the couple two bicycles and pointed out several picnic spots worth seeing. The offer was accepted. Madame had obviously finished what she had been expected to do.

'I must dash off now,' she said, and added with a hearty laugh, 'My husband is very jealous. He'll think I have eloped with the butcher.' Then she continued, with a wink, 'He's a cracker and I am just waiting for him to say the word! My husband grumbles about too much meat and I tell him he shouldn't kick a gift horse in the mouth.'

Philip and Fleur had a good laugh. Fleur said, 'Most men like plenty of meat.'

'Yes dear,' affirmed Philip. 'There's no accounting for taste. Perhaps her butcher likes his oats.'

'Yes. And I know someone else who has his fair share!'

With that, Philip chased her around the table, and finally caught her on the couch.

A knock on the door saved her bacon. It was Madame Benôit with the two bikes. Philip thanked her and said they would make good use of them.

The rest of their honeymoon was spent touring the beauty spots Madame Benôit had suggested. Her description didn't do them justice. They were indeed beautiful, most were by the riverside. Philip and Fleur, when they weren't romping in the grass, were walking by the river, discovering the wild life which abounded everywhere. The river banks were home to many creatures. Voles in particular seemed undisturbed by their presence, as they swam along carrying materials to their nests. Waterfowl and moorhens were plentiful. The little dabchicks were a delight to watch as they dived down in search of food.

The lovers walked miles along the banks of the river, arm in arm, as though without a care in the world, quite content to walk and enjoy the twittering of birds and the occasional song of the thrush or blackbird, and their own billing and cooing.

Philip and Fleur.

Fleur was very adept at choosing the right kind of food for picnics. Her sandwiches were always fresh and appetizing, with always a little left over for the birds. After such a banquet of goodies, all Philip and Fleur wanted was to lie together, eyes closed, and listen to the babble of water and the chorus of songbirds, with the occasional plop of a vole as it plunged into the water.

Time passed all too quickly, and towards the end of their honeymoon Fleur became a wee bit anxious and needed Philip's reassurance. Philip had no idea of his training programme, or where it would take place, but he promised to come home whenever possible, and he would move heaven and earth to be home when the baby arrived.

Their last duty before returning to Paris was to return the

cycles to Madame Benôit and thank her for the loan of them. She refused point-blank to accept payment; however, Fleur insisted on her accepting a box of chocolates, for which she thanked them profusely. Madame Benôit told Fleur not to bother cleaning round as that was her job, and that she would be in later to do her weekly chores.

Everything loaded on the car, Philip and Fleur set off to waves and good wishes from Madame Benôit.

'Are you happy, dear?' Philip asked.

'Yes, indeed. Partings always leaves me a little sad, but it will soon wear off.'

Philip gave her knee a little squeeze to reassure her.

The journey was pleasant but uneventful. They arrived home in Paris to lots of hugs and kisses from Lucile. She had been busy cooking and the table was set for a sumptuous meal, even a bottle of champagne and a centrepiece of exquisite flowers whose fragrance set the seal of welcome. Fleur gave Lucile a special warm-hearted hug and kiss.

The meal was a huge success and by the time coffee and liqueurs appeared it was getting late, and eyes began to droop. Lucile was still chirpy, but the strain of the journey was having its effect on Fleur and Philip. Lucile suggested that they should toddle off to bed and leave the washing up to her.

Fleur and Philip slept like logs. Lucile woke them at seven with a cup of tea. Lucile knew that Philip had to present himself at the Academy that morning.

After a hurried breakfast, Philip said his goodbyes to the two girls, grabbed his weekend bag, which contained his personal kit, and dashed off to catch his bus.

Fleur was sad and tearful.

'Don't worry, Fleur, Philip will be back as soon as possible.'

Lucile made coffee, and brought in biscuits and gave Fleur a kiss and a little cuddle. She soon brought back a smile.

17

Philip arrived punctually at the Academy and reported to the recruiting officer as ordered. On greeting him, the officer enquired about his wedding. 'You managed to get your affairs straightened out then?' he asked.

'Yes, sir! Everything has been sorted out. I have no more worries.'

'Good! The next thing is to get you settled in. Tomorrow will be a busy day. You'll wonder if you are coming or going, but don't worry, after a couple of weeks you'll fall into the routine.'

Philip was then handed over to the orderly sergeant, who escorted him to the squad sleeping quarters.

'Here we are, sir! Choose any of those beds,' he said, sweeping his arm around in a vague direction. 'Tomorrow we'll start getting you into shape,' he called out, with a backward glance and a knowing smile.

At six o'clock sharp the following morning, Philip's eardrums were momentarily shattered by the blast of the trumpeter sounding reveille, followed by the raucous voice of the duty sergeant. After roll-call and breakfast, events happened in quick succession, commencing with drawing kit and equipment from stores, medical and dental inspection, followed by treatment where necessary.

After a few days, and the squad being pronounced fit, training proper commenced. By this time the squad had more or less cottoned on to the rigorous routine and the austere, crowded sleeping arrangements not to mention the foul atmosphere generated at night, the heavy breathing and snoring and the odd nightmares.

After a few weeks of training, the feeling in the squad became friendly. The squaddies knew one another and the squad began to function as a unit, helping one another in true comradeship.

Philip began to acclimatize to service life, but he missed Fleur. He missed the touch of her soft warm body beside him at night. He sent, and received, several letters each week. Lucile rarely missed adding a page or two, and Philip marvelled how alike Fleur she had become. She had blossomed out so much in looks and stature that one could easily take them for twins; even their writing was similar.

Leaving square-bashing, gymnastics and route marches behind, and having shaken off the aches, pains and stiffness, the squad became more involved with the techniques and the principles of war: the supply systems, medication, map reading, the treatment of prisoners of war, manoeuvres and the use of ground cover to advantage.

All this warlike stuff gave the squad ample exercise, bolstered further by gun-drill on the 75-mm field guns. Later came the movement of gun batteries, the selection of suitable gun positions offering maximum cover against attack with minimum exposure. This was associated with a bit of brain work, working out from the survey map the angles and ranges to put the guns on target.

Philip, with his Sorbonne education, had no trouble in lapping up everything that was thrown at him. Towards the end of his training he had the opportunity to prove himself, which he did with flying colours. He led a battery of 75-mm guns in and out of action. He had a turn at OP – observation post work – working out all the angles and calculations and passing them on to the guns. It was all make-believe at this point. Philip was congratulated on his achievement and very pleased with himself. The thought at the back of his mind was a disturbing one, that the next time would be for real. The squad passed out with full honours and was granted a week's leave. Philip was pleased as Punch, and hastened to let Fleur know.

It was now May 1940. On the tenth of May, Holland, Belgium and France were invaded, on the very same day that

Winston Churchill became Prime Minister. The so-called 'Phoney War' was over. The lull, as well as giving Britain and France breathing space to muster troops, to back up the weak line from the west point of the Maginot Line to the coast, had given Germany time to mass her spearhead of Panzer units, backed up by dive-bombers of the Luftwaffe and her mobile 88-mm all-purpose guns.

The long-awaited blitzkrieg was unleashed. Belgium's antiquated army had no answer to it. The might of the German army and the dive bombers cut through the defences like a hot knife through butter. The Dutch were forced to surrender and Queen Wilhelmina fled to London. This was followed by the sudden surrender of King Leopold. The French 7th Army was forced back to Antwerp.

Fleur was at the end of her pregnancy when she received Philip's letter. He had written whenever he could to Fleur, but leave had been impossible. Now that the long-awaited letter and the good news had arrived, Fleur became over-excited, to the alarm of Lucile. Lucile got her to bed and applied cold compresses to her hot forehead. She seemed to be going into labour. Lucile became anxious; this was a new experience for her. She got into a panic and called the doctor.

The doctor was met by an apologetic Lucile, but he reassured her she had been right to call him. As it was Fleur's first child, he would send her to hospital.

By the time Philip arrived, Fleur was resting intermittently between labour spasms, in hospital, and it looked as though Philip would have to spend his leave going back and forth to see her.

Lucile excitedly told Philip the good news. She congratulated Philip, and gave him a big hug and kiss. 'Oh, how like Fleur Lucile has become,' he thought.

'We've just time to have tea, Philip, then we'll go and see Fleur. I've got all her clean clothes ready, and a couple of books, though I think she'll be too excited to read.'

Lucile put on a nice tea; even so, neither Philip nor Lucile could muster an appetite to do it justice.

Philip hailed a taxi, and half an hour later the two were at Fleur's bedside. She had had the baby and now she was peacefully asleep. The nurse suggested it was best to let her rest and beckoned Philip and Lucile to come and see the baby. Looking down at the wee figure, snugly wrapped and sleeping peacefully in its cot.

'*Oh c'est très joli, Philip! Regarde ses petits poings.*'

'*Quel genre?*' asked Philip.

'*C'est une fille, Monsieur! Comme elle est jolie, n'est-ce pas, Monsieur?*'

'*Oh oui, jolie comme sa mère, n'est-ce pas, Lucile?*'

'*Oui Philip, tu as raison.*'

The following morning was one of excitement. Philip and Lucile had little appetite for breakfast. Both were anxious to get down to the hospital as soon as possible, nevertheless they sat down to coffee and croissants. Their last mouthful was suddenly interrupted by the doorbell ringing. Lucile answered it. It was *le facteur*. He handed an official-looking letter to Lucile. It was addressed to Philip.

'I don't like the look of that, Lucile,' he said. 'Put it on the fire,' he added jokingly.

Their elation was instantly shattered. It was notice from his unit, ordering him back immediately. They left everything as it was and hastened to the hospital, not wanting to lose a second with Fleur.

Fleur was sitting up in bed feeding the baby as Philip and Lucile were ushered to her bedside. Fleur looked lovely, her face full of love and devotion. She flushed a little as the two homed in on her.

'What a beautiful picture you make my dear,' declared Philip. 'How are you, my love?'

'Oh now, I am very well – especially now that you are here.'

Lucile and Philip had discussed the devastating letter, and decided not to mention it. Lucile said she would break the sad news to her the next day, though she would make light of it, and disguise somehow the real portent.

* * *

Philip, arriving back with his unit, soon found out the reason for his recall. The German 3 Panzer Corps had established a bridgehead over the Meuse, and reinforcements were urgently needed to stem the advance.

He was glad that Lucile was there to look after Fleur and the baby. Lucile was a very practical young lady and he had every confidence in her. As he was leaving the house, Lucile said, 'Don't worry, Philip, go and do what you have to do, and leave the rest to me.' She then gave him a big hug and lots of kisses, as Fleur would have done, and as Fleur would have wanted her to do.

The war news was worse the next day. They were told as they were leaving that the Panzers had made two more bridgeheads over the Meuse and were advancing on Louvain, Namur and Dinant.

Further south, as though unstoppable, three Panzer corps, Guderian's 19th, Reinhardt's 41st and Hoth's 20th, were sweeping through the Ardennes in south Belgium and Luxembourg. The Belgium Army had little option but to withdraw to the Meuse, leaving roadblocks to slow down their advance. This then was roughly the position as Philip's squad set out to join various units of the French 7th Army.

The squad had all been given officer rank. Philip was now a *Capitaine*. He and two others, Albert and Henri, were sent north to join the artillery units of the French 7th Army at Breda. The three never reached Breda. The German armies were pushing west and south-west. In a victorious mood, they swept aside all opposition causing almost a panic situation.

As Philip and his two companions approached Antwerp, they met units of the French 7th Army in full flight, going south and west to the coast. Luckily they met an HQ Artillery Colonel, who gave them a rough idea of the situation and dropped them off at an artillery battery fighting a rearguard action.

'I'm afraid you are being dropped in at the deep end,' said the Colonel. 'The officer over there by the guns will take care of you, and good luck.'

The gun position officer was in the thick of it. His voice rang out at the end of each barrage, relaying to the guns orders sent down from the observation post.

Casting a critical eye over the three new faces, he asked, 'Any of you experienced in OP work?'

'We have all done some practical work, but not for real,' Philip said.

'Right! You come with me, Captain.' To the other two he said, 'Do you think you two lieutenants can manage the gun positions down here for a while, while I take the Captain up to the OP? Be guided by Bombardier Cross,' he said. 'He knows all there is to know about staff work.'

With no time for discussion, orders were coming down fast and furious from the OP as the guns switched from one target to another.

Every now and then a salvo of enemy shells would plummet down, off target, but too near for comfort. Occasionally small bands of infantry would filter through the position, helping along wounded comrades. Sometimes they would impart scraps of useful information.

At the OP, after a quick introduction, Philip found himself in the midst of a foray, observing and passing on information, orders and corrections to the guns. Philip now felt part of the war, and doing his bit. Out in front he could hear the shells he had ordered whistle overhead then observe where they landed. If they were on target he would order so many rounds of gunfire. This could be with various calculations such as sweep and search, in which case the range would search up and down say, 25 yards, and the angle, right or left a few minutes. In this way there would be a bigger area covered by the shots. This would be used if, say, infantry was scattered over a large area.

The war was hotting up. The gradual withdrawal of the French 7th Army was turning into a rout. Various factions of the 7th were streaming past Philip's position in ever-increasing numbers. The gunfire was horrendous and the rumbling of the tanks ever closer. The racket going on was now added to by the dive-bombers of the Luftwaffe.

By this time the Major was back at the OP with Philip. The

OP had not been discovered but the gun position had, and the guns were feeling the might of the Luftwaffe. By the time the Luftwaffe left, two of the four guns had received direct hits, destroying them and killing seven men and wounding two others.

The Major and Captain Pipkin-Brodeau arrived on the gun position as the seven casualties were being laid out together and the two wounded were being patched up and put into the lorry, which doubled as a gun tower.

Philip stepped out of his truck, slipped and fell headlong on the ground. He looked round with surprise, which quickly turned to nausea and disgust as he floundered about in the entrails of his dead comrades. Philip, not yet hardened to the indecent, vulgar realities of war, retched and threw up.

From that point onwards, the troop movement was south-west. Through German strength in every armament of war, the French, the Belgians and the British Expeditionary Force were being squeezed in ever greater concentrations into the coastal areas.

The German advance was fearsome and relentless. Brussels was taken on the seventeenth of May and on the twenty-second General Guderian's Panzers were advancing northwards to attack the British troops in the Channel ports of Boulogne, Calais and Dunkirk. The stranded forces queued by the thousands along the beaches, hoping the navy would rescue them.

At Boulogne, six British destroyers evacuated some 4,000 troops under heavy fire. That day two French destroyers arrived to assist in the evacuations. They were sunk.

At Boulogne, some 5,000 British and French troops were captured. At Calais, the British troops rejected a call to surrender and resisted several attacks. This probably influenced the remarkable evacuation when, on the twenty-sixth of May and the following week, the strangest armada of ships, boats, small sailing boats, and in fact anything that could float or be towed, crossed the channel to pick up the bedraggled remnants of British and French forces.

During an horrendous week, when some 400,000 troops stranded on the beaches were intermittently shelled and bombed, 338,226 were rescued by the strange medley of small boats, and the gallant men who brought them across.

The OP staff reached the guns as they were being limbered up – hooked to the limber – prior to moving off to another position. They were on the point of evacuating the position, when a sudden deafening hail of 155-mm howitzer shells plummeted down, turning the gun positions into humps and hollows.

'Oh be Jesus,' screamed Paddy, the Irish GPO's assistant, clamping his hand over his arse. 'I've shit myself! You had better drive, sir, while I clean myself up,' he said, looking round for something suitable.

'There's no *Daily Telegraph* here,' said Philip. 'Take a few pages from that Bible, I'm sure God will forgive you.'

Philip, leading his two 75-mm guns, did what he could in fighting a rearguard action. The nearer they got to the Channel ports, the more difficult it became. The roads became clogged up with vehicles, some burnt out, some without petrol. Philip tagged on to a convoy just as a squadron of Stukas flew down the column, machine-guns blazing, leaving some vehicles in front and some behind alight. Luckily, Philip's little group escaped the bullets; however, they were in the middle of an inferno, with no hope of getting out with the guns. They did the only thing possible, as did others who shared their predicament. They scrambled up the bank side and broke through the hedge.

Philip led his men down to the beach at Dunkirk, and joined the queues that had been formed. They felt like sitting ducks, and as the Stukas dived down on them, naked and vulnerable. Only training and experience saved them from running as the Stukas screamed down in a nerve-shattering dive. It seemed impossible for them to miss. The soft sand took much of the shock; nevertheless there were casualties, which kept the medics and willing helpers busy.

There was wild cheering as the ships of the Royal Navy appeared on the horizon, and then, as a dark mass of small ships advanced beyond the naval vessels towards the shore, there were gasps of amazement.

The troops lost no time in wading out to meet the hotchpotch of little ships which went back and forth to the larger vessels with their cargo of sodden soldiers. It was hours before Philip's little crowd were helped aboard a small motor boat. The large craft, loaded to capacity, had weighed anchor and were heading for England. Undaunted, the little craft carried on to land them at Dover.

At Dover, the naval vessels and little ships were given a warm welcome. Clean clothes, food and drink were doled out to the soldiers. Then their particulars were taken. Finally they were given leave passes, railway warrants and money, and sent home. The French troops were found shelter and processed in the same way.

Philip explained to the officer in charge that he had dual nationality, that his mother lived in Derbyshire and he would like to stay with her until he was called for further service. The officer was nonplussed and called for advice. After discussion and a phone call, Philip was treated as the English, and allowed to go.

18

Philip's mother Mary was now firmly established as mistress of Slippery Edge Farm of Ashover, Derbyshire. Lots of changes had taken place since owd George and Sara Pipkin, Mary's parents, had met their death in that motoring accident on the notorious Slack Hill.

Mary's brother Robert and his wife Sally had returned to their own home, The Gables, situated on the hillside overlooking Ashover village. Most of Slippery Edge Farm's land had been rented out. All that was left now was the farm and outbuildings which housed chickens, Clare the mare, ducks, the odd goose and a pig or two.

Benny had retired, Tommy had found another job. Sammy Mottishaw, who, sadly had just lost his mother, still worked at the farm. Sammy now lived alone at the little cottage. He was finding it very hard fending for himself. Sammy had been, and still was, a very good worker, and Mary could not help but feel sorry for him. She kept an eye on him, and made sure he fed well. When she cooked, and that was most days, there was always a steak and kidney pie or hotpot for him, and maybe a cake or two.

Sammy was always grateful to Mary. There was nothing he would not do for her. He secretly adored her from afar and was always at her beck and call. They had a very good working relationship. He did practically everything on the farm regarding the stock and Mary did the buying-in and the accounts.

Being wartime, there were many restrictions and rules to follow. Most things were rationed and it was up to everyone to do their best with their gardens to produce food, hence the campaign – Dig for Victory. Lots of parks and small plots of land which had never seen a spade now sported cabbages and vegetables of all kinds.

Sammy was not to be outdone at 'doing his bit'. His cabbage patch, as he called it, flourished. The pigs and chickens did their best, not forgetting Clare the mare. Sammy liked nothing better than sorting his cabbage patch out. He kept himself and Mary well supplied with greens, potatoes and fruit, and from his special corner he grew a mass of flowers. Sammy really enjoyed gardening, and was never happier than when he could present Mary with a big bunch of flowers, as he had done that evening.

He was smiling to himself as he walked up Slippery Edge Lane, carefully clutching a large hot meat and potato pie wrapped in a thick cloth. It was his favourite meal, and the very thought of it almost made his mouth dribble in anticipation of tucking into it.

'Hello, Sammy!' a young soldier in a strange uniform greeted him. 'Don't you remember me?'

Sammy studied the face, then suddenly a look of recognition spread across his face. 'Why it's Master Philip! It's nice t' see thi. Miss Mary will be surprised. She's in t' house, and set on makin' a meal. Tha's come just reight!'

'That's the best news I've heard this week, Sammy. I'm famished! See you tomorrow. You can show me round the farm then. Bye, Sammy!'

'So long, Master Philip.'

Philip gave a lively knock on the door. It opened almost immediately.

Mary stood back in amazement. 'Oh Philip! Come in.' She held him at arm's length. 'Let me look at you!' she said. 'You look fine!'

Then with a whoop of joy, they were locked in an embrace of tearful contentment.

'Oh Philip, it's marvellous! It's been such a long time, and now you're a married man. I was so sorry not to be at your wedding, but never mind, you are here, so you can tell me all about it. First of all, we'll have dinner. Sit down and I'll bring it in.'

Philip was enjoying his meat and potato pie. He was too ravenous to speak. Mary was contented just to watch him enjoying his food and did not interrupt him until he sat back in his chair with a satisfied look on his face. 'I really enjoyed that, *Maman*.'

'Great, Philip! I enjoy watching people who enjoy their food, particularly food I have cooked.'

Over coffee, Mary asked, 'Did you enjoy your stay in Marseilles?'

'Yes! Marseilles was just the same as I remember it. We enjoyed going round the parks as you and I used to. We even fed the ducks!'

'How did you find your dad?'

'Oh, he is in good health and enjoyed our company. Of course he was working during the day, but he made up for it in the evening. He took us out somewhere different each evening. His factory now turns out tanks instead of tractors. I got the impression that he was a little dissatisfied, or perhaps a better word would be frustrated. He was itching to play a more active part in the war. He asked me to tell you that he would most likely go back to where he was born, the little village of Maisons Blanches or Troyes, and hoped you would find him there when this war was over; but if he could he would come to England. He sends his best love to you, and says you are never out of his thoughts, and hopes that one day we shall be together once more.'

Mary could not hold back the tears, and Philip, himself very upset, put his arms around her to comfort her and passed his handkerchief to her to dry her eyes.

Of course Philip did not realize the import of the mention of Maisons Blanches.

Mary, now composed, asked about Fleur and Lucile. 'They are both fine *Maman*, and Fleurette! She's beautiful! I miss them terribly.'

'*Est-elle sage?*'

'*Oui Maman, elle est une ange.* I am a bit worried about them now that the Germans have broken through our lines. There seems little to stop them reaching Paris.'

'By the way, Philip, you haven't told me yet how you came to be here.'

'Well, as you know, *Maman*, I left the Sorbonne and went to L'Académie Militaire. From there, after training, I was drafted to the Seventh French Army, fighting by the side of the First British Expeditionary Army. I was supposed to join the Seventh at Breda. Actually they were in retreat, and I joined them at Antwerp. I joined an artillery unit. From then on we fought a rearguard action. There was no stopping the Panzers and the dive-bombers. We pushed back to the beaches of Dunkirk, together with the British.

'There were several thousand British and French troops on the beaches. The bombing and strafing by the Luftwaffe was terrible. There was no shelter or cover, we were sitting targets. The navy did a good job, escorting thousands of small boats as near as they could to the shore. Then the small boats came back and forth to the big ships loaded with men.

'It was a sight I shall never forget. The boats appeared on the skyline like a big dark cloud. As they came closer, well! It's a wonder you didn't hear the shout that went up. The big ships stayed on the horizon, and the little boats, of all shapes and sizes, came close and loaded up with sodden soldiers. Many swam out and others waded out. Many were drowned, others were taken prisoner and many were killed or wounded. The war is only just starting, and I shall be called back any time. In the meantime I am going to enjoy myself.'

'Oh love! It must have been awful for you. Make the best of your holiday! By the way, you can use the car. I don't use it much so I have a few petrol coupons saved up. All this rationing, coupons and dockets, makes life tedious. We have to budget carefully.'

'Hitler's got something to answer for, one of these days, *Maman*. I hope I am there to see it. I am sure there would be plenty of volunteers willing the pull the trigger or devise a more fitting end to such a monster.'

Elevating the conversation to pleasanter thoughts, Mary suggested letting Robert and Sally know the good news. 'I'll give them a ring at once, I'm sure they will be in,' said Mary, calling the operator.

'Hello, Sally,' she said, once the connection was made. 'I have someone here anxious to see you and Robert. Is Robert there?'

'Yes, he's here. We'll be with you in a jiffy, Mary. Nail him to the floor if he tries to leave!'

'Perhaps Robert will take you for a gallop,' said Mary. 'He still keeps two horses. Sally rides too. Poor old Clare is getting a bit long in the tooth for galloping about. I only keep her for old times' sake, and because Sammy likes her. She follows him everywhere, as does Flash and the little pig we keep – Sammy calls him Pongo. When you see him, you'll understand why.'

'That can't be very profitable, *Maman*.'

'No, it isn't, Philip. I think I must be as soft-hearted as Sammy. He talks to them as if they were his own flesh and blood. They are bonded to him. It would break Sammy's heart if anything happened to them. Anyway, Sammy's got so little in this world that I haven't the heart to deny him that small favour. It keeps him happy, and he makes good use of the manure on his cabbage patch, as he calls it.'

Robert and Sally arrived in quick time, and Mary, like a good housewife, had the kettle on the boil, cups and saucers on a tray and a plate of home-made cakes to pass around.

After the usual greetings to Mary, Robert and Sally rushed across to Philip and made a great fuss of him. Naturally they were both keen to know everything from A to Z.

Robert, who was a part-time RTO – Railway Transport Officer – at Chesterfield Station, was very anxious to know how things were going in France. What could he say?

'Bloody awful, disastrous, Uncle Robert. We are outnumbered, outgunned, outmanoeuvred and outwitted. I think the Germans did as the British thought they would do. They pushed through Belgium and swept round the western end of the Maginot Line and the coast. It was the weakest and most obvious point to attack.'

Robert then asked a flurry of questions which were outside Philip's knowledge of the situation.

'My word, Philip,' he said. 'You've had a lucky escape. It must have been terrible on the beaches.'

'It was bloody awful! That's the only way I can describe it. I wouldn't like a repetition of that fiasco.'

At that moment Mary entered with her tray of tea, which put paid to the bloody war conversation, much to Philip's relief. Talk turned more to the family and domestic side of life, which continued until it was time for Robert and Sally to leave. Robert was due to do his stint on Chesterfield Station.

The next morning, Philip wrote a long letter to Fleur, not knowing whether she would receive it, the situation regarding post being fluid and uncertain, but he felt better when it was finished. He had, at least, the satisfaction of knowing that he had done his best.

He felt the need for a quiet stroll through the leafy lanes to think and review his situation. He explained his idea to Mary, who said the walk would do him good.

'Perhaps I could take the car tomorrow. Better still, I would like to take you out for a meal, if you know of a place. With all this rationing, I'm a little out of touch with what is possible. I believe when you visit friends, it is polite and acceptable to take along a contribution to any proposed meal.'

'That is correct, Philip, but it is not quite like that. One can still eat out within reason, the menu is of necessity restricted and varied according to availability. It is all a question of having what is on offer.'

'Shall we take a chance on it then, *Maman?*'

'Yes Philip, that will be fine! Life today is all chance, *n'est-ce pas*, Philip?'

'*C'est bien comme ca, Maman.* But never fear, our luck will see us through.'

'Your confidence gives me hope, Philip.'

19

Philip set out for his stroll, taking with him his letter to Fleur to post. Instead of going up Slippery Edge Lane, he decided to take the path through the fields to the river, then follow it as far as the Butts Pastures, and take the gentle climb up to the village.

This pleasant stroll along the babbling waters of the Amber was just what he needed. It was leisurely and refreshing, and conducive to clear thought and inspiration. It gave him the opportunity to regulate his thoughts in some semblance of order.

Arriving at the Butts in a better frame of mind, he reached the main road and made his way to the post office to carry out the pressing priority, which was to post his letter to Fleur. Philip renewed his acquaintance with the postmistress, who, thankfully, was too busy to ask too many questions. He affixed his stamp, gave his letter a quick kiss and dropped it in the pillar box.

Feeling once more on top of the world, Philip continued his stroll around the quaint little village of Ashover. Hearing the clanging of metal and seeing the wide-open doorway of Jack Straw's blacksmith's shop, and the bright glowing forge being blown up by Willy Blossom on the bellows, made Philip pause awhile.

It was Jack Straw hailing him from his old armchair that drew Philip inside. Jack remembered him coming with Robert's horses to be shod.

'Take thi' weight off thi' feet a minute! Sit thi' sen down,' said Jack, indicating a vacant chair. 'It's a long time since I saw thi'. How t' world treatin' thi'?'

'Oh, I can't grumble, Jack,' he lied. 'What's tha' doin' sittin' down?' he continued, letting Jack know that he hadn't forgotten his Derbyshire dialect.

'I'm retired now, tha' knows. Owd Willy there is boss now! I only come down to cheer him up. Truth is, I can't keep away. I keep Willy company, and keep in touch with mi' friends. I live up yon,' he said, pointing up towards Ashover Rock. 'Trouble is, there's no bugger up there to talk to.'

'So you're retired now, then?'

'Ay! I was findin' it a bit hard goin', so I decided to hang up mi' hammer an' tongs, an' give Willy a chance. Anyway, my owd, are tha' goin' t' ave a drink wi' mi'? I allus keep a bottle or two in mi' owd cupboard over yon.'

'That's very kind of you, Jack. You're not goin' to get me drunk, are you?'

'Nay, mi' lad! Thi' mam would soon be after mi'.'

Jack called over to Willy. 'Ha's tha' got a minute, Willy? Come an' join us! I'm just havin' a drink wi' Philip here. Tha' remembers him, doesn't tha?'

'Cos I do! Tha' lookin' well, Philip. I haven't seen a uniform like that before! Is it French?'

'It is, Willy. I am half French! I could have joined the British Army, but it's the same war, isn't it?'

'Anyway, here tha' are,' rejoined Jack, offering Willy his drink. 'Get that down thi'. It'll put a bit o' lead in thi' pencil.'

'Thanks Jack, I'm just about ready for a break. Cheers!'

It must have been one of Willy's slack days, because they sat at the little table as though in a café. Philip asked about one or two people he remembered. Then he asked about owd De'ath, the undertaker.

'Is old Mr De'ath still around?' he asked, trying to add his little pennyworth to the conversation.

'Oh ha!' said Jack. 'He's gettin' an owd man now, tha' knows. His son Percy does most of t' business now, while poor owd man De'ath walks about like death warmed up. He's a poorly man, tha' knows, an' owd bobby Pringle, who was a policeman, reckons he'll be makin' a box for himself afore long.'

'Owd bobby Pringle's a comical owd bugger when he gets

goin',' commented Willy. 'When he pops in here, it's like a bloody pantomime. People stop an' wonder what's going off. It's a wonder I ever get any work done at all.'

'I can see you have a wonderful time together,' remarked Philip, in a burst of laughter.

'Tha' can say that again, Philip,' said Jack. 'It's what makes t' world go round. We only come this way once, we may as well make t' best of it.'

'I can't fall out with that,' said Philip, and added, 'Well, time's getting on and I had better make tracks. Thanks for the drink. I've really enjoyed your company. I'll pop in again before I have to go back to wherever that may be, if I may?'

'Pop in any time, Philip. You'll find us here almost every day. If by chance we don't see thi', we wish thi' the best o' luck. Look after thi' sen, lad, an' take care, and remember me to thi' mother.'

'You can be sure of that! Well, goodbye to you both for now.' And with that, Philip took his leave.

Strolling along by the church, he mused to himself, No one would know there was a war going on. He called at the newsagents and bought a daily paper, and promised himself to keep up with the news.

After dinner, Philip and Mary spent the rest of the day with Robert and Sally. Sally and Mary got on very well together. Both being farmer's daughters, they had a lot in common. They had even gone to school together. Very little happened in Ashover that escaped their attention, and while they were catching up on local gossip, Robert and Philip were discussing the latest war news, so the four were fully occupied.

There was no heartening news in the papers, all doom and gloom, in fact. The British and French troops were being pushed back to the coast everywhere. Any craft that could float headed for England. Most of the French Navy sailed for English ports. Ships that could not sail because of repairs or other reasons were scuttled to save them being used by the Germans.

* * *

After a week at Slippery Edge Farm, the suspense of the expected recall increased by the day. Although each extra day was a bonus to be with his mother, it felt more like a reprieve from the executioner's block. Philip was reduced to a state of nervous excitement every time he saw the postman approaching, and gave a sigh of relief when he passed. It was not that Philip was afraid, it was just the awful suspense.

It was therefore with a sense of relief and excitement that Philip eagerly pounced on the fateful letter when at long last it slipped through the letter box. He gazed at it, and turned it over in wonder. It was from the War Office in London. Philip's hands trembled as he hastily tore open the letter. It was a summons to attend an interview at the War Office, together with a travel warrant. He read it through a second time, but it gave no clue of its significance, only that he had to be there at eleven o'clock the next morning.

Philip told his mother and showed her the letter. She tried to hide her concern and said, 'Well, you know, they have just realized that they can't win the war without you. So go to it, lad, and do your stuff! We'll all be gunning for you! You know that.' Mary gave him a big hug to hide the tears that welled up in her eyes. 'We're all proud of you, Philip, and I know your dad would be too. Let's have a big celebration tonight. I'll invite Robert and Sally, and anyone else you would like.'

He didn't have to give the matter much thought. 'I'd like Sammy to be invited. He's looked after your interest for a long while. He's trustworthy and devoted to his job, and I have every confidence in him. I'm sure he will always be on hand for you, *Maman*, should you by chance or misfortune be in need of help or something.'

'You're right, Philip. He is very dependable. I'll do as you say.'

Mary asked Sammy if he would like to come to Philip's going-away party.

'Oh! I don't know, Miss Mary,' he said. 'I feel a bit shy with lots of people at parties.'

'Well, Sammy, Philip especially asked for you. You'll know everyone there. Philip will be disappointed if you don't come.'

'I wouldn't like to disappoint Master Philip, I'd like to come, Miss Mary. I'll put on my Sunday Best and have a bath and shave. I'll look smart for Master Philip, I haven't worn my Sunday Best since Mam died. It's exciting, Miss Mary!'

'Now, Sammy, get your work done early. Let me know when you've finished. I'll take a quick look round, then you can go, and be back here for seven o'clock. Oh! And here's your tea.'

'Thank you, Miss Mary,' he replied in his usual polite manner.

Come seven o'clock all the guests were relaxing in the armchairs. To make a party of it, owd Jack Straw and Willy Blossom had been invited, and owd Benny had been prised out of his retirement chair to be present. That made eight in all. A nice round number.

The table was a credit to Mary and her culinary prowess. It looked inviting, with plates full of bite-size sandwiches and dishes of mouth-watering goodies, and a selection of wine brought in by Jack and Willy. To crown the display was a large bunch of mixed flowers brought in by Sammy from his cabbage patch.

Mary invited everyone to be seated and Robert said a few words and proposed a toast to Philip. 'Now,' said Robert, 'I don't want to see anything left on the table! *Bon appétit*! Come on, Sammy, don't be bashful, get stuck in,' he added, more in line with Sammy's comprehension.

Everyone did justice to the table, helped on by the flow of wine. The party proved friendly and agreeable with lots of chit-chat, questions and answers. Owd Jack Straw kept the party in stitches with his tales and witticisms.

'I haven't seen Joe Tight lately,' said Robert. 'Is he still around?'

'He doesn't get out much these days,' replied Willy Blossom. 'He'll be counting his money! He's got a bob or two, tha' knows.'

'I reckon he has too!' offered Jack Straw, who knew a bit about everyone, and what Jack Straw didn't know, wasn't worth knowing. 'Owd Tighty was always a tight-fisted owd bugger,' he added. 'I reckon he'd skin a fart before parting with it.'

This remark threw Sammy into a fit of uncontrollable laughter, which spread like wildfire.

'Tha're a one, Jack!' said Sammy, wiping the tears from his eyes. 'Anyway, he's got nobody to leave it to, an' he allus said as his coffin would be lined with pound notes and thrippeny bits.'

'Why the thrippeny bits, Sammy?' asked Jack.

'To put in his Christmas puddin'' roared Sammy.

No one seemed to want to break up the party, until Mary said, 'I think we had better call it a day. Philip has got to catch an early train, so I think we'll have to let him get his head down for an hour or two. He doesn't want to be clapped out for his interview, does he?'

Everyone agreed. After taking half an hour saying goodbye, Jack, Willy, Sammy and Benny set off up Slippery Edge Lane, singing fit to wake the dead. By the time their voices were out of earshot, Philip was in bed, and Mary, Sally and Robert were just putting the last of the crockery away.

'I think everyone enjoyed themselves,' said Robert, 'and I bet those four "Melody Boys" up the lane there will have thick heads in the morning.'

'Well,' said Mary, 'they enjoyed themselves, and a thick head is a price that sometimes has to be paid.'

Robert and Mary put on their coats and made to leave. Then Robert said, 'Would you like me to call and take you and Philip down to the station, to see him off? The four of us can go, if you like.'

'Yes, that would be nice, Robert,' replied Mary. 'Half seven, then. Goodnight Robert, Sally, and thanks for everything.'

Robert gauged the time nicely. There was no long delay. The train was just steaming and screeching to a halt as the four negotiated the last step up to the platform. There was no luggage, so a quick kiss and a handshake, and Philip was on his way. They all waved until he was out of sight.

Come on, Mary,' said Robert, giving Mary a little squeeze. 'Put a brave face on it! Philip is a strong fine man. He'll come through it, if anyone does, and I've given him a few tips, so try not to worry, dear.'

Mary pulled herself together, and lost herself in the small talk that followed. By the time they reached Slippery Edge, Mary was more composed and her old self again. She had one consolation: at least Philip was in England instead of France. He might be able to come home from time to time. It was an encouraging thought.

20

The Germans' relentless advance continued through northern France, causing grave concern. They were getting too close to Paris for comfort. Many Parisians were leaving Paris and moving south, and each day that passed the exodus increased, reaching almost stampede proportions. Fleur and Lucile were at their wits' end to know what to do for the best. It was at this point that Fleur's guardian angel Annette, who had provided Fleur and Philip with a honeymoon cottage, once again came to the rescue. She offered Fleur, Fleurette and Lucile accommodation in a little cottage near the Spanish border, and quite near Annette's second home in Bayonne. The generous offer could not have come at a more opportune moment.

'*Oh Annette! Comme tu es une ange! Comment peux-je jamais te repayer?*'

Fleur and Lucile gave Annette a fond embrace.

'*Ne t'en pense rien. C'est ma plaisir.*'

Annette also offered them transport with her family, an offer Fleur could not refuse.

The two families loaded the truck with the bare essentials. It was to be driven by Annette's brother, with a couple of children for company. The rest of the families filled the family car, which followed on behind.

The big guns could be heard, as their little convoy drove out of Paris, to join the flood of like-minded people travelling on all roads heading south.

They escaped by the skin of their teeth, for the next day, the fourteenth of June, the German Army entered Paris. But they weren't out of the woods yet.

The journey south was horrendous. It was bad enough just slowly threading one's way through the hotchpotch of traffic. There were vehicles old and new trying to filter through the human carnage, all with one aim: to put as much distance as possible between themselves and Paris.

There were horses, donkeys, even goats and dogs pulling anything on wheels. They were loaded to capacity, and all giving their last ounce of strength toward the general flight. Everyone was carrying or pushing something. There were handcarts and wheelbarrows. Some people were carrying suitcases, some with mattresses on their heads. It was pitiful seeing old folk and little children struggling along carrying something, however small, 'doing their little bit'.

It was heartbreaking, seeing all this trail of humanity, and being unable to help. Fleur and Lucile's eyes looked sore and dry. Their tear glands had ceased to function.

As if this movement was not enough, the Luftwaffe kept up a harassing attack, bombing and machine-gunning indiscriminately along the winding, wearying columns, leaving in their wake a trail of dead and wounded. It was heart-rending to see children clinging to their dead mothers. It was all too much for Fleur as she clung to Fleurette.

Eventually, after struggling along all night, the cars and trucks left behind the thousands of poor, miserable, ill-fated people. It wasn't easy to leave these unfortunates, but to stop would only cause more congestion.

After two days and nights of pure hell, the journey became less fraught with danger, even pleasant, compared with what had gone before. Even so, nothing could dispel the anxieties and the future uncertainties as the trucks and cars travelled into the unknown.

At least Annette and Fleur with their families had a destination to their flight. They had provided well for their journey. They had food and drink, a stove, and cooking paraphernalia. Annette's brother Henri, a very resourceful character, had loaded ample of the necessities of life, and dispensed with all luxuries and frivolities.

There was little real sleep had until the fourth night, when Henri found a secluded site to set up camp. The strain of the journey was beginning to show on every face. Henri decided that time should be spent on having a good hot meal followed by a good night's sleep. He had had the good sense to bring along a small selection of medical things in case of emergencies. He was prepared to dole out a sleeping tablet to anyone who could not sleep. Actually it proved unnecessary. A hot meal, the cool air and the silence of the night did the trick. Henri made sure that everyone was asleep before he settled down.

Refreshed, the two families began to stir as the morning air began to warm. Henri had been busy with the stove, and now the welcome smell of cooking and the fragrant odour of fresh coffee soon aroused the interest of everyone and brought them to the table, which was in this case the tailgate of the truck. In spite of the traumatic events of the past few days, everyone was eager to eat.

The meal was simple, satisfying and there was plenty of it. The morale of the party had improved, and afterwards the children were encouraged to run about and play and exercise themselves, ready for the last stage of the journey. Lucile and Annette folded the blankets and stowed everything away on the truck, while Henri attended to the vehicles and Fleur saw to the needs of Fleurette, who was as good as gold. The last ten minutes or so was spent chasing the children around to get rid of some of their energy.

Everything and everyone refreshed and replenished and everyone now a little out of breath, the two vehicles set off, and the party settled down to the long journey ahead.

The remainder of the journey was tiring but uneventful. They arrived at St Palais, a small town in the Basses-Pyrénées. Annette gave Fleur and Lucile a tour of the cottage, pointing out the stock of provisions brought in for such an emergency as this.

'Oh Annette, chérie! Nous te serons obligées pour toujours. Merci bien.'

'Ça ne fait rien! Je prie Dieu que nous tous survivrons.'

Fleur and Lucile, tears streaming down their faces, gave Annette a big hug and smothered her in kisses. Naturally their kisses extended to Henri and the children. They departed with lots of waves until the night swallowed them up.

Left by themselves, it seemed strange and lonely. The cottage was outside the town. Tucked away in one of the many valleys in the lower Pyrenees, it was quiet and remote from the rumble of traffic; but at that moment the only thing on their minds was to see to Fleurette and get to bed. Lucile explored the kitchen, and discovered an old oil stove. There was plenty of oil, and after fiddling about with it, she managed to get it going. She soon had a kettle of hot water. She found two hot water bottles and placed one in each bed. There was no cot for Fleurette so Fleur made her nice and snug with pillows in her own bed. Fleur and Lucile had hot drinks and biscuits and went to bed.

They awoke the next day to a lovely sunny morning, spoilt by the clump, clump of marching feet, bringing them back to earth and stark reality. Fleur leapt out of bed, and peeped through the curtains and saw what she rather expected. It was a troop of German infantry. Whether they were on a training march or moving nearer to the coast was a matter of conjecture. Turning the matter over in her mind, it was fairly obvious that the Germans would occupy all coastal areas, though at this point they would not expect any serious threat of invasion from Britain. The reverse was more of a possibility; nevertheless, the thought of being surrounded by Germans was a difficult pill to swallow. Lucile was a little perturbed and apprehensive.

'Don't worry about it Lucile. We'll just go about our business as though nothing has happened.'

'We have little choice, Fleur! Actually, little has happened in this part yet,' she said, with a strong emphasis on the 'yet'.

During the night something had been niggling Fleur at the back of her mind. She scanned her thoughts. She felt it was something to do with Philip. So much had happened during the past week or so that she found it difficult to assemble her thoughts objectively. She persevered and deliberated long and hard. Eventually the mist cleared and her recall snapped into place. It was the last letter from Philip, saying that he was in England, and if she ever received it, would she pass on the news to Charles, Philip's father. She reacted at once, calling to Lucile to search for paper and envelopes.

'Here they are, Fleur! Also two stamps. Who are you writing to?'

'It's to Philip's father, to let him know that Philip is in England.' Do you think there is a post now, or will the letters be censored?'

'I think it is quite likely, but it may not have happened yet. Do be careful, Fleur! Write as few words as possible, and nothing incriminating. If he gets the letter, at least he will have our address. He may find a way of getting in touch with us. I think he is very resourceful and quick at putting two and two together.'

Fleur wrote simply; she gave the name and address, and said Philip was staying with his mother at the farm, adding: 'Please call and see us sometime. Fleur'.

'I think he will read enough into that to be curious enough to find a way, don't you, Lucile?'

'That's fine, Fleur! I see you have put "at the farm" instead of "England", which could have raised eyebrows.'

'Now we had better face the outside world again, and find a post office and see if the postal service is still functioning,' said Fleur.

'That is a good idea. I'll finish off dressing Fleurette, while you get ready. We'll discover St Palais together.'

St Palais looked a very ordinary small town, surrounded by a panoramic view of hills and distant mountains. The town itself was busy, with people milling around doing their shopping. The only disturbing sign was the sprinkling of the field grey of the Wehrmacht. Most of the crowd was Spanish-looking, which one would expect, as the town was so near to the Spanish border.

Fleur asked the way to the post office, and was directed there. She was rather surprised, but heartened, that it appeared to be functioning as normal.

'Well, here's hoping,' said Fleur, as her letter dropped into the box.

They made a leisurely stroll around the shopping area, bought bread, butter, milk and a few other necessities. A very nice lady, captivated by Fleurette's charming smile, gave her a piece of chocolate. The lady chatted awhile with Fleur and Lucile. Apparently she lived close to the cottage, a neighbour, who had noticed the girls setting off. Moreover, she was a close friend of Annette's, and enquired about her. She said her name was Madame Pinson, a widow, and, Fleur gathered, a wee bit lonely. She offered help if needed, and invited them to coffee. The girls thanked her for the invitation, then made their way back to the cottage.

'How pretty and friendly that lady is,' observed Lucile, and added, 'I feel less lonely now Fleur. Don't you agree?'

'Yes, indeed.'

Fleur and Lucile were happy to have made a friend, and in a short space of time, they had gathered a small group of friends. They all had one thing in common, that was the fearful war situation. With scant regard for the Germans, they were apprehensive of the outcome of the war, and really alarmed at the inability of the British and French to hold the line.

21

Charles, Philip's father was still in Marseilles. His factory was still turning out tanks, but now that France had capitulated and was under the thumb of the Nazis, it was almost certain that the tanks would be used against Britain. This prospect was abhorrent to Charles, whose mind was working round a plan to leave the factory and a way of escaping to England, or at least finding some way of helping the British. Britain was going to need all the help it could get to overthrow the Nazis.

The only way to get to England was to beg, borrow or steal a boat. Charles was no sailor. He would need a partner who could handle a boat, and navigate. An idea came to him. There must be sailors, or better still skippers, who, like himself, felt frustrated and helpless at seeing their country humiliated and plundered. Charles decided to spend time around the docks, in cafés, cabarets. Surely he would eventually find what he was looking for. He spent weeks, and all his spare time, touring the docklands. He met lots of people, but the right person with the ability and guts to join him was like finding a grain of sand in a bag of sugar.

He shammed sickness to augment time to pursue his idea. He searched and searched until he was at the end of his tether. He felt weak, sick and hungry. He almost stumbled into a café, all thought of his quest forgotten, and fairly collapsed in a seat, dog-tired, physically and mentally drained. What little concentration he had left was centred on a good meal. He ordered a bottle of wine and a large meal. Charles was so weary, he was only half aware of the rather unkempt person sitting opposite.

He looked as exhausted as Charles. He was making good headway into his meal. Half a smile crossed his weather-worn face as he glanced across at Charles.

'You look like I feel, *Monsieur*,' he said and continued, 'Fed up with the world, and who can blame you. My son got rounded up with the English at Dunkirk. I expect he will be in England now.'

'What regiment is he in, *Monsieur*?' asked Charles, with a hint of curiosity.

'He is in the artillery with the Seventh French Army. I believe they were on the British right flank.'

'Well,' said Charles, with a flash of interest, 'that is a coincidence, my son too is in the Seventh, also in the artillery, and now in England. His mother, my wife, is English, and she too is in England. Her parents were killed in a motor accident. She has taken over the running of the farm, and I am planning to join her when I retire. This damned war has upset all our plans, now I don't know what the future holds. I'd give my last centime to be with her now.'

'*Monsieur!* We are birds of a feather! I too would join you in your wish. I have been wondering and dreaming how to get to England to be near my son, but it seems impossible, and must remain just a dream.'

'Don't give up, *Monsieur!* You know the old saying, nothing is impossible, if you think hard enough, and long enough about it. By the way, I am Charles Pipkin-Brodeau.'

'And I am Albert Dutton.'

They shook hands, and their conversation became warm and friendly. Their ideas ran parallel and their conversation set the seal of friendship. Time passed quickly and most of the customers had left. Charles and Albert were so wrapped up in their talk it came as a shock to find that they were the only two in the café and the proprietor was anxiously tidying up – another way of saying 'Time, gentlemen'. They took the hint, and bid goodnight to the owner and left.

'Well, Charles, it's been very nice talking to you. We must meet again.'

'As a matter of fact, Albert,' said Charles, 'I was about to invite you round to my house for a drink and a bit to eat. That would give us chance to continue our discussion.'

Charles gave Albert his address and they agreed seven o'clock the following evening would be fine. They shook hands and parted.

Arriving home, Charles was surprised to see a letter on the mat. He tore open the envelope. It was a brief note from Fleur, telling him that Philip was staying with his mother, which he already knew, having had a letter from Philip. It pleased him to note how she had framed her words without mentioning England.

Charles noted the address, and quickly consulted his map. He saw that St Palais was in the Basses-Pyrénées and near to the Spanish border. Charles knew that Hitler had helped General Franco to power, but now it seemed that Franco was doing his best not to get involved in this multinational war. He would probably return any escaped prisoners to Gibraltar, to curry favour with England, perhaps with an eye on Gibraltar, which had always been in dispute.

Charles, now in bed, mulled over Fleur's letter, her address and the chat with his new-found friend Albert. Charles always intended to end his days in the village of his birth, Maisons Blanches. His thoughts turned to Philip and the terrible events leading to the fiasco on the beaches of Dunkirk. There must be lots of British soldiers still in France hiding away in all kinds of terrible places, perhaps hoping to reach Spain but lacking the know-how and any sort of help. He thought how nice and helpful it would be if he and his friend could somehow evolve a plan to help these wretched people to filter through to Spain and Gibraltar.

He gave up much of his sleep wrestling with his muddled thoughts, which somehow seemed to be pointing a way. His mind overstretched and exhausted, he at last fell into a heavy slumber. He awoke with a start as he handed over his first escapee. He felt surprisingly fresh and excited. He would put the thoughts of his muddled dream to Albert. Perhaps between them, they could come up with a feasible plan.

Living alone, Charles had most of his meals in the town. He

had never aspired to be a cook, and preferred to eat out. Now that he had invited Albert home, he felt obliged to entertain him properly. With this in mind, he sought the advice of his local café. He was soon put at ease.

'*Pas de problème, Monsieur,*' he said. '*Chaud ou froid?*'

'*Froid, je pense, a sept heures.*'

'*Très bien, Monsieur. Laissez-le à moi!*'

Albert and *la serveuse* from the café arrived almost together. The table was set with wine and two glasses. By the time Albert had shed his coat, *Mademoiselle* announced that the meal was ready. The girl left with a generous tip.

Charles poured drinks, then without undue ceremony the meal began. The atmosphere was free and easy, and between mouthfuls, Charles explained as best he could the muddled thoughts that his mind had been trying to assemble in some sort of order.

'I think it may be possible for us to get through to Spain and Gibraltar and maybe England. It may cost a bribe or two! As for passing soldiers through, that's a different kettle of fish.'

There was silence for a moment or two while Albert mulled over the idea, and munched a cream cake. Charles could see by his facial expression that some idea had been given birth; he waited in hopeful expectation.

'Leaving us out of it,' he said, 'don't you think it would be more helpful, as you said, to the war effort, if we could somehow smuggle young British, French or Belgium soldiers out, so that they could carry on the fight? After all, we are much too old to be dashing around with a rifle.'

'That's a brilliant idea, Albert. Of course you are right. If we could only bring that off, it would be a great, praiseworthy achievement. Right. Agreed! Now we have to work out the practicalities. Are you prepared to start immediately?'

'Yes, Charles. The sooner the better! I have money and a cheque-book. Hopefully we shall be able to draw on it.'

'My situation is the same. Let's hope for the best! I have a letter here from my daughter-in law. She, her baby and sister have moved from Paris, and now live in St Palais, in the Basses-Pyrénées.'

Charles spread out his map and pointed out the exact spot.

'I propose we start from there, and work northwards until we have established a chain of safe houses willing to give help to escaping prisoners or anyone fleeing from the Germans. My car is loaded with petrol, sleeping bags and an amount of food. Perhaps we ought to take spare underclothes. Can you think of anything else, Albert?'

'No. Oh, perhaps a torch and matches?'

'Good thinking! We'll do that. We'll sort out other problems as they crop up.'

'When do we start?'

'As soon as possible. Tomorrow suits me. How about you?'

'Right, Charles! Tomorrow it is then!'

'Shall we make it eight o'clock?'

'That's fine. I'll be here on the dot!'

'We'll drink to that! And here's to success.'

They were both excited. They tossed back their drinks, shook hands and parted.

Neither slept well, which perhaps was not surprising, but at eight o'clock sharp Charles let out the clutch and they were off. The sky was blue and cloudless, not too hot, and ideal for travelling. The journey took them to Avignon, Toulouse, St Palais, some 300 miles and 9 hours' travelling time, during which time Charles and Albert got to know each other. They arrived in St Palais at 7 p.m., having stopped twice for refreshments and changed drivers several times.

Fleur had the surprise of her life when she replied to a knock on the door.

'*Oh Mon Dieu,*' she exclaimed in amazement. '*Entrez, Papa.*' She called him Papa now, a little endearment to which he responded with a tender kiss. Charles introduced Albert to Fleur and Lucile.

Fleur said, 'Please take a seat. You must be tired after such a long journey, Lucile is just about to get a meal.'

'You have just come right,' said Lucile. 'The meal will be ready in fifteen minutes. Perhaps you'd like to freshen up?' she continued, pointing the way to the bathroom.

Charles was just about to make apologies for crashing in on their meal, but Lucile forestalled him. 'There's no problem! There's enough for four!'

Then Fleurette trundled in with a shy little smile on her face.

'How pretty she is, Fleur!'

'It's your Grandfather! Come, Fleurette give him a little kiss!'

Charles held out his arms. She allowed him to pick her up and give her a little cuddle. She put her arms around his neck and gave him a wet kiss. This welcome surprised him, but made him very happy.

Over dinner, Charles told the girls about the factory, and that in the present circumstances, the tanks being produced would almost certainly be used by the Germans. Charles said he couldn't bear the thought of making tanks, perhaps to kill his own son. Albert, who was in a similar situation to Charles, said he felt the same, and would do anything to get rid of the Boche. He told them about his son, who, like Philip, was in England, and probably in the same unit.

Charles outlined his plan to organize a route of safe houses from where the fighting was, down to St Palais and beyond to the Spanish frontier.

'Albert and I propose to start here, if possible. Have you any idea of the local feelings, Fleur? Are they pro-German?'

'I think you will find they are anti-German. They have vivid memories of the German bombing of Spanish towns. For example, Madame Pinson, a friend of Annette's who owns this cottage, is very anti-German. It was the Luftwaffe who killed her husband in Guernica during the Spanish uprising. She would do anything to even the score, even find safe houses near the frontier. I'll introduce you.'

That did not happen, for the sharp eyes of Madame Pinson had noticed the arrival of two smart-looking gentlemen, and as evening was turning to night she sensed that Fleur, who had no spare rooms for visitors, would welcome a way out of her predicament. In neighbourly fashion, she popped along to see if she could help out in any way. Fleur answered the door and invited Madame Pinson in.

'Oh Fleur!' she said. 'I saw the two gentlemen arrive, and knowing the limitation of your house, I was wondering if you would like me to offer accommodation to them. I have plenty of spare rooms. They are there, and free for the asking. I'll be glad to help out. To tell the truth, you would be doing me a favour. I get so lonely, all by myself in a big house. I crave company, and like to feel I am helping someone.'

'We haven't discussed the question of staying the night. It is very kind of you, Madame Pinson. I've a feeling they might take up your offer.'

'I won't stay, Fleur. Just send them along if they accept. In the meantime, I'll get a room ready just in case.'

'Goodnight Madame Pinson. You're an angel!'

Charles and Albert had weighed up the position, and had accepted the fact that they would have to sleep rough, either in the tight confines of the car, or on the hard-baked terra firma, neither of which held prospects of restful sleep. So when Fleur explained Madame Pinson's offer they were overcome with gratitude.

'I hope this is a good omen for our campaign!' exclaimed Albert, who didn't really relish the idea of sleeping rough, though he realized that their chosen course would be anything but a bed of roses.

Fleur took Charles and Albert along to Madame Pinson's house. She introduced them, then bid them goodnight, and left them to her tender mercies. Madame Pinson was goodness itself. She had made up a couple of beds in one of her many rooms, and soon reappeared with two hot drinks.

'I'll leave you now, gentlemen. Until tomorrow then! and sleep well.'

Charles and Albert felt totally at ease with Madame, and felt certain that their plans would be safe with her. Her extreme loathing of the Nazis, and what they stood for, guaranteed it, and enhanced their trust and reliance in her. The two felt happier and less alone in their struggle against the enemy. Tired and travel-weary they settled down. Their talk became intermittent and ended in whispered ideas, and finally the two succumbed to blissful slumber.

The next morning they woke up bleary-eyed, to find Madame Pinson standing at the door with a tray of coffee and croissants. She smiled as she greeted them.

'Good morning! You have slept well?'

'Yes indeed! Like the dead!'

'I have made up something for your lunch, you said you wished to make an early start,' continued Madame Pinson.

'Yes, *Madame!*' replied Charles. 'We have a long journey ahead, and thank you for looking after us. We hope you have luck with your friends near the frontier. That would be a great step forward. We shall be in touch with you later.'

'I think we have made a good start,' remarked Albert, 'Here's hoping our trip north will be as successful.'

Charles and Albert said their goodbyes to Madame, and called on Fleur and family to say goodbye. Charles was enchanted by Fleurette's lively chatter and could not resist picking her up for a special cuddle and a big kiss.

As they drove off to waves and cheers, Albert noticed a rivulet of tears tracing the contours of Charles's cheeks. He guessed that he was wondering if he would ever see her again.

'Charles,' said Albert, 'You're a sentimental old fool, like me! I am glad I'm not alone. When the chips are down, this old country means a lot to us. It's our reason for being here. I am glad we are two old fools together.'

Albert patted Charles on the shoulder.

'Come, Charles,' he said, 'let's concentrate on the journey and our plans. This is not the time for sentimental thoughts. Look to the future and leave the past to history.'

'Sorry, Albert! You're right, of course,' he replied, putting his foot down to demonstrate his determination not to be deflected from their chosen goal.

Time had rushed on apace. The Blitzkrieg was taking its toll on London and other English cities, with massive damage and thousands of casualties. Hitler, backed up by Hermann Goering, was convinced that Britain would capitulate. He hadn't reckoned on the tenacious spirit of the British people.

Italy's Benito Mussolini, watching from afar, saw Germany as an odds-on favourite and plunged Italy into the war on his side. In matching Marshal Balbo's – and later, Marshal Graziani's – army of 236,000 well-armed troops against Britain's 36,000 troops, he had misjudged the well-trained, elite 7th Armoured Division – the Desert Rats. After playing a game of cat and mouse to gain time, the 7th Armoured Division launched an attack which sent Graziani and his troops reeling back towards Tripoli.

The change in the fortunes of war coincided with Charles and Albert's journey up to Troyes. They had recruited several safe houses, whose owners promised to recruit some of their most trusted friends who had suitable facilities. After a very long and tiring journey they stopped for the night near Auxerre, and the following night just south of Troyes. Charles felt a tinge of excitement as they entered his native territory but, after two long gruelling days' travel, they had one thing on their minds which superseded all else – a good night's sleep. They had a hot drink to relax their travel-weary bodies in restful slumber. All tucked up, and snug for the night in their sleeping bags, sleep was instantaneous, and soon they were snoring like a couple of pregnant pigs.

After what seemed like minutes, their slumber was suddenly shattered by a low-flying aircraft. Simultaneously they sat bolt upright and wideawake. The erratic spluttering of the engine seemed to indicate a lack of fuel. The pilot was obviously fighting to keep the engine going and hoped to find a landing place before it gave up the ghost.

'It's out of petrol!' offered Albert as both rushed to dress. There had been British sorties over France, but there was no indication as to its nationality. In any case it was a pilot in distress, and for a moment, war was put aside. Here was an airman needing help, and help was what he would get, whether English, French or German.

Charles and Albert were now dressed. They tried to get some indication of direction. The engine started cutting out for longer periods. A crash seemed imminent. Then it happened! It wasn't a crash followed by an explosion or fire, as one would have expected, but it was more like an elephant crashing through the undergrowth.

The two pinpointed the direction, and ran towards it. Other people could also be heard making for the crash. It seemed to develop into a race to get to the scene. The noise got louder as the would-be rescuers converged on the plane. Charles and Albert ran, scrambled over fences and forded a stream. It was then that they noticed torches flashing here and there, which seemed to be concentrating on one particular point. They quickened their pace and were soon rewarded by the sight of the plane, and by the time they arrived they were two of a dozen or so. The first glimmer of dawn was appearing. The plane was a British fighter, out of petrol and a long way from home. The crowd seemed to know each other, and were discussing how to get enough petrol to get the plane back to England.

It was at that point that Charles piped up and offered a couple of gallons from the reserves he was carrying in the car. Charles's offer started the ball rolling, and one by one the others came forward with offers. The total amount fell short of what was required, according to the pilot. It was decided that everyone would try to persuade their local petrol stations to help.

It was almost daylight when the pilot suggested pushing the plane a few yards to a clump of trees protruding from the wood, and breaking a few branches to camouflage it from prying eyes. The group set to work, breaking leafy branches. The job was done in half an hour, making it difficult to spot from the air. Pierre suggested that they all meet in the café nearby, at eight in the evening to report on the petrol offered. Maurice volunteered to feed and shelter the pilot, whose name was George Swift.

It was then that Charles finally recognized his cousin. He had been looking hard at him for some time, looking for some trait or sign of recognition. Then François stood rubbing the lobe of his ear. This jolted Charles's memory. Charles called over to him. He too had been uncertain, but now he rushed over to Charles.

'Charles!' he exclaimed in astonishment. 'What a surprise! I have been watching you for some time. It's ages since I last saw you, and I wasn't sure. It's great seeing you again, but how did you come to be here?'

'Oh François, it's a long story! Perhaps we'll have time to chat tonight in the café.'

'I'll look forward to that, but where are you staying?'

Charles gave him a brief outline of their plans, and explained that they were sleeping rough by the side of their car and hoped to reach Troyes and finally Maisons Blanches the next day.

'Oh Charles! Don't do that! I'll go back to the car with you, then we can drive to my house in the village. We have plenty of room and you can catch up on your sleep.'

They did collect enough petrol, though it took a few days and a lot of hard work, carrying it through the woods and fields. In the end the pilot managed to take off, and months later they heard that he successfully landed his plane at Biggin Hill in England.

Charles and Albert were found a rented cottage on the outskirts of the village. From there, with the help and cooperation of the few who helped to get George Swift and his Spitfire back to base in England, and encouraged by their success, their plans really took off.

22

Back in England, Philip's interview at the War Office in London was a success. He had examinations in German, English, French and Italian. One could say he was the pick of the bunch – not an altogether enviable position to be in. He was congratulated and was welcomed into a new 'secret group' now taking shape in the remote Highlands of Scotland.

Arriving there, Philip was soon thrown into the thick of it. The first priority was to reach maximum fitness. This was achieved by gymnastics, running, jumping, rock climbing and all the things that left you stiff and sore and wishing you were still at home with your mam. Then came unarmed combat and the use of the knife. As a reward, or a form of relaxation, there was sport of all kinds. Philip, being a keen sportsman and having had his army training, was already fit, or at least he thought he was, until he was introduced to the squad of muscle-men who put them through hell and made muscles ache which they didn't know they had. It was a harrowing and sometimes an agonizing experience, all in the cause of fitness.

On reaching the end of this course, there was an air of expectancy; perhaps there would be a bit of relaxation or even a spot of leave. But not a bit of it. What they had undergone was only one part of the course. Now came the lighter side of their training, though equally important: map-reading, tactical groundwork and camouflage. Then came a study of wireless – faults, maintenance and repairs – and communication. Then came the scary bit, parachute jumping. It was a case of not being the one to show fear. They egged one another on, and in the end all passed out.

The climax to all this was a lively get-together with drinks and refreshments, and a few speeches by the Colonel and training instructors. Afterwards the real party began, with dancing, singing and turns, by anyone boasting a bit of talent. As the night wore on, so the songs and jokes became smuttier. The company was more or less equal, and by the end of the evening, the crowd dispersed in ones and twos in good heart, with lots of giggling, laughing and the occasional squeal. It was a jolly end to a strenuous course. The next day everyone went off on a hard-earned week's leave.

A week's leave soon passes; no sooner have you shaken hands with everyone, than you are shaking hands again and saying your goodbyes. It was like this with Philip. The days in between were spent with his mother at Slippery Edge Farm, doing the rounds of the family. Philip wrote to his father and Fleur. There were no replies. Of course he did not know of the changed circumstances. The lack of communication was devastating. Philip was at his wits' end to know what to do. In a way, he was pleased when his leave was over. In Scotland he would have too much to do, and it would take his mind off private matters.

In Scotland there was a revision of all the training that had been done. 'Practice makes Perfection' was the slogan on the lips of every instructor. There was a spate of lectures and demonstrations. Then they had an intensive course on explosives, detonators, fuses, and how and when to use them. Then came mine detection and how to lift mines by the use of knife or bayonet.

The war had now progressed to the benefit of the Allies. The Lend-Lease act of America had come into force, and America had started to rearm. Britain's losses of ships were being replaced and everything necessary to conduct a successful war began to flow across the sea. The balance of power began to shift in Britain's favour.

It was now January 1942 and Operation Torch, the invasion of French North Africa, had reached a successful conclusion in carrying out a giant pincer movement, trapping Rommel's army into surrender at El Agheila. This left the Allies free to land troops in Sicily.

It was at this point that Philip in Scotland, feeling a little bored with all the repetitive training, was suddenly hauled out of the classroom and told to report to the office.

Philip's heartbeat did a lively tattoo as he entered the office. All the bigwigs were sitting at the table. Philip had never seen such a display of pips, crowns and red tabs before. He surveyed with apprehension the sea of stern-looking faces and felt it hard to cancel the call of nature. The only likeness to this scene that he could recall was the court martial of Nurse Edith Cavell during the First World War, who was shot as a spy. He gave a little shudder at the thought of it. Then the Brigadier spoke,

'I suppose you are wondering why you are here?'

'Yes, sir!' he replied. 'But I suppose you are going to tell me?'

This reply raised a few eyebrows and the Brigadier said, 'Quite! Well, Captain Pipkin-Brodeau, we have a very important mission, which requires a person fluent in Italian. You appear to be the only one in your group with this qualification. It will mean a parachute drop, and the object will be to blow up a gunpowder factory. According to information, the factory doesn't appear to be particularly well guarded, but it is a dangerous mission.'

He paused awhile, to let the information sink in.

'Well, Captain, do you think you are up to it? You have been temporarily transferred to British HQ.'

'I'll do my best, sir. Where in Italy is the powder factory?'

'It is in the long valley from Pescara to Sulmona, not far from Sulmona railway station. Do you know that area, Captain?'

'Like the back of my hand, sir. I have cousins in the area, where I used to spend holidays as a child.'

'Do you think anyone would recognize you?'

'It's some years since I was there. I don't think I would be recognized, though perhaps a bit of make-up would help. Better be safe than sorry.'

'The plan is to drop you and four men, all experts in every art of combat and fully trained in explosives and survival. You will be in charge, Major Pipkin-Brodeau.'

Philip looked in surprise at the Brigadier, thinking it was a tease or a slip of the tongue, or maybe a sweetener.

'Your promotion will be posted up in Brigade Orders tonight,' he said with a crafty smile and twitch of his moustache. 'It's our way of showing our appreciation.'

It didn't fool Philip, though; he would call it 'a bit of soft soap'.

'I shall leave you to plan the exercise,' he continued, 'the time and place of the drop, and the amount of explosive, fuses and detonators. There'll be enough rations for two weeks. You will be in civvies, of course, so don't get captured! Getting back to England via Switzerland or France or by whatever means will be up to you and your ingenuity. By the way, you will have a wireless to get in touch if necessary. We could make other drops, if need be. Can you think of anything else you may need?'

'I would like five Italian uniforms, preferably medical – RAMC equivalent.'

'That shouldn't be too difficult. Leave it with me. Let me have your plans as soon as possible.'

'Certainly, sir,' said Philip. He saluted and marched out.

Philip's first step was to introduce himself to the four chosen men and brief them on the exercise. They were to meet every day for training and discussions. Philip was very pleased with the choice of men; they looked tough and reliable, with a broken nose and a few scars and bruises to show for it. They used an old disused farmhouse nearby to practise wiring up and using various methods of detonation.

Unfortunately Philip couldn't remember much about the construction of the buildings, but he seemed to think they were of wood encircled by a mound of earth.

Major Philip Pipkin-Brodeau and his four cut-throats, Sergeant Bob Cook, Corporal George Treadwell, Private Ray Shorthouse and Private Sam Slater, worked long, hard and enthusiastically for the next fortnight, with little or no thought for anything else.

The last week's training was done at night. It was realistic and really a dummy run of the real thing. The old farmhouse represented the explosives factory. The exercise had to be carried out as quietly as possible. They all carried clickers, the only form of recognition.

As soon as it was dark the exercise began. The five approached the farmhouse as soundlessly as a tiger stalking its prey. Sergeant Cook stood by to give covering fire if things went wrong. Corporal Treadwell gave the two privates equal lengths of fuse and detonators with the dummy explosive charges. The dummy charges were set and the two ends of fuse were brought together. The Major tied the two ends together, then when the four were ready, the Major lit the fuse, and the five ran like the very devil. Clear of the target, they sat on the grass, and soon they heard the detonators explode, almost simultaneously, as was expected. They gave a little cheer, knowing that the next time would be for real, with a big explosion as the charges went off, and hopefully the whole caboodle.

Come morning, all the equipment, clothes, tools and everything to do with the proposed action were neatly laid out for checking. The Major handed the checklist to Sergeant Cook with specific instructions to ensure that everything tallied with the list.

'Will do, sir,' he said, and added, 'Don't you think, sir, it would be a good idea, to take along a chain-breaker? There may be fences, gates and padlocks to force before we reach the actual building.'

'That's an excellent suggestion, Sergeant! I don't know what I should do without you! You're worth your weight in gold.'

'I'll remind you of that, sir, when we reach the first bloody great padlock!'

'You do that, Sergeant! There'll be a bloody great pint for every one we have to break – and the same goes for you three too.'

That evened the score, and brought a smile to the other three, and a bit of lip-smacking.

'Right now,' ordered the Major, 'you get on with the checking, while I go and see the Brigadier. He may come back with me, so no messing about. Understood?'

'Yes, sir! Understood!'

The conference with the Brigadier was short and to the point. At the close of it, everything was Go! Go! No time to mull over the arrangements. The timetable was set, with hardly time to scribble goodbye letters.

The next morning at the crack of dawn the five, with pack and baggage, were whisked off south by air, to catch the specially prepared plane fitted with expendable fuel tanks to complete the journey.

'Bugger me!' exclaimed Sam Slater. 'They didn't give us time to back out.'

'You wouldn't have backed out in any case, would you?' asked his chum, Ray Shorthouse – 'Shortarse' for short – with a worried expression on his face.

'Of course not, Shortarse,' Sam replied. 'I'm only here to look after thi', I promised thi' sister that I'd get thi' back, even if I had to carry thi'.'

'Well, Sam, I hope tha' doesn't go back on thi' word. She'll duffy thi' up if tha' did, and that would be after she'd snatched thi' goolies.'

23

The five settled down well during the flight, making light of it, with lots of joking and small talk. One would have thought that they were setting out on a holiday to some idyllic island in the sun overflowing with dusky maids blessed with nothing more than a sarong or a straw skirt, instead of perhaps a journey with no return. But that's how it was in the British Army: light-hearted jokes and banter to add a bit of cheer to a depressing situation, to hide their own doubts and feelings. Once faced, however, with the realities of whatever hellish assignment they were destined to undertake, they would carry it out with the utmost vigour.

The drop was calculated to coincide with the fading light of day. Everything had been checked and rehearsed en route. Now, as dusk approached darkness, the five pushing away the butterflies, lined up and, one after the other, plunged into space. The five parachutes opened and quickly disappeared into the void.

The minds of the five soon turned, with a little apprehension, to the job in hand. There was no easy landing. It was just the reverse. The vista was lunar, with a scattering of rocks of all sizes in this part of the mountain. There was no sign of life, just a deathly silence. No lights, just blackness.

Using clickers, the five quickly came together. Luckily, there were no casualties, only a few bruises. It was very cold, and teeth chattered, prompting Shortarse to remark, 'It's cold enough to freeze your goolies, Sarge.'

'Tha're not wrong there, Shortarse. I reckon we ought to be issued wi' little sheepskin bags to put 'em in.'

'Tha're reight there, Sarge, but not so little! Don't forget Sam. Tha' wouldn't want him to be left out in t' cold, would tha?'

'No, but he shouldn't grow so much!'

'He reckons it's his mam who insists on him taking codliver oil.'

'Well,' said Sergeant Cook, 'that goes to show that you can't have it both ways.'

As a boy, the Major had spent some time in these mountains, but it was now so dark, it was impossible to locate anything recognizable. Snow covering the mountain decided them to do the only sensible thing. They found the lee side of a rock face and did what they could with the equipment and parachutes to make themselves as comfortable as possible until daylight. Sleep was too much to hope for.

Huddling together under the parachutes created a modicum of warmth, but the situation was anything but conducive to sleep. It was therefore a blessed relief when the first streaks of light appeared over the horizon. No one seemed to want to take the initiative, then Private Sam Slater blew in his mate's ear. 'Are tha' awake, Shortarse?'

'Course not!' came the instant reply. 'Tha'd better brew up, seeing as tha're the first awake. Then wake mi' up.'

'OK, smarty! Where's t' meth tablets?' he asked.

'It's all together, just under the edge of the parachute. Over there,' he said, pointing a finger in the direction. 'Come on, Sam, don't be all day about it! My mouth tastes like a duck's a—'

'All reight, Shortarse, fill thi' gob wi' t' snow!'

Private Sam Slater was soon handing round mugs of tea.

'Here you are, Major,' he said, handing Philip a steaming mug. 'That'll get the circulation going, sir,' he added with a smile.

'Thank you, Sam, you've just about saved my life!'

The five sampled their hard rations to fortify themselves for whatever lay ahead. Breakfast over, the Major outlined the day's programme.

They were on Monte Marone, and their first objective was to

march northwards and secrete themselves on the adjoining mountain, Monte Maiela, which overlooked the Sulmona valley and Sulmona itself. The Major knew that, from the summit of Maiela, one had more or less an aerial view of the town, the station and the nearby explosive plant.

With this in view, the party divided their baggage as equally as possible amongst themselves. The Major took his compass bearings, and the five set off.

'The snow isn't very deep, sir,' observed Corporal Treadwell.

'That's a blessing, Corporal. I hope there'll be even less in the valley.'

Not to be outdone, Private Shorthouse continued, 'And there aren't many people about, sir.'

'Now that's a very good observation, Shorthouse,' exclaimed Major Philip. 'I hope your powers of observation will have improved by the time we reach the powder factory.'

'Oh, don't worry about him, sir. I shall be keeping an eye on him. I promised his sister that I'd look after him.' Sam added with a sigh, 'Of course, sir, I didn't know, at the time, what I was taking on!'

'Well, Slater, we all make mistakes,' replied Major Philip, tittering with amusement.

This back and forth humorous taunting seemed to make light of their struggle to reach the summit of Monte Maiela, but eventually they arrived there, more than pleased to shed their loads. By this time the sun was rising, and radiating a bit of warmth.

'Rest here awhile,' ordered Major Philip. 'I'll do a little recce to recapture the feel of the mountains, and perhaps rediscover some of our old hideouts.'

Half an hour later he was back. 'I can hardly believe it,' he said. 'I found the waterhole! And from there, I found the cave as easily and as naturally as I used to. Right, men! Pick up your gear. We'll use the cave as our headquarters. There's plenty of room to sleep and store our supplies. Take note of where it is. If any of you become separated, make for the cave and waterhole. That will be our rendezvous. I don't suppose many people know of its existence.'

The cave was ideal, well sheltered from the prevailing wind and not easy to find. The waterhole was near, and was equally inconspicuous and could be a life-saver, declared Major Philip.

'Fortunately this place is as unattractive as it is inaccessible. I think we should be safe here, so long as we do nothing stupid to attract attention, like lighting fires or shooting at wolves; so let's play it cool! Right?'

'Right, sir,' was the concerted reply.

'Now, Private Slater, Sammy! How about a brew-up? Then we'll consider our next move?'

With a mug of tea and biscuits, they sat around to discuss the main issue: to find an accessible route to the powder plant.

'I have given much thought to this question,' announced Major Philip. 'I really could do with someone who knows a bit of Italian, *ma non fa niente*,' he muttered, more to himself than to his audience. 'This is really a job I must do myself, so here's what I propose. I'll take Corporal Treadwell with me, and leave Sergeant Cook in charge here. Just below the summit,' he said, pointing towards a point in line with Sulmona, 'there is a hermit's house and chapel, from where there is a route which snakes its way down the mountain. This path is used occasionally by the hermit and his donkey to carry food and necessaries back to the hermitage. I know the hermitage, and the hermit, even the hermit's girlfriend, and listened to the many lurid details of shocking incidents, but that's by the way.'

'Oh go on, Major,' urged Private Sam Slater, all agog. 'Tell us all the lurid details!'

'Perhaps on our way home. But I don't think you are old enough, Sam, and I don't want to be the one to destroy your illusions! Remind me on our way home.'

'I will, sir. To be sure I will! I will!'

It was agreed that the Major and Corporal Treadwell would follow the hermit's path down the mountainside. In a suitable hiding place, Corporal Treadwell would be left to observe the Major's progress and take a compass bearing for future

Hermit's house and chapel.

reference, just before he disappeared from sight, owing to distance or light.

'I shall find the best route across the valley, to skirt the town, arrive at the station, and finally, the explosives factory. Hopefully having arrived there, I shall then decide how best to carry out our mission,' explained the Major. 'I hope to return by the same route, pick up Corporal Treadwell and return here. Is that understood?'

'Yes, sir,' they replied.

'Having climbed the mountain a few times in my youth, I can tell you that it's no picnic,' commented Major Philip. 'By the time we get back here, the Corporal and I will be exhausted and hungry. Our bodies will need revitalizing for the real thing. That's where you come in, Private Slater, with your culinary acumen.'

'Leave it to me, sir. Perhaps you can tap your hermit friend for a bottle of Chianti. That would set the seal of excellence on our meal.'

'Now there's a thought, Sam,' he replied. 'I'll see what I can do.'

It was afternoon when the Major and Corporal Treadwell set off down the mountainside to reach the hermit's path. They had dined well on bully-beef stew and biscuits, with lashings of sergeant major's tea – sweet and milky – so the two felt reasonably fit and high-spirited. They were kitted out in Italian medics' uniforms, so their presence, if noticed, would cause little or no surprise.

Three-quarters of the way down, they came to a little hollow surrounded by scrub, which gave cover from the path, and an open view of the valley.

'This is ideal, Treadwell,' declared the Major, pointing out the direction he would take. 'I should be back here by dusk, depending on how things go.'

The Major set off at a smart pace, while Treadwell put a few finishing touches to the camouflage. Satisfied now, the corporal settled down for a long vigil.

The Major quickly disappeared from view, not to reappear until he was making his way across the valley. Treadwell kept a check on his movements and recorded a compass bearing from time to time on his progress. Finally he disappeared altogether.

Out of Treadwell's view, the Major met one or two people, who passed the time of day with him and commented on the warm weather.

'Buon giorno, Signore. Comè fa caldo!'

'*È vero!*' replied the Major, mopping his brow with his handkerchief to emphasize his agreement. Passing under the arches of Porta Vecchia, a medieval aqueduct, he continued as far as the railway. Just beyond was the explosives plant. Without creating suspicion, he wandered around as if going about his business but now and then cast a keen eye over the plant. There didn't seem to be a guard on the place, as one might have expected. He could see one or two people moving around. Some appeared to be walking along putting their coats on, as if their shift was over.

'Oh yes,' the Major said to himself, as his heart beat a little faster.

The few people walking out of the factory grew to a small crowd as it approached the gate. As the last of the workers left, the Major sought the obscurity of a clump of trees, from where he could observe the factory to advantage.

Soon, however, daylight began to fade and observation became more and more difficult, to the point where his imagination began to play tricks on him. Then a few lights were switched on, and a light came on in a small hut, out of which came a man carrying a lamp. He walked along to each building in turn, stopping for a few seconds, then moving on. It appeared that he was locking up. Lastly he stopped by the main gate. By the rattle of the chain, it seemed that he was securing the gate with chain and padlock. He was soon walking back to the hut. He disappeared inside and closed the door, and a quiet mystique shrouded the factory.

The Major walked cautiously around the mound of earth surrounding the factory. He came to the gate which was chained and padlocked. 'So far so good,' he murmured to himself. Being encouraged by the apparent lack of security, he ventured to walk round again, but this time between the mound and the chain link fencing. There did not appear to be any problem about entry. The chain-breaker would make light work of the fencing, even the chain holding the door.

There was no sign of any other guard. The one in the hut was probably enjoying forty winks. The Major walked slowly away, leaving the factory to its peace and tranquillity.

As he made his way through the archways of Porta Vecchia and on through the edge of the town, he came upon a solitary wine shop and purchased two *fiaschi di Chianti*. *La signora* looked faintly surprised, as though she was trying to recall where she had seen that face, or a likeness, somewhere before. He spoke the local *dialetto*, so there was nothing there to cause suspicion. Yet he felt there was something that puzzled her.

The Major left the shop with a slightly worried expression, but his high spirits caused by his success soon pushed his unease away. He set off with a will, towards Monte Maiella; nevertheless, from time to time he was plagued by the face of *La signora* in the wine shop. He could not get her out of his mind. Try as he might, she returned.

The Major skirted the town, crossed a river and the main road to Pescara, on the coast. Now he was nearing the mountain, passing on the way the civilian prison at Bardia and the little village of Fonte dell' Amore with its POW camp. Climbing the foothills to the mountain proper, he rested awhile at the monument of the Italian poet Evidio.

He was pretty well exhausted by the day's strenuous efforts. His mind drifted to the point of slumber. He'd been recalling his early youth in Sulmona, and his schoolfriends. Then suddenly the face of Filomena, his childhood sweetheart, flashed upon the screen of his mind. He was amazed, astonished beyond belief. The face was the one he had seen in the wine shop. There was no doubt about it, it was Filomena. His heart missed a beat and his face burned with the memory. Her mother and brother used to run a smallholding in 'contrada cantone' near the little village of Intro d'acqua. He recalled the hours spent together in the vineyards, gathering grapes, trampling them in bare feet, and doing all the outrageous things teenagers do.

All the reminiscence of his youth seemed to reinvigorate him. He set off at a cracking pace for the hermit's path. It was quite dark now and the only guide to his direction was his position in relation to the lights surrounding the prisoner of war camp and the lights from the civilian prison at Bardia, but this was sufficient to work out roughly his direction. It was no easy climb, particularly with a *fiasco* of Chianti in each hand. He was sorely tempted to sit awhile and quench his thirst and rid himself of one of the bottles. But no, Major Philip Pipkin-Brodeau had more self-control than that. The thought in his mind was for the welfare of his men.

It was a stiff climb to reach the hermit's path, but he made it, and marvelled that his two bottles were intact. In spite of the cold wind blowing, and whether it was the exertion of the climb or the excitement of the success of his quest is debatable, but he was lathered in sweat. He kept going until he reached Corporal Treadwell, who was shivering to the chatter of his teeth.

The Major flopped down beside him. He shed his coat and put it round Treadwell's shoulders. Decorking one of the bottles, the Major passed it to him. 'Take a good swig of that, Treadwell. It'll warm you up a bit! Has anything happened while I was away?'

'Not really, sir. Oh, the girl with the donkey came up to the hermitage.'

'Has she gone back yet?'

'No, sir. I reckon she's staying the night. It's too dark now to be wandering about the mountain, and I don't suppose the donkey would think much of it either.'

'You're right there, Treadwell. The dirty old bugger! He has a beard down to his goolies. You'd never think he could perform.'

'Well, sir, you never can tell, with all this invigorating mountain air, and the milk and honey, and who knows, perhaps ginseng root and Spanish fly.'

'Well, Treadwell, I never thought you were an authority on such matters, but then with a name like yours, it's understandable!'

Losing no time, they picked their way up the steep, stony path. There was one solitary light in the hermitage as they passed by.

'I expect the old hermit is in bed,' suggested Treadwell.

'If, as you say, one of his maids is still with him, he's every reason to go to bed. He has a bevy of beauties to pay him visits, known locally as the Bouncy Babes of Maiella. After all, what would his life be like bereft of excitement? It appears that his donkey is not the only one with a liking for oats.'

'Well, sir, I don't think he'd like turning her out with a donkey at this time of night. It's dark, and she wouldn't like it.'

'I am sure she wouldn't, Treadwell. And I don't suppose the donkey would be in raptures about it either.'

The route above the hermitage was rocky and hazardous, with no worn path. In the dark it was a question of clawing one's way upwards, forever upwards. After what seemed an eternity, they eventually reached the summit. Their troubles, however, were not yet over but, working methodically to right and left, they came to the hide and the three parachute-shrouded bodies.

The Major and Corporal Treadwell helped themselves to biscuits and bully beef and Chianti. It must have been the sweet scent of Chianti that invaded their nostrils, for the three slumberers were soon wide-awake and holding out their mugs.

'Oh, this is great,' the three sleepy voices chorused.

Soon there was a flurry of questions from the three, but the Major silenced them, saying, 'Let's all get some sleep now. Tomorrow we'll discuss our plans. It will be a long, hard day, I promise you, so get your heads down and get some sleep while you can. So, goodnight everyone! Sleep well.'

The grotto lapsed into silence and sleep.

24

Miraculously the five were awake at the crack of dawn. Private Sam Slater was already coaxing the primus into flame. The Major was turning over his plan of action in his mind. This was the day when he hoped that everything would go well and end in success. The remaining three were just hoping Sam Slater would get a move on with the tea.

'Come on, Sam! What tha' playin' at?' complained Ray Shorthouse, and rabbited on about his bad luck at having such a lackadaisical sod for a mucker.

Whereupon Shortarse threatened him with a mug of icy water.

'*Pace!*' called out Sam, airing his only word of Italian.

The horseplay ceased as mugs of hot tea were passed around.

'Now that we are all reclining comfortably,' announced the Major. 'I'll explain the plan for the final attack on the gunpowder factory.'

He drew a plan of the factory, and explained how it was protected by a mound of soil.

'Fortunately there is only one person on night watch, who seems to spend most of his time in a small hut. The gate is chained and padlocked, but I imagine our chain-breaker will deal with that. We cannot carry much more than the essentials for blowing up the factory. Take full canteens of water and a day's rations. If necessary, we can live off the land or by our wits – beg, borrow or steal. Don't worry, I am very resourceful when it comes to bargaining with the farmers, and don't forget we have money. We'll make our way down the mountain in the early afternoon, or earlier if it turns misty. I have found a good hiding place near the railway. It's a large cane-break. It won't be comfortable, as the ground is wet and infested by mosquitoes. The less time we spend there the better! At least we can leave food and things not needed for the explosion. Now, are there any questions?'

'I've one question,' said Shorthouse. 'What will happen to the chappie in the hut?'

'That's something that's been troubling me,' replied the Major. 'I really think his future will be in the lap of the gods. Perhaps the shed will protect him, particularly if he's asleep on the floor. I really think we should forget about him, and concern ourselves with the job in hand, and thank our lucky stars that there is only one guard. Now, no more sentimentality! Keep your mind on the job. 'What's the weather like, Sergeant Cook?'

'It's misty, sir.'

'In that case, I suggest we take advantage of it, and make our way down. There's plenty of cover around the foot of the mountain. There are trees, bushes, hedges, orchards and vineyards everywhere. Be cautious. If we meet someone, try to act as naturally as possible. You all know how to say *"buon giorno"*, *"buona notte"* – good day and good night – and walk on, and leave the talking to me. Understood?'

'*Si, Magiore,*' mumbled Sergeant Cook a little shyly.

The mist was ideal, and looked as if it would remain so, until they reached the valley. They followed in the steps of the Major as he zigzagged down to the hermit's path. The path was well worn, but rugged and varied in steepness.

'This is a piece of cake!' exclaimed Sergeant Cook. 'It's not as bad as I expected, and certainly nothing like the way up.'

'Tha's reight there, Sarge,' agreed Shortarse. 'If I'd known about all this trampin' up and down, I'd have asked mi' mam to make me more jam butties.'

'Why, does goin' downhill make thi' hungry, Shortarse?'

'Ay, it does, Sarge. Even breathin' brings on hunger pangs.' He added, with a little demonstration, 'It makes me fart too.'

'I had noticed, Shortarse! I bet thi' mother had trouble wi' thi' when tha' were sucklin'.'

'Oh, don't be daft, Sarge. I hadn't any teeth then!'

'Well, all I can say, it was a good job, an' no mistake.'

This is how it went on, all the way down, and all agreed that it made light of the journey.

As often happens, one counts one's chickens before they are hatched. And so it happened that day, for as they reached the last yard or so, Shortarse stubbed his foot on a tuft of weed and fell arse over bollocks.

'Trust thi' to make a balls-up, Shortarse! Where are all those fairy steps tha' uses in t' ballroom?' asked Sam Slater. Then in a more sympathetic tone, 'Are tha' hurt, Ray?'

Ray Shorthouse tried to stand. He yelled out in pain. 'I think my leg's broken!'

This immediately caused a panic. The Major hurried back to see what had happened.

Poor old Shorthouse was laid out. The Major, and Sergeant Cook, both first-aiders, examined his leg, foot and toes. It was decided that the ankle was damaged in some way. Shorthouse couldn't bear to put his foot to the ground, let alone put his weight on it.

'That's buggered it up good and proper,' commented Sergeant Cook.

There was no better comment from the Major. 'We're in a real pickle now,' he said. Then he added in general, 'Scout around and find, or cut, two strong straight branches which we can use as splints, while I puzzle out the best thing to do.'

'Well, we could put him out of his misery,' offered Corporal Treadwell jokingly.

'Oh, tha' can't do that, Corporal,' chimed in Sam Slater, 'I promised his sister to get him back safely, even if I had to carry him.' Then he added, 'It looks as though I shall have to carry him now. That'll teach me not to make rash promises.'

The Major considered leaving Shorthouse with food and water, and collecting him after the explosion, then changed his mind. 'No, we'll take him with us. I'll have to find a doctor to see to him. Then we'll think of what to do for the best.'

Using two strong branches, Shorthouse's leg was bound and immobilized, then, taking turns, he was given a pickaback. He was no feather, and the journey proved exhausting, and it was with a sigh of relief that their burden was lowered to the ground in the middle of the cane-break.

They had taken a chance in crossing the rail track that no one would see them. They saw the signalman walk along the line, but he seemed too preoccupied to notice them. After all, they were to all intents and purposes five medical soldiers carrying a wounded comrade.

Now safely hidden from prying eyes in the middle of the large cane-break, it was a question of wait and see. They kept a watch on the railway line. Their one fear was that the signalman would phone for help. Nothing happened, then a train rumbled south loaded with tanks to stem the British advance.

Everything was quiet now. Sam fussed around his mucker Shorthouse, making him as comfortable as possible. Luckily they had brought insect repellant, which was now being used. It kept the insects at bay, but at a price. It was debatable which of the two it irritated the most. Sam, like a good housewife, soon had the tea water on the boil. It was very welcome, but the monotonous diet of biscuits and bully began to pall.

The cane-break was perhaps a mile or so from the outskirts of the town, and little further from the wine shop the Major had visited. He had thought a lot about the girl who had served him. He had the feeling that there was a sort of semi-recognition between them, and the more he thought about her, the more sure he became that she was Filomena, his childhood sweetheart.

The Major decided to go and buy wine and maybe bread. Naturally his team were all for it, though he didn't tell them the whole story.

It was early dusk when he set off in the footsteps of the men who had been working on the land, and by the time he reached the wine shop they had all dispersed.

It was only after that first encounter that both had pondered to the point of conviction that their hunch was correct.

The Major contemplated the window for a moment, to whip up enough courage to enter. The loud clanging of the bell almost shattered his resolution, but as the girl entered, their eyes met in a flash of recognition. In a trice the girl was in his arms, smothering him with kisses. 'Oh Philip, it is you?'

'You remember me, Filomena?'

'How could I forget you, my love? You are in the Italian Army?'

'Yes.'

Philip had to be sure of her allegiance before trusting her, although he was 99 per cent sure she would not give him away.

'What do you think of the war, Filomena?'

'The war is a disaster for Italy, and the world. The fascists are bad as the Germans. The majority of our people did not want a war.'

Filomena had blossomed into a glamorous beauty whose charm and seductiveness weakened the legs of the strongest. Like a rosy ripe apple, she was there to be plucked. Philip, not one of the strongest, was susceptible to rosy apples, and trembled excitedly in anticipation of the first nibble.

Filomena matched Philip's desire. She quickly turned the notice on the door to *chiuso* and whisked Philip into the lounge, where, under Filomena's voluptuous spell he collapsed onto the large settee.

Filomena made no bones about it. She was ripe, and Philip hungry. She said laughingly, 'You undress me, and I'll undress you!'

This rang a bell in Philip's dim past. 'Fancy you remembering that! It was by Lake Scano, wasn't it?'

'Yes, and I won!'

'I had a little difficulty with your knickers, my fingers were all thumbs.'

They both laughed excitedly and the little game was on. Clothes and buttons flew far and wide. Filomena won again. Philip lost by a knicker, which he peeled off with great ceremony and fascination. He gave her a playful smack and chased her round the room, and caught her trying to disappear under the table. They frolicked about, then suddenly Philip remembered the reason for being there. He remembered his men in the cane-break, and Shorthouse with a damaged foot. They all depended on him. He became unsmiling and serious, which Filomena noticed at once.

She flung her arms around him and whispered gently, 'What's the matter, my love?'

'There is something I must tell you. Do you really want the English to win?'

'Yes,' she replied, 'with all my heart! I hate the Germans. I hate Mussolini, and what he has done to my country, and my people.'

'What would you say if I told you that I was working for the English, and that I was here on a mission to cause damage?'

'Oh *caro mio!* I would help you if I could. I'd do anything for you, you know that. Before you go, please let me have your baby. It would always remind me of you. I know I cannot have you, but strange things can happen in wartime, and who can say, or know, the outcome. As long as I live, I shall always be here for you, if you ever want me.'

Filomena burst into tears, and clung to Philip as if life depended on it.

Philip was absolutely certain of her trust. He consoled her and told her as much as he could, after which she commented, 'But Philip, if you do what you have to do, and escape over the mountains, I fear for your lives. The first thing that will happen will be thousands of soldiers swarming over the mountains, with spotter planes to direct them. I have seen them carry out this when POWs or prisoners from our local jail escape. The one with the damaged leg would have little chance, and would slow you down. Don't do it, *caro mio!* I have a better plan.'

Filomena was as wise as she was beautiful. They both sat on the couch; she drew a large blanket over their nudity, and continued to expound her plan. She pointed out that she had several rooms, a cellar and a false roof with a small recess which would be hard to find. There was a small secret door on the inside of a large built-in wardrobe which matched the woodwork and would withstand the closest scrutiny.

'You could do what you have to do, and return here. I can prepare the room with blankets, food and drink. If danger threatened, I could give a warning knock. You would then have to be silent until the danger was past. As for your wounded comrade, I will look after him. I have done some nursing, also I have a doctor friend who, I am sure, would help me, if necessary. If it is a sprain I can treat it with rest and cold compresses. I have done nursing in Sulmona hospital. If it should be more than a sprain, I shall see my doctor friend. What do you think, Philip?'

'You are as wise as an owl. I like it very much! I'll do it. I must return to my men tonight to let them know my plans. I'll take them a couple of bottles of vino back, to keep them happy.'

'Why not bring them back here tonight? I'll arrange the accommodation. Bring everything with you! You will all be able to have a good rest and set out tomorrow night, all refreshed and fit, and your journey will be halved. After you have done what you have to do, come back here. I'll have you all safely hidden away before the alarm goes off. Trust me, *caro mio*.'

'Now we have a couple of hours before I have to go,' said Philip, giving Filomena a little squeeze. 'I wonder what we can do to while away the time?'

The answer came as Filomena pushed Philip down on the couch. 'Don't tease,' she said, pushing her hand down his thigh. 'You know what I want, Filippo!' she hinted, cuddling close to him.

'Oh what I have to do for King and Country,' teased Philip.

'And for Italia,' countered Filomena, as she pointed his tool in the right direction.

'Filomena,' he said, in all seriousness, do you really want me to give you a *bambino, cara mia?*'

'Yes, yes, Philip! With all my heart! I shall always have a part of you to cherish, my love.'

They spent a rapturous two hours together, and Filomena

was overcome with joy. Hopefully she had now the makings of what she wanted most in life. Only God could create the circumstances to bring Filippo back to her, to make her life complete.

Philip set off with his two bottles of vino. He was almost mobbed for his trouble as he parted the canes to gain entrance to the hide.

Nothing had happened apart from the villagers who came and went, from their work in the fields.

Philip was pleased to see that Shorthouse was much better for his rest, and the cold compresses had brought down the swelling in his leg.

'Do you think you are able to walk on it now?' he asked.

'If I have to,' Shorthouse said, 'I bloody well will do!'

'Good show!' said the Major. 'That's the spirit!'

The bottles were passed around, while Philip explained the plan of action, not forgetting to point out Filomena's part in it, which met with whole-hearted approval.

'I expect you will all be glad to see the last of this mosquito-ridden place.' To which they all nodded approval, between guzzles of vino. 'Right then,' he continued, 'here's the plan. We'll set off in an hour's time. That will give me time to get my breath back.'

'He can say that again,' whispered Sam Slater, with a knowing wink.

'Did you enjoy yourself, sir?' asked Shorthouse, who was more interested to know the Major's goings-on than his plan. That would unfold as it went along.

'Yes, Shorthouse. It was a welcome surprise after several years.'

'I bet he dipped his wick,' whispered Sergeant Bob Cook.

'Well, he certainly looks shagged out,' whispered back Treadwell, looking a wee bit envious.

At long last, without too many interruptions, the Major finished his monologue. 'Now, Sergeant Cook, I want you to check that everything is evenly distributed among the four of us, leaving Shorthouse to struggle on as best he can with his leg.'

'Oh, I think he'll make it, sir! We'll have to watch him, though,' he replied with a playful smile. 'He's a crafty old bugger, sir. We'll have to watch he doesn't swing it.'

'Don't worry, Filomena will soon sort him out. He'll be so cheesed off with making gnocchi and polenta and fetching water from the well – carrying it on his head, of course – that he'll be pleading to return to duty. Right! If there are no more questions, we'll move as soon as Sergeant Cook has checked everything.' Then, more seriously and showing a bit of concern he turned to Shorthouse, 'Are you quite sure you are fit enough for the journey? It's about two miles.'

'I'll give it a go, sir. I'll make it, sir. If only to get Filomena's attention,' he replied, with a crafty wink and a smile.

'Good show, Shorthouse! You're made of the right stuff!'

They set off at a leisurely pace, in consideration of Shorthouse's lameness. It was dark and eerie as they made for the lane leading to Filomena's wine shop. The only noise was the distant barking of farm dogs. On a less serious quest the journey could have been enjoyable. Shorthouse surprised everyone. He must have been in pain, but like the good soldier he was, he suffered in silence.

Filomena's house was in darkness, for obvious reasons, but she was anxiously waiting by the open back door. As they arrived, one by one they slipped through the doorway and were ushered into the lounge. Filomena locked the door and switched on the light. Without more ado, Filomena put everyone at ease, and the Major introduced his squad.

To get everyone settled quickly, she led them up to the secret room where all their kit was dumped. She explained everything to them, especially the drill if anyone should come to search the house. The Major insisted on a dummy run, to familiarize everyone with the layout of the house and the drill. This exercise took ten minutes, which the Major thought was too long. With a bit of extra planning and getting the sequence right in the form of a drill, the time was reduced to six minutes, roughly the time it would take Filomena to slip her dressing gown on and come downstairs to the door.

Major Philip discussed with Filomena whether it would be better to delay the operation by one day, so that they could be properly rested, and give Shorthouse a little more time for his leg to recover. He explained that having a full team would increase their chances of success.

Filomena at once saw the wisdom of this, and agreed immediately, no doubt thinking about the possibility of another night with Philip.

She examined Shorthouse's leg, and satisfied herself that it was only a sprained ankle. She fetched a bucket full of ice-cold water from the well, and set Sam Slater on to slap a cold compress on his ankle every five or six minutes.

'I'll have you as fit as a fiddle by the morning. I want you to take it in turns throughout the night to change the compress,' said Filomena in Italian, encompassing with a sweep of her hand, the three likely lads, and adding, 'You'll see to that for me, won't you, sergeant?'

'Certainly, Filomena! Rest assured, he'll be there at the double tomorrow night.'

Shorthouse's face fell. 'That's not fair,' he said. 'I thought Filomena was going to nurse me back to health. I doubt that I shall be fit by tomorrow if it's left to Sam. He'd too ham-fisted to nurse anyone! He's a disgrace to the medic's uniform he's wearing.'

'Tha' knows what thi' sister said. I promised to keep thi' on t' straight and narrow, look after thi' an' get thi' back home, even if I have to carry thi'. So stop thi' blitherin', an' stick thi' leg out!'

There was a lot of good humour that night. The boys enjoyed the Italian food created by Filomena, who was a talented cook, and the Policelli went down well too. Come 10 p.m. eyes began to feel heavy and by 11 p.m. the lads were all snug in the secret room and snoring as gently as babies. The Major was in the small room on the first floor, next to Filomena's – privilege of rank?

The rhythmic snoring filtering down from above was a signal to Filomena to do a little bed-hopping. She fitted in nicely to the contours of Philip's body. Because of Philip's anticipated combat on the following night, Filomena cut down his rations to one long lingering bout of lovemaking, which ended in blissful sleep.

Filomena and the Major were down stairs by 8 a.m. They had coffee and toast and by 9 a.m. Filomena was serving in the shop. The boys were still driving the sheep home – they slept on as arranged. The Major wondered if Filomena had slipped them a Mickey Finn, they seemed so peaceful.

Philip, in the lounge by himself, had time to ponder the wider aspects of what he was doing. He felt terribly guilty about the turn of events. It was marvellous, though unexpected, to find Filomena, and though her help was expedient and welcome, there was a smattering of regret for taking advantage of her good nature. Philip's mind drifted back to Paris, Fleur, Fleurette and Lucile. He collapsed in an agonizing flood of tears. He would have to tell Fleur the truth, however hard that would be. He could only hope that she would forgive him. He cursed the war, and Hitler and his whole satanic regime. Lots of strange, regrettable things happened during wartime, when each day could be your last, and each day alive was a bonus. With all this on his mind, Philip thought that perhaps a quick death might be the answer and the justice he deserved.

Filomena, entering the lounge, broke the Major's train of thought.

'I'll make some coffee,' she said. I think it's time your "medicos" had breakfast. They must be starving!'

'I'll give you a hand, Filomena. Just show me what to do.'

Luckily, no one came into the shop for a while, which gave Filomena and Philip time to prepare a meal and rouse the 'Sleeping Beauties'. The Major cautioned his party not to talk above a whisper, but to come down quietly for breakfast. He placed a bucket of water and a towel and soap for them to wash the sleep from their eyes.

25

Today was the day of action. Shorthouse's ankle was fine, according to Shorthouse, who did not want to be left out of the fracas – besides, he would never be able to face them at home. They were now rested. They had eaten well, drunk well but not to excess, and slept well, and were now raring to go.

Filomena understood their pent-up feelings and encouraged them to play games. She produced cards, dominoes and one or two unknown games. They relaxed and obliged by playing cards, at which they were all adept.

It was after a sumptuous dinner that the Major took control. He chased them upstairs to give them their final briefing.

Everything set to go, they assembled by the back door, loaded down with equipment, explosives, detonators and fuse wire; Shorthouse was nursing a light machine-gun, in case of an emergency. It was hoped to be an unnecessary precaution.

Filomena sent each one off with a kiss and a hug, and wished them success. She led them along a short cut to the lane leading to the station. She gave Philip a huge lingering kiss and a warm hug.

'*Buon fortuna*, Filippo,' she said, overcome with emotion. She turned back towards her house, her eyes streaming with tears. 'Come back to me, *caro mio*. I will look after you all.'

It was dark as they parted; only a few pinpoints of light pointed out the direction of their objective. The Major felt confident that the workers would have left the powder factory by the time they arrived there. His prediction proved correct. As the Major crept forward, the last of the workers were passing through the gates, followed by the nightwatchman, who hastened to fix the chain and put on the padlock. He repeated the previous night's performance just as the Major had hoped, and disappeared into his cabin. Motioning his men forward, the Major whispered what had happened, and pointed out the nightwatchman's cabin.

They approached the gate. Two men held the chain and padlock. Then Corporal Treadwell used the chain-breaker, which was covered over with an old blanket to muffle the snap of the chain.

It went without a hitch, and soon the five were carrying out the drill they had practised for hours, placing the charges, detonators and fuse wires.

The whole operation went like clockwork. The four withdrew cautiously through the gate, followed by the Major, who had set the delayed fuse for half an hour. The gate was closed and the chain and padlock replaced to look as it had looked originally.

The five hurried along as noiselessly as possible until they reached the well which had featured in their plans. All the surplus bits and pieces from the operation were now tied to the heavy chain-breaker and dropped into the well, where they quickly disappeared beneath its murky water. Losing the cumbersome weight, they felt as though walking on air, though now, as the minutes ticked by, their anxiety rapidly increased.

There was a lot of air activity that night. The German transport planes had been passing over in a ceaseless convoy all day rushing their troops south to stem the Allied advance. There was still a lot going on above, as they waited with bated breath for the explosion which would mark the destruction of the explosives factory and the success of their mission. The half-hour was up, and no explosion. The atmosphere was tense to breaking point, and the five were biting their nails in puzzlement, wondering what they had done, or not done. Each one, in his own mind, was going over his own part in the action, then suddenly to their great relief it happened. The sky for miles around lit up in an almighty flash. This was followed by a tremendous explosion, which reverberated through the

Explosion at the powder factory.

mountains and made the earth tremble. The powder factory was no more.

Their job was done, but they felt little satisfaction. They had carried out their orders to the letter, but there was no real jubilation, and when the dust had settled and they realized the havoc and destruction they had caused, they each, in some strange, mysterious way, reflected simultaneously on the same subject. What had happened to that poor innocent watchman, just doing his job?

There was no time to mull over his fate. The only redeeming

factor was that his cabin may have been strong enough to soften the strength of the explosion. They had enough to worry about with their own predicament. Suppose the shock of the explosion made Filomena change her mind about helping them? Her village could be swarming with police and soldiers. The very thought was unthinkable! The Major disregarded it out of hand.

'Right!' he said. 'Let's get back as quickly as possible. No talking, and if you hear people coming towards us, take cover until they have passed. There are bound to be people rushing out to find out what the noise was, and to see the damage or offer help. Hopefully the explosion will be blamed on the air activity – a stray bomb, perhaps.'

Fortunately, they didn't hear or meet anyone. Of course, sensible people would take the main road to the station. They wouldn't be skulking about, down lanes and muddy fields. It was as they cut across a vineyard to reach the lane that they came upon Filomena, hidden in the shadows of a leafy tree. She broke cover and came towards them. She gave an audible sigh of relief as she counted and saw a 'full house', and sank into Philip's arms.

'I have been very frightened for your safety.' She clung to Philip, kissed everyone in turn, then led the way back to her house.

There was nothing incriminating to hide away except for the snub-nosed machine-gun, which was Shorthouse's baby and never far away from his tender care. He was a deadly shot, but they all hoped he would never have to prove it, in any last-ditch effort to escape.

Filomena, always looking on the bright side, had mentioned everyone in her prayers for good measure, and in anticipation of her prayers being answered had laid on a lavish dinner *à l'anglais*, with lamb, potatoes, peas and all the trimmings like mint sauce, and, of course, wine.

They were all ravenously hungry and thirsty after an exhausting day, with all its pitfalls and uncertainties. They weren't out of the woods yet, not by a long chalk! To say it was a celebration was a little previous; nevertheless, it was a very welcome surprise.

The explosion of the gunpowder factory had certainly

stirred up a hornets' nest, and as Filomena had rightly predicted, the next day Sulmona was buzzing with activity. Italian and German troops were everywhere and Filomena had heard on the grapevine that Field Marshal Kesselring had arrived with some paratroops and set up his headquarters in Introd'aqua, a small mountain village about 2 miles from Sulmona.

Spotter planes were searching the mountains, in close cooperation with the mass of soldiers poking into every nook and cranny. It was four days before the search was called off, during which time the American Air Force bombed Sulmona twice with 42, and then with 67 Flying Fortress bombers. That caused a panic and helped to divert attention from the mountains.

Lots of things appeared to be happening far too quickly to be assimilated by the brain. According to Filomena's source of information, the British had landed troops at Salerno, and Canadian and Polish troops had surrounded the Germans in Monte Cassino. The great marshalling junction at Foggia had been repeatedly bombed, causing severe disruption to the transport of German tanks and artillery.

The war seemed to be getting closer to them by the day. Filomena appeared to be stuck with them for the moment. She didn't seem to mind, but the group was fearful for her safety.

The Major decided it was time to go. In all conscience he felt unable to let Filomena take any more risks. He told her of his decision to leave that night. She was very upset, but the Major was adamant. Filomena was in a silent mood as she closed the shop. She told them to help themselves to food as she had some business to see to, and off she went.

It was late when she returned, by which time everyone was getting anxious. The group were packed up and ready to leave. Two of the Major's men had been posted some way past the house, to give warning of anything unusual.

It was near midnight and the Major was near the point of having to make a decision when Shorthouse came in to say that

Filomena was coming, but she had someone with her. This caused a stir. The Major quickly grasped the situation. He placed Shorthouse in the corner behind the couch, with the machine-gun. The two entered. Filomena was at first shocked to find herself looking down the barrel of a gun; then with a smile on her face she introduced one of her many cousins. She quickly explained that Pepino was a mountain guide, and that he knew every track, cave or cranny, and that he had crossed Monte Maiela and Monte Morroni more times than he could remember.

Filomena stressed that he was most experienced and utterly trustworthy. He had recent experience in guiding groups of POWs across the mountains and knew the Germans' disposition and their likely moves.

Pepino was very friendly, and very confident and professional as he explained his plan. They were to go that night, as the Major had already decided. Pepino explained that the journey would be very hard and extremely exhausting, as there was still plenty of snow, and it was very cold; frostbite was a danger to be guarded against. For this reason the trek had to be done quickly with as few stops as possible. If all went well, they would be in British hands in 12 hours. Pepino stressed the point of keeping tabs on one another, and told of men straying off the track and being found waist-deep in snow and fast asleep, which could have been a sleep to death. He emphasized the importance of helping one another. A helping hand or even an encouraging word could work wonders in boosting morale.

While this pep talk was going on, Filomena had been busy in the kitchen finishing off what she had already started that morning. By the time the talk was over, Filomena had a hot dinner laid on. At least they would set off with full bellies.

26

It was later than anticipated by the time they set off. It was a tearful parting for Filomena, but she put a brave face on it. A bit of emotion spilt over as Philip and Filomena said their goodbyes. Everyone congratulated Filomena on the nice meal and all she had done for them, not forgetting the extreme danger she had run in helping them.

Everyone felt sad for Filomena, who was losing the love of her life. She had never recovered from her rapturous days at school with Philip, and his occasional holiday visits. She adored him and would always be there for him. But his path in life had led him in other directions. He realized that Fleur was made for him. The war had turned their lives into a turmoil, but whatever happened, he would always be wedded to Fleur and Fleurette.

With Pepino and the Major in the lead, the six set out on their hazardous journey. They were reasonably clad for the trek, and carried enough food for the estimated 12-hour trek.

The night was bright, with a touch of frost, which made for brisk walking to keep warm. There were few people about to notice the three pairs walking along at varying intervals but keeping in sight of the couple in front.

Pepino led them through the quiet streets of the outskirts of Sulmona. The few Italian and German soldiers they passed seemed oblivious of their presence and anxious to reach their destination, perhaps a warm bed or a comforting fire. It was that kind of a night.

They soon left the town behind for the snow-covered foothills. There, they turned right to face a gradual climb. They walked and climbed for several hours, which seemed eternal. Their walk became monotonous and dreamlike, and time lost its meaning as they placed one weary foot in front of the other like robots. Talking had long since faded, and the only audible sound was the crunch, crunch of boot on snow.

It seemed a lifetime before Shorthouse and Slater, the last pair, had caught up with the other four who had called a halt. They took this opportunity to refresh themselves with food and drink, while Pepino, between mouthfuls, explained through the Major that they were above the small town of Paleno, and that they now had to descend the mountain to cross the river and carry on along the foothills. It was at this point that they all changed their socks after massaging their feet. The socks from their trousers pockets felt warm and comforting, thanks to the caring wisdom of Filomena.

There was no time to dwell on this little comfort. '*Andiamo!*' said Pepino. They carried on as before, only this time it was downhill.

At times they followed Pepino's example, and pulled the tail of their overcoats between their legs and swished down the mountain on their arses, like kids at Christmas. It was exhilarating but hazardous, trying to avoid trees and bushes. They were all fairly lucky, apart from Sam, who lost his sense of direction and balance and straddled a small tree and put his marriage prospects in jeopardy. It looked comical, but they were too tired to laugh, though Shorthouse got a little of his own back, for a change.

'Trust thee to get thi' cock in t' way. I don't know what mi' sister'll think o' that.'

'Oh, stop thi' whittlin', clever clogs, an' keep thi' hands on thi' goolies or tha' might finish up a eunuch!'

Descending the mountain offered a little *divertissement*, and a break from the upward grind. The town below looked peaceful enough. They made their way along a quiet road which led to the bridge. Pepino called a halt and told them to hide behind a low wall, while he went on alone to reconnoitre the bridge. All was well. Pepino beckoned the party to join him. This they did, but as they left the bridge, there was a sudden splutter of a machine-gun, which came from an island in the middle of the river. Pepino started running and beckoned the others to follow. They ran like the very devil, but faster. They ran and walked alternately for an hour or so. Of course Pepino knew where he was going. He disappeared into the woodland which came down to the river.

If they thought the first part of the journey was hard, they were in for a shock. Pepino was a hardened mountaineer, having served in the 'Alpinis' – a crack mountain regiment. He had leg muscles of iron. He urged them along at a cracking pace. They followed, their leg muscles objecting to the point of seizure, and chests fit to burst. They put their trust in Pepino and soon found themselves in an obscure derelict cattle shed, one corner of which had a bit of roof intact. They huddled together like a bunch of clapped-out ponies fighting for air.

Pepino disappeared for a while, then reappeared in a surprisingly cheerful mood. He said they were lucky, though they didn't feel it. He said they hadn't been followed, but a ski patrol had just glided down the mountainside. Apparently he had just managed to drop behind a bush as they shot past.

'Tha' looks like bloody Santa Claus!' uttered Shorthouse, with a grin.

Pepino smiled, but didn't know why.

'Credo che staremo qua uno momento per mangiare!'

Shorthouse smiled, but didn't know why! But he did catch the last word – *mangiare* – which he did know: food. That brought a twinkle to his eyes as he grabbed his haversack.

Pepino had said, 'I think we'll rest here awhile and eat.' They were cheering words, which brought immediate action. The meal finished with Filomena's fat roosters looking like something the vultures had left behind, and a couple of sad-looking bottles of vino.

'My word! I was ready for that,' sighed the Major, adding another bottle to the pile.

They all took the opportunity to change their socks again and give their feet and legs a good massage. It was only a little thing, but in their condition, it took quite an effort; however, the results were well worth the trouble.

They set off again with renewed spirits. Pepino had explained, and demonstrated with a stick on snow, the route they had taken and what to expect on their next and, hopefully, final lap. He pointed out that they still had a lot of climbing to do, and a difficult mountain stream to cross. He was pleased with their progress so far, and instilled in them a note of encouragement and confidence.

Much of the remaining route was shielded by trees. They made full use of them. It was daylight now, and the distant rumble of shell-fire told them they were nearing their goal. In spite of the activity, Pepino insisted that they were fairly safe in that area; nevertheless, they kept their eyes peeled.

The six slipped and crunched ever upwards in the snow. Like automatons, their movements became mechanical, but sluggish and painful. No one felt inclined to talk, and as they progressed, their minds became numb. They concentrated every ounce of strength forcing one painful, weary foot in front of the other, until, exhausted and spent, they shuffled and stumbled to a halt on the rocky lip of a raging torrent.

'This is the mountains stream,' croaked Pepino with a sigh of relief.

'Bloody hell!' interjected Shortarse. 'Aren't we lucky it's only a mountain stream!'

'The worst is over,' continued Pepino, and added with a crafty smile, 'once we are on the other side.'

They sized up the gushing torrent from different angles, none of which instilled enough confidence to have a go. The angry water cascaded in pent-up bubbly foam as it escaped around the large conical-shaped boulders. They looked on in amazement at one another. Who was going to be the guinea pig? Silence! Then Pepino, who had crossed many times, though, he admitted, not when it was as bad as today, explained how to cross, and demonstrated with his arms and legs how to grapple with the huge boulders. Then to everyone's surprise, he took a running jump, hands outstretched to encircle the pointed top of the cone.

'It's easy! Now! One at a time. Come, Majore!'

The Major, to show an example, took a mighty leap, and

almost dislodged Pepino, who grabbed and held on to him. They still had a few other rocks to grapple with, but not quite so formidable as the first.

They all managed without getting too soaked. That is to say, all but Shortarse, who fell between two rocks and had to be hauled out by the scruff of his neck.

They collapsed in the shelter of a huge pine. Poor old Shortarse exclaimed as he started to wring out his clothes, 'I'm bloody soaked to the skin!'

Whereupon Sam retorted, 'Thi' mam allus said tha' were a bugger for wettin' thi' sen!'

They rested awhile, drying off around a little fire Pepino had made. The rest thought it was testing providence. Sam said, 'It's playin' wi' fire!' They were fairly well sheltered, with the hot embers of the fire still throwing out a bit of heat. Pepino judged it reasonably safe to stay a while longer and eat the remainder of the food, but to keep a bit of wine for the last lap.

'It's much easier from here on,' declared Pepino. 'There's one more hill to climb. Then it's downhill to the river, then we follow along its bank until we meet British troops at a little village called Casoli.'

This news gave them something to chew on. It gave a glimmer of hope, but if only it would loosen their cramp-prone muscles. Pepino, in his experience and wisdom, suggested having a good massage and a few loosening-up exercises. With his encouragement and demonstration, they willed their aching muscles to respond. It was a painful experience to start with, but they did benefit from it.

They put on a bold front and breasted the hilltop in fine style. Now it was a case of free-wheeling down to the river. They hadn't been told how far the river was, and were rather expecting to see it laid out before them as they topped the rise. Long before they reached the bottom of the valley, they found their ankles, and a different set of muscles came into painful use. It was difficult to choose which was the more painful, going uphill or down. Each was a crippling experience.

After what seemed a lifetime, they had the heartening sight of water sparkling in the sunlight, like finding an oasis in the desert. They did their best to give a cheer, but like the poor devils in the desert, their best was a weak frog-like croak. Nevertheless, the sight brought a sparkle to their eyes and a stimulated heartbeat.

Reaching the river wasn't the end of their troubles by any means. Even though the bank was fairly flat, there remained a good many miles of hard slog. Ten hours of non-stop tramp. Because of crippling fatigue, it was increasingly necessary to call a halt for a breather. Over the river there was a ding-dong of a battle taking place between opposing artillery batteries. They really felt now that they were walking into the thick of it, especially when a couple of stray rounds fell into the river in front of them, much too close for comfort.

'That's not bloody fair,' said Shortarse, popping behind a convenient bush to crap and finish off what the shells had started.

'I can't take thi' anywhere without thi' disgracin' thi' sen,' chided Sam. 'I don't know what thi' sister will say when I tell her,' he added, with a cheeky grin.

Changing the subject, Treadwell said, pointing to the river, 'Look there! That shell in the river might have saved our bacon!'

There were several quite sizeable fish floating on the surface. Pepino cut a long stick and fished out three big ones. Smiling, he said, holding up the fish, '*Mangiare più tardi.* To eat later.'

In spite of the sporadic bursts of gunfire, the six made their way along the river bank. The odd round or two which came their way did little damage, but helped them to forget their aches and pains for a moment and, like a kick up the arse, put a little more pep into their pace. Soon the stray shells were exploding behind them.

The trail went endlessly on, and it wasn't until they came to a bridge that the party came to a sudden halt.

'Halt! Who goes there?' The order rang out crisp and clear.

They stopped in their tracks, looking round.

'Advance one, and be recognized!' Whereupon the Major went forward to the bridge, waving his white handkerchief. He explained that they were British soldiers of a demolition squad, returning to their lines after completing their assignment.

The sergeant was a member of The Royal West Kents. They shook hands and the sergeant beckoned the rest of the party to join them. Soon the six were warming themselves by a crude stove made from petrol tins and nursing large mugs of hot tea. In no time at all a lorry arrived to take them into Casoli, where the headquarters was situated.

After being interrogated by the Commanding Officer, the five said their thanks and goodbyes to Pepino and wished him a safe return. Then they piled onto the waiting truck to take them to Salerno. There, they were given new clothes, a good hot meal, with wine and the comfort of a blazing fire.

Come evening, they were given a large empty room in the village hall. There were palliasses, pillows and blankets. Dog-tired, with sore feet and aching muscles, they were soon peacefully asleep, and they slept the clock round. It was only the nagging pangs of hunger that eventually roused them.

The cookhouse staff must have taken pity on them, for they had everything they would expect of a good English breakfast. With that under their belts, they ventured out along the beach.

'There's been a rare old rumpus going on here,' said Sergeant Cook.

They surveyed the aftermath of the battle which had taken place along the seafront. There were both German and British tanks, guns, vehicles and equipment of every kind scattered about everywhere. Repairable British tanks were being moved to workshops, and a burial party was carrying out the gruesome task of registering and burying the bodies.

That evening, after receiving cigarettes and goodies from the Red Cross, they were given tickets to Tommy Trinder's Ensa Show. That was their last night in Italy.

The following morning they were driven to the airfield, where they boarded an RAF plane for England. From the airport, the five were taken to London and direct to the War Office, where they were congratulated on a job well done and debriefed on the way the action was carried out. Their documents, leave passes and travel warrants were already made out and handed to them with their pay.

Before parting for good, the five went out for a meal to Lyons Corner House. They all exchanged addresses and promised to have a reunion after the war.

They all went their own ways, except Shorthouse and Slater, who lived in the same Yorkshire town of Ilkley.

27

Major Philip Pipkin-Brodeau, feeling a little bit sad at the parting, made his way to St Pancras Station, and went to the telephone kiosk. There was no way of getting in touch with Fleur, Fleurette and Lucile. Paris was out of the question – it was still occupied. He didn't even know if they were still in Paris. They could be anywhere.

He did know where to find his mother, so he phoned Slippery Edge Farm in Ashover. It seemed a lifetime since he was last in Ashover.

At last a voice answered. 'Hello, Mary speaking.'

'Hello, Mam. *C'est Philip ici, je parle de Londres. J'attend le train à Chesterfield.* Oh! My train is just in, see you in three hours, all news then, must go! Bye for now, Mam.'

Philip dashed off to catch his train. It was overflowing with soldiers and kitbags. He almost entered a third-class in the scramble, then checked himself just in time to remember the crown on his shoulders. He extricated himself from the maddening crush, and found a nice corner seat in a first-class compartment. He had managed to get a daily paper, and settled himself down to catch up on the news. Lots had happened since he was last in England. Soldiers were everywhere. The whole population seemed to be in some uniform or other, and catching some of the conversation, it became obvious that the Allies were tooling up for the invasion of Europe. Troops he noticed from the carriage window all seemed to be heading south.

Philip's eyes soon became weary from reading, and maybe a little from the journey, and in spite of the lovely young lady opposite trying to play footsie with him, the rhythmic motion and the sound of wheels on steel soon lulled Philip into a dreamy, contented slumber.

Philip did not realize how much the military mission had taken out of him, plus the slog over the mountains and perhaps, his bit on the side – though Philip would never regard Filomena as such. Nevertheless, all this had taken its toll. To put it bluntly, Philip was exhausted and in need of time to recuperate.

He slept the sleep of the dead, much to the disappointment of the lovely young lady opposite with the itchy foot and doubtful intentions. After about 150 miles of sleep, Philip awoke with a start, as he felt the sudden braking and the train coming to a halt, and saw all the passengers gathering their belongings and making for the exit.

'This is Chesterfield, sir,' said an old lady in passing, realizing that Philip had just woken up.

'Thank you, madam,' replied Philip. 'I must have dropped off.'

He made a scramble for the exit. The first person he clapped eyes on was his mother, who had a puzzled look on her face, wondering if Philip had missed his train. Her face brightened and her eyes sparkled in recognition as Philip, the last one to leave the train, suddenly stepped straight into her arms.

'Oh Philip!' she said in surprised relief. 'I was just thinking you had missed your train! *Comment vas-tu, mon cher?*'

'All the better for seeing you, Mother!'

Mary had come by car; she had been economizing on her petrol allowance in order to have plenty for Philip to enjoy his leave when he came home. Of course it had been a great surprise when she heard his voice on the telephone. Until that moment she had no idea where he was or what he was doing, though she half suspected it would be something important, otherwise he would have been in touch with her. Mary had the good sense not to question him too much. If he had something to tell her, he would do so in his own time.

Philip picked up his holdall, his only item of luggage. Mary snuggled her arm through his as they made their way to the car. She drove over the cobbled road which wound its way past the old Crooked Spire.

'Mother, it seems ages since I saw the Crooked Spire! Nothing seems to have changed.'

'Oh, hardly anything! Apart from the blackout and dimmed lighting, which are a necessary nuisance. You'll find shops and cafés more limited as to what is available. You'll be lucky if you can find an orange or a banana for sale. Nevertheless, we manage! You'll find lawns and parks, and any spare land, now growing vegetables and greens. The slogan today is "Dig for Victory". Of course, the farmhands eligible for call-up have now been replaced by girls of the Land Army. They do a really good job.'

'How have you coped with the bombing?' asked Philip.

'It hasn't been too bad here. We had two dropped in Clay Cross and one or two in Tupton. After Clay Cross works, I suppose. I feel sorry for people in London and the thickly populated big cities. They are feeling the gruesome horrors of war, night after night. The casualties are horrific! It certainly reminds us that there is a war on!'

'The real war will start when we invade Europe,' said Philip, and continued, 'I am fearful of that. The casualties will be catastrophic on both sides. I shudder to think of it. Let's not dwell on it, and let's enjoy ourselves while we can.'

'Yes, you're right, Philip. Let's enjoy your leave and think of nice things.'

'Let's talk about the farm. Have you much stock these days?'

'No, just a few hens and a couple of pigs, and of course Clare. She's getting a bit long in the tooth now, but she's one of the family. I keep her for Sammy's sake. He's as devoted to her as I am. He rides her now and then, and she follows him around like a dog, as do the pigs, given the chance.

'Sammy's on his own now. He was devastated when his mother died. I feel really sorry for him. He was so distraught, he ran away one day. Robert found him on the moors and brought him back, and saw to the funeral. Since then I've taken Sammy in hand. I see he gets a good meal every day and generally keep an eye on him. Everything is running quite smoothly now. Most of the land is rented out and Sammy's plot makes me almost self-sufficient.'

'How are Uncle Robert and Sally?'

'Oh, they are fine. I see quite a lot of them. They both still belong to the choir. Robert still rides, and takes Sammy with him quite often – that is, of course, when he isn't on duty at Chesterfield Station, where he enjoys doing his bit as a RTO. But enough of the war. I've saved enough petrol coupons so that we can travel around, and perhaps catch up with relatives and friends. The car is yours for your leave, so feel free to enjoy yourself. If you do that, I'll be happy.'

'Thanks, Mam! We'll enjoy it together. I'm in need of a rest and a break.'

Philip enjoyed the journey to Ashover. Nothing had changed. The countryside looked just as quiet and peaceful as he remembered it. Soon Mary was turning down the lane to Slippery Edge Farm. Sammy was by the gate to welcome them. Clare, nuzzling his neck, looked up in surprise.

'Hello, Sammy!' called out Philip, shaking him by the hand. 'I'm terribly sorry to hear about your mother, you must miss her terribly.'

'Yes I do, Master Philip. These things happen you know, and we who are left just have to get on with life. It's nice to see you again, Master Philip.'

Mary and Philip disappeared indoors. Mary, as was the custom, put on the kettle to make tea. Philip noticed that the table was already laid. There were four cups and saucers, and by the time the kettle was on the boil, Uncle Robert and Sally were crossing the threshold. There were welcoming handshakes all round and a big kiss from Sally. Mary appeared with a tray. '*A table*,' she invited, whereupon everyone sat down.

'Help yourselves,' encouraged Mary, as she made to pour the tea.

Philip, always polite, thanked his mother for laying on such a sumptuous meal, and thanked Uncle Robert and Sally for joining them.

'You don't think we were going to be left out of it, Philip,' joked Robert. 'This was all planned months ago! Wasn't it, Mary?'

'Of course it was. The only thing was, we didn't know when!'

The four settled down to do justice to such a spread, as questions and answers passed from one to the other.

This was the kind of reunion with the appropriate lavish meal meant to be lingered over. When at last it was over, as generally happens, the two women volunteered to clear the table and wash the pots, while the two men volunteered to serve the drinks and put the world to rights.

That evening was one of the many evenings spent together, sometimes at Robert's, often playing cards or dominoes, other times just chatting and enjoying one another's company.

Daytimes were spent visiting friends and relatives or making trips into the countryside, with the occasional picnic or meal out. Philip managed to get in a bit of riding with Uncle Robert and Sammy. They all enjoyed the exhilarating gallops along the valley, by the riverside. It was refreshing and sharpened the appetite, which pleased Mary, who liked to see her cooking appreciated.

Come Saturday, Philip, feeling the need of younger company, asked his mother if she minded him taking the car into Clay Cross to the tanner hop at the Brotherhood Hall. It was a wooden construction. The floor was reasonably good for dancing, especially when dusted with chalk.

Philip, by chance – or that's what he would say – met one of the Marriott girls shopping and invited her out to the dance. She accepted eagerly. It was at a previous tanner hop that he had met her. On that occasion they had missed the last bus and walked through the fields back to Ashover. This time they did it in style in Mary's car.

It was obvious as he came down for breakfast that his evening at the tanner hop had been a success. He was bleary-eyed and dreamy, and his mother resisted making any comment.

It was that morning, having a quiet breakfast with his mother, that their conversation touched on personal matters.

Several times both had been on the point of asking, 'Have you heard or seen anything of Dad?'

It fell to Mary finally to ask this anxious question.

'No, Mother,' he said. 'I've been wanting to ask the same question. The last time I spoke to him, he was still in Marseilles and working at the factory as usual. But I must say he wasn't very happy. He was toying with the idea of taking a more active role in the war. What he meant was anybody's guess. That's as much as I know, and not much help, I'm sorry to say. If I get to know any news of him, you'll be my first priority.

'It is much the same with Fleur. I have no idea where she and Fleurette and Lucile are. I wrote to her when in France, but had no reply, which at the time, when the Germans were pressing hard and our positions were in disarray and fluctuating, was not surprising. I don't think there is much chance of finding out anything until we make a landing. Then there will be all hell let loose! I'm very worried, Mother. There's no way of getting to know anything. Everything is hush-hush. Perhaps I'll try the Red Cross. When I reach my unit, I shall leave no stone unturned to find out what has happened to them, and Dad.

'I am in the French Army, and only seconded to the British Army. Don't worry about it, Mother! I shall find a way, if there is a way. I feel that everything will turn our right in the end.'

'What are you doing this morning, Philip?'

'I think I'll have a stroll down the village and see a few friends, and have a good think about my situation and a way to get to France. Perhaps this cool, fresh breeze will blow away a few cobwebs and produce clear, inspired thought.'

Philip set off at a leisurely pace. It was a good mile and a half into Ashover, the way he planned it, which gave him ample time to grapple with his thoughts. But try as he may, he felt trapped in a web of circumstances with no escape and no answers. Eventually his thoughts strayed to Fleur, Fleurette and Lucile. He tried to imagine what it would be like to meet them all again. What would he say to them? He pictured Fleur and Lucile, with pretty Fleurette running into his open arms. He felt her soft warm face on his cheek and a little hand twiddling his ear, and tears of happiness streamed down his face. His mind strayed into a world of fantasy.

Suddenly a voice cut across his thoughts. 'Hello, Philip. Did you really enjoy the dance?' Then with a closer look, 'Have you been crying?'

'No, Molly, I've just caught a fly.' Then, blinking and giving his eye a wipe with his handkerchief, he declared it felt much better. 'Yes, I did enjoy the dance. And how about you?'

'It was lovely, Philip. I enjoyed every minute of it! And it was nice to be driven home, even though the car got a bit hot and had to rest halfway to cool off,' she added, with a coy little smile.

'I'm sorry I didn't notice you coming towards me. I was daydreaming as usual. I'm just strolling down to the village to meet a few natives.'

'Will I see you again before you leave?'

'It's hard to say, Molly. I'm expecting to be called back any day. I always give a sigh of relief when I see the postman pass, and so does Mother. I hope I'll be able to take you again to the dance. It was fun, wasn't it?'

'Yes, it was great.'

There was no one around. Philip gathered her to him for a hug and a kiss. 'That's just in case,' he said, with a smile, and added, 'Keep your fingers crossed! You never know.'

'I always keep everything crossed – you know that, don't you?' she called back over her shoulder, with a cheeky smile.

Philip, deep in thought, continued on his way. He was thinking about the good old days when his grandparents, George and Sara, were alive. As he turned the corner leading up to the church, his eyes were drawn to the flower display in the corner shop window. The thought of his grandparents and the flowers beckoned him into the shop. He chose a large bunch of mixed sweet-smelling flowers, and continued slowly and thoughtfully up the hill towards the church. The church yard was tidy, and the graves well cared for, borne out by the display of freshly cut flowers. Philip tidied the vases on his grandparents' graves, discarding the dead flowers and replacing them with his fresh ones. He stepped back to admire the effect of his handiwork, muttering to himself. 'I'm sure Grandad and Grandma would be pleased.' Satisfied, he stood there for several minutes, head bowed in reverence. He uttered a little prayer to the vision he had of his grandparents sitting in their armchairs by the fire, the cat and dog lying peacefully in their usual places. That is always how he would remember them. Philip felt at peace with himself as he walked slowly away. He strolled along thoughtfully back to Jack Straw's blacksmith's shop, wondering if he would still be there.

It wasn't long before he could hear the tap-tap of hammer on iron, as something was being fashioned into shape. Sure enough Jack was there, sitting in the same spot as Philip last saw him, even at the same table, with a bottle and glasses.

'There you are, Philip,' he said, greeting him. 'I've set the table ready,' he added, pointing to the bottle and glasses. 'I heard you were home. I was hoping you would give us a call.'

'I'm pleased to find you still here, looking fit and well, and I see Willy Blossom is still knocking hell out of his horseshoes.'

'Oh ay, Philip. He's a good chap at his job.'

'So he should be. Look who trained him.'

'Well, I've always done my best for him, and I'm pleased with the result. Anyway, sit thi' sen down, an' tell me how things are with you. There th'are, get that down thi',' he ordered with a smile, then he called over to Willy, 'Come on and join us.'

'It's just like old times,' said Willy. 'Nothin' much changes!'

The three chattered away for a good hour, and the empties on the table stood in testimony to friendship.

Philip asked about Prospero De'ath, one of the oldies in the community.

'He popped off suddenly – a heart attack, they said. He was on his way to measure up poor old Mrs Grimshaw from School Lane. She'd been hangin' on for ages. Prospero's son has taken over the business.'

According to Jack, young De'ath had the same solemn countenance and adeptness with his tape measure as his old man, and as keen an eye for prospective customers.'

'He fair gives me the shudders, the way he look me up an'

down when he comes in here. I'm sure he has all my measurements in his little notebook.'

'Oh don't worry, Jack! He'll have a long time to wait. Anyway, how's bobby Pringle? Have they fixed him up with a car yet?'

'I asked him the same question the other day when he popped in for a chat. He said, "Not bloody likely! I can't even get a new gear wheel for this owd bone-shaker. There's a couple of teeth missing on the gear wheel. I go along with a jerk, on every revolution of the wheel. It's like being on a cranky-horse on t' fairground. It's never gone right since I ran into Sammy's bloody runt."'

'By the way,' said Willy, 'how is Sammy getting on? He was really overwrought and confused when his mother died.'

'Oh, he seems to have settled down,' said Philip. 'Mother keeps an eye on him and makes sure he has at least a good meal every day, and gives him a few cakes and titbits to take home. Sammy is very easygoing and takes a real interest in the few animals and poultry, and his flower and vegetable plot is a real credit to him. He keeps Mother's house amply provided with flowers, not to mention fruit.'

The talk went on and on, and the time slipped by unnoticed.

Philip, suddenly aware of niggling hunger pangs, wound up the conversation, thanking Jack and Willy for their hospitality, and made his goodbyes, with a promise to call again if time permitted.

Feeling well informed and refreshed, he called in for a paper and returned home by the shortest route, going through the fields and following the river to Slippery Edge Farm. He loved this walk, and was beginning to feel the benefit of his holiday. He cherished a hope that the postman would pass by the farm for at least a few more days.

He arrived home feeling full of beans and as hungry as a horse.

'Good timing, Philip. You must have heard the pots rattling! Dinner is just ready for serving. Did you enjoy your walk?'

'It was great. I gathered all the latest news and tittle-tattle from Jack Straw. He's a scream and no mistake!'

Philip took one look at his mother, and saw she was red about the eyes, and that all was not well.

'What's wrong, Mother?' he asked.

She found it hard to reply, as she fumbled in her pocket to withdraw the telegram, bringing to an end Philip's leave and her hopes.

Philip read the telegram and the brief instructions with dismay, more for his mother than for himself. He was realistic and knew that each day without news was a bonus, that it was just a matter of time to this fateful day.

He was to leave tomorrow for Greenock, in Scotland, and was to report to the RTO, who would give him instructions and arrange transport to his unit. It all smacked of hush-hush, and set Philip wondering what the powers that be had in store for him.

Philip put his arms around his mother to comfort her. 'Try not to worry, Mother,' he said. 'It's not the end of the world! And I'll be able to get a leave from there. Now let's sit down and enjoy this nice meal you've cooked.'

Each getting a grip on their emotions, they sat down and talked about everything under the sun, rather than what was uppermost in their minds. Later, Robert and Sally came down for a farewell drink. It helped to smooth over the sorrows of tomorrow.

Uncle Robert offered to drive the four of them down to the station to give Philip a good send-off. It was greatly appreciated and would make the parting less emotive.

28

Philip wanted to say goodbye to Sammy, so immediately after an early breakfast, he took him a mug of tea and had a few words with him.

'Sammy,' he said, handing Sammy his mug of tea, 'I'm leaving this morning, and I just wanted to have a few words with you before going, and to say goodbye. It may be a long time before I return, and I want you to promise me to look after my mother while I'm away. Will you do that for me?'

'Of course I will, Master Philip. I'll look after her as long as I live. Miss Mary is like a mother to me. I'll never let her down. Don't worry, I'll still be here when you come back!'

'I hope so, I do hope so.'

He shook hands with Sammy, who was trying hard not to show the tears that were clouding his eyes.

'Goodbye, Sammy,' he said.

'Goodbye, Master Philip, and try not to worry, and come back safely!'

At eight sharp, the four waved goodbye to Sammy as they set off for Chesterfield. There was no heavy luggage to lug around, Philip's impedimenta consisted of his holdall.

The train was on time, which thankfully avoided long, lingering goodbyes. Just time for a quick handshake, a big hug and kiss for Mary and Sally, and Philip was on his way. Apart from reading his newspaper from cover to cover, and making a pig of himself with Mary's generous packet of sandwiches, his journey to Greenock was uneventful. The latter part was an uncomfortable sleep which left him with a stiff neck and a cramped leg. It was therefore with a sigh of relief when at long last the train applied its brakes to puff and shudder to a stop in Greenock Station.

The RTO was pleasant, but brisk and to the point. There was no information forthcoming, beyond saying that he would organize transport as requested. He couldn't give the destination or how long the transport would be. Philip, somewhat taken aback, wandered into the restaurant to wonder what all the secrecy was about. He bought a book and a meal, and settled down to await being paged. He was not in the best of moods.

Back in Chesterfield, Mary, Robert and Sally left the station a little saddened, though doing their best to keep up a light-hearted conversation. Robert had to go on duty, and was a little pressed for time. He was obliged to rush back, drop Mary off, and dash back to Chesterfield, to his part-time job as RTO.

Mary, back home, felt weary and forsaken. She was worried about Philip. He hadn't told her about his job, and Mary suspected it to be secret and dangerous. He was like his father, who wanted to be in the thick of it. Charles was in France somewhere. She felt he was dead, a feeling that had haunted her for months. She made herself a cup of tea, which did little to alleviate her tormented mind. Overcome with all her anxieties, she burst into tears of despair.

She was still crying when Sammy, hoping to cheer her up, arrived with an armful of beautiful mixed flowers.

Seeing Mary in a distressed state, he came in and closed the door.

'Whatever's the matter, Miss Mary?' he said. He was visibly shaken. He had never seen her cry. Out of his depth, he trembled; his eyes filled with tears in sympathy, but he was at a loss to know what to do.

Mary stood up, wiping her eyes. Seeing Sammy in tears with his armful of flowers touched her emotions profoundly.

'Come here, you big softy,' she said between her sobs. She held out her arms invitingly as he was drawn towards her. She held him in a close embrace; putting her lips close to his, she whispered, 'You and I are birds of a feather, both alone in the world.'

Sammy didn't quite understand the import, but he gradually overcame his fear and shyness. He felt the closeness and the warmth of her body, and responded to her kisses. Her delicate perfume excited him. He felt his manhood rising to the occasion, but this was a new experience for him, and he was incapable of taking the initiative.

Mary, sensing his gaucheness, slipped her hand down his thigh and grappled with his flies. She had to undo all his buttons before, with a gasp of wonder, she held a handful of throbbing delight.

Sammy, in his innocence, was like a lamb being taken to slaughter. Mary drew him to the couch. His face was one of amazement as she slipped off her knickers and lay down. She had to do everything for him, but he soon cottoned on; but then, to Mary's ecstasy, he performed like a bull at a gate. This was his first sexual experience, and as for Mary, it was her most pleasurable encounter since Pierre the milkman in Marseilles.

In spite of Sammy's bashfulness, he had certainly lifted Mary out of the doldrums and caused her to examine herself, her life and her direction. There were too many ifs and buts where Charles was concerned. He was in France, keen to get involved in the fighting, and could be dead. She had no communication with him, and there was no way of knowing until after the war was over, and that could drag on for years. As for Philip, his life was clothed in secrecy, and his silence regarding his part in the war spelt danger. There was no address to write to, and no communication allowed.

Mary decided to live her life in today's situation, and not as it might be at some hypothetical date in the future. Mary was no chicken now; life was slipping by and tomorrow might be too late. Let the future take care of itself.

She laid tea for two on the kitchen table, then went down the yard to call Sammy, who appeared in a flash.

'I've got tea ready, Sammy. Come inside for it today. I want to have a talk with you.'

'Right, Miss Mary. I'll just wash my hands first.'

He entered the kitchen sheepishly, half expecting to be in the doghouse, but Mary's smiling face soon allayed his fear.

'Sit down, Sammy,' she said, indicating a chair, and passed him a cup of tea.

Sammy was quick to notice it was a cup and saucer, and not a mug.

'Help yourself to whatever you'd like,' she said, with a wave of her hand.

'Thank you, Miss Mary,' he replied, choosing a sandwich.

'Now then, Sammy,' she said, 'There are one or two things I would like to put to you. First, from now on call me Mary.'

'Yes, M-Mary.'

'Now that you are on your own, like me, how would you like to live here? There are several bedrooms – you could have one of those. What do you think of the idea?'

'I'd like it, M-Mary.'

'Oh good. I have other ideas too. If this arrangement suits you, you could sell your cottage, which would give you a tidy sum of money to start a bank account for yourself. I wouldn't want rent. This is a big house and I find it lonely here on my own. I know I have a cat and dog. I talk to them, but it's not the same as having someone to talk to. I would feel safer too if you were staying here. I'll look after you, and I'll make sure you have nice, well-fitting clothes to wear. I'll feed you and do your washing. Now what do you say to that, Sammy?' she asked, with one of her sweet, disarming smiles.

'I don't know what to say,' he replied, choking with tears. 'Nobody has ever wanted me, or ever given me as much thought as you, Mary. There! I've said it – Mary! I think it's wonderful! I'll look after you to the end of my days. Thank you, Mary! You'll never regret it.' He sobbed into his handkerchief, to hide his emotion.

'Oh Sammy! Don't cry! Come here and let me give you a little cuddle.'

* * *

Philip, at Greenock railway station, was anything but pleased after the RTO's cold, uncommunicative reception and the hours spent waiting for transport. At last he was paged on the tannoy, ending his annoying wait. He picked up his holdall, fixing the RTO's eyes with a withering glare, and marched out of the station to the awaiting transport.

The driver saluted and opened the door.

'What kept you?' demanded Philip, giving vent to his frustration.

'Sorry, sir, but I came as fast as I could, and as soon as I could.'

'Sorry, driver! I've been waiting for hours here, kicking my heels, but I shouldn't be taking it out on you. Have you eaten?'

'No, sir.'

'Right, pull into the first restaurant. I'm starving, and I expect you could do with a meal too.'

'I won't say no, sir. Thank you very much, sir.'

It wasn't long before a likely-looking place came into view. The driver turned in and found a vacant parking space.

'By the way, what's your name, driver?'

'Summers, sir. Private Summers.'

They found seats and ordered their meal.

'Where are we making for, Summers? Does it have a name or is it a secret?'

'It's supposed to be secret. It's nothing but a mass of wooden huts surrounded by barbed wire and patrolled by guards. All the activity is behind closed doors. It's called Peak Point. It's miles from anywhere. It's frightfully hush-hush, and that's about all I can say. No one seems to know what's going on, and you need a pass to go to the toilet,' he added, with a witty smile.

'It sounds an exciting place. I can't wait to get there!'

'It's like a POW camp, sir, but not so noisy. Whatever goes on, it's very quiet. It's more like a morgue and very eerie at times.'

Arriving at Peak Point, the vista was just as Summers had

described. It was like the back of nowhere, as silent as a graveyard, with not even a bird in sight.

Hell, thought Philip, nothing here to get excited about. He dismissed Summers, and made his way to the gate. The guard saluted, received Philip's papers, and handed him over to the duty sergeant.

'Will you come this way please, sir,' he said, standing aside to let Philip pass.

He was directed to the Colonel's office, where he tapped on the door.

'Enter!' said a commanding voice, and Philip opened the door. 'Come in, Major Pipkin-Brodeau, take a seat,' he said, pointing to a vacant chair. 'I've been expecting you. As a matter of fact, I'm just browsing through your record. You are just the kind of person we are looking for. I see you are fluent in several languages. A polyglot, no less! I understand French is your natural language?'

'Yes, sir. I was born in Marseilles. My mother is English and my father French.'

'So far, so good,' said the Colonel. 'Now I'll come straight to the point of why you are here. Our contact man with the French underground movement, the Maquis, has been taken by the Gestapo. I won't try to pull the wool over your eyes. He will be shot, and maybe tortured first. So you see, the Gestapo may have forced vital information from him which could prove fatal to anyone taking his place. Whoever does take his place must be on his guard always and trust no one. Now, Philip – do you mind me calling you Philip?'

'No, sir.'

'Well, Philip, if you wish to change your mind, now is the time to do it. This commission is for a volunteer. What is your answer?'

'I am French at heart, and my answer is yes.'

'Jolly good show, Philip, and the very best of luck. And by the way, on tomorrow's orders you will find your promotion to Colonel. Congratulations,' he said, shaking Philip's hand. 'That is all for now. I hope to see you in the mess tonight.'

'Thank you, sir. I'll be there!'

* * *

The course was tailored to Philip's particular requirements. The language part was skipped. There was a rundown of the workings of the organization and the pitfalls to be avoided. The main part was wireless communication, coding and decoding, the administration of airdrops, and the safe hiding and distribution of arms, ammunition, explosives or whatever.

Philip did not let his excitement at returning to France interfere with his course. His reason for volunteering to go depended on its success. His yearning for news of his wife Fleur and family, and of his father, hinged on the outcome of his task.

The course was short and very concentrated, owing to the urgency of replacing the poor devil taken by the Gestapo. Luckily Philip was the kind of person with a voracious capacity for absorbing detailed information, someone who could quickly weigh up a situation, make a quick balanced judgement and decide the appropriate action to take. His bravery and courage had already been demonstrated and were never in doubt. He exuded confidence in his command of people, and earned their trust.

Colonel Philip Pipkin-Brodeau, totally immersed in his course, had little time for pleasure, and the only relaxation he allowed himself was to write to his mother. His news was very restricted, which caused him to invent interesting events or situations to bring a smile to his mother's face. All their mail was strictly censored and routed through the War Office, which did nothing to allay his mother's fears and premonitions. She was no fool, and realized that Philip was in the thick of it – where he would want to be. She wondered sometimes why she had had a son, and not a daughter.

With two months' intensive training into the world of wireless and radar, coding and decoding, Philip felt full of self-confidence and ready to play his part in the rescue of airmen shot down and prisoners of war on the run. He felt proud and honoured to be trusted with the organization of airdrops and the distribution of arms, ammunition and explosives to the

Maquis and the French Resistance. He had learned as much as possible about the most trusted members and a few of their names, and he had been warned about the German wireless detection vans and their skill in plotting radio transmitters.

The members and staff of Peak Point gave Philip a smashing party the night before his departure. He had not been a regular frequenter of the mess because of his commitment and dedication to his course; everyone admired him for it, and crowded round to wish him loads of success and a safe return. Philip was touched to the core by the overwhelming warmth shown to him.

He had already had a course of instruction in parachuting, so it was no daunting surprise when during his last briefing he was told that he was to be dropped in a wooded area north of St Palais in the Basses-Pyrénées. This part of France was new to Philip, but with the up-to-date maps issued to him, he would soon get his bearings. He had already committed to memory a few of the safe houses in the area, and of course he knew about the capture of the poor devil whose place he was taking, who controlled the radio link with England.

Philip did not know how far the rot had set in. He did know whether the Gestapo had invented lots of ingenious ways of extracting information from prisoners. He would have to be very wary about trusting anyone, an unenviable situation for anyone to find himself in. He gave an involuntary shudder as his mind flashed over some of the methods the Gestapo might be trying out at that very moment on the hapless radio operator.

It was Philip's task to re-establish radio contact with England and repair the linkage of safe houses for RAF crews and POWs on the run. He had already come to terms with the job, although the thought of what was involved, and the undeniable danger in every step, brought a little flutter of butterflies to his tummy. He knew from experience that once safely on the ground, he would feel more in tune with his mission, and steadfast in what was expected from him.

29

The crucial day arrived, and for Philip it was go, go, go. At the crack of dawn he was discreetly whisked away by car, southwards to an undisclosed RAF airfield. He was dressed in civilian clothes of French origin, as was firmly established by an odd tatty label still attached to his jacket. His pockets contained his identity card, a cigarette lighter, money and a few odds and ends one would expect to find. His identity was described as Philip Brodeau, easily verified by his certificate of education.

That evening, as dusk was falling, decked out in flying kit and parachute, he was driven out to the runway and the awaiting Lysander.

'This is it,' he said to himself, as he settled in the cockpit. At that moment he felt a flush of pride at having been chosen for such an important mission, and vowed not to let himself or his superiors down.

The engine was warmed up and throbbing rhythmically as the chocks were pulled away. The Lysander soon picked up speed and lifted off, to level out at the required height and disappear over the horizon.

The pilot kept up a conversation to pass the time, not forgetting to keep his eyes skinned for enemy aircraft, and Philip made sure the pilot didn't drop off to sleep. He thought it a good recipe to keep both on their toes. Actually Philip was able to learn quite a lot about the dropping area and the distance to certain towns and villages. It was obvious that the pilot had done this journey before. He said there were few Germans in this particular area, but plenty along the coast, but he pointed out that there was always a chance of finding a fighter on your tail.

Lady Luck must have been shining on them, for the skies remained clear. It was not until they were over France that they saw what looked like a rocket attack on a train. It was dark, and Philip could only guess what was happening by the long streaks of light and flashes of explosions; but of course, with his experience the pilot must have witnessed many such scenes.

The remainder of their journey was plain sailing, almost enjoyable. Approaching the dropping zone, the pilot gave Philip some last-minute instructions about the drop. There was to be a second parachute with a canister of equipment, wireless, small arms, ammunition and food. He said the area was well wooded with bushes and scrub, and that there should be no problem in hiding all the evidence of the drop.

'Take it for granted,' he warned, 'that people hearing a plane will search the vicinity, for one reason or another. We are approaching now. Remember what I have said – remove any evidence, then put as much space between you and the drop as you can before dawn. Here we are then! Good luck! Get ready, go!'

Philip plunged out into space, and plummeted down. With a sudden jerk, the chute opened, and Philip gave a sigh of relief. 'So far, so good,' he told himself. As he floated down, and in spite of the darkness, he had a cringing feeling of being watched by a thousand eyes. He felt naked and vulnerable. In the last minutes, everything that the pilot had said, and his training of dos and don'ts, flashed through his mind. Then in the last seconds he became aware of the ghostly shapes of trees and bushes leaping towards him. Then, with a sudden thud and a roll, he was safely down.

He allowed himself a moment of elation, then sprang into action. He quickly gathered in his parachute and slipped the harness. Looking around, he saw his other chute flop down as gracefully as a ballerina. He gathered it in and released the canister. His eyes settled on a clump of bushes, a likely spot to hide his parachutes. He made his way towards it. It seemed ideal for the purpose. Time was of the essence, he did his best with the situation as it was. He stuffed the parachutes and the canister out of sight and added a few branches to complete the job. Satisfied with his camouflage, he carried his small attaché case, in which was hidden his radio, and headed north. He munched a few biscuits and some chocolate to keep himself going until he found a suitable place to have a meal.

Reaching the outskirts of St Palais in the early morning light, he searched for somewhere to hide his radio until he had found a safe location to set it up. He wanted somewhere where it would be easily retrievable. The attaché case was small, battered and inconspicuous. The hedge and path he was following led to a gate, a road and, beyond, rows of houses. There was no sign of life anywhere, and the last thing he wanted was to be caught with a radio transmitter. He laid himself alongside of the hedge, and with his knife dug a hole big enough to hide the attaché case. Fortunately the ground was soft and sandy, and in no time at all the radio was fitting snugly in the hole. He quickly covered it over and placed a large stone on top. Philip then walked to the gate, counting his steps, 12 in all, and made a mental note of it. He carefully noted the street – Rue de la Gare – and the number of the house opposite the gate. Number seven.

Now free of the radio, he walked nonchalantly along the street, as though without a care in the world. It was still early, with few workers going about their business. Philip decided to break the ice. He stopped a middle-aged man and asked him if he could recommend a restaurant nearby where he could get a meal at a reasonable price.

'*Oui! Certainment, Monsieur,*' he replied, and directed him to the next street. Philip had plenty of francs, and felt quite at home with the language.

It was light and eight o'clock as he reached the café. It looked smart and inviting as he entered. The girl who served him was smartly dressed in a pretty uniform, with a headband and a pink ribbon tied in a bow. She gave a coquettish smile of welcome as she invited Philip to a table. He responded with a little sparkle in his eyes which sent a message of approval.

He was soon sitting comfortable with his coffee and croissants. He eyed up the girl, and pondered how she could fit into his scheme of things. Philip would not have given her a second thought, had she not flashed him a bewitching smile every time she appeared in his field of vision. She was obviously smitten by him.

Philip flagged her down as she was passing, and ordered another coffee. The coffee arrived, which gave Philip the chance to work his charm on her.

'Are you working all day?' he boldly asked.

'Not today. I finish at midday. Why do you ask?'

'I am at a loose end, and I was wondering if you would like to show me your beautiful town. I am a stranger here. I come from Marseilles. I decided to get out of it before the Americans attack, as they surely will.'

'Yes, sir! That would give me much pleasure!'

So it was arranged that they should meet at the café at 12.30.

Philip wandered around St Palais to familiarize himself with the general layout, but at 12.30 sharp he was standing by the restaurant, just as the girl came out of a side entrance.

They greeted each other in the traditional French way, with a little kiss on each cheek.

'Let me introduce myself. I'm Philip Brodeau.' He dispensed with the 'Pipkin bit' – too much of a mouthful, he thought.

'And I am Madeleine Renard.' She added, 'This is my mother's restaurant. I live here. Can you ride a cycle?' she asked.

'Yes,' he replied.

'Wait a moment,' and she disappeared, to return with two bicycles.

They cycled around, with Madeleine pointing out places of interest. Then she led the way along a towpath by the river. After a while they dismounted and pushed the cycles up the hillside away from the river to a shady clump of trees, to relax a little. Madeleine was a great conversationalist and exciting to be with. They lounged, side by side on the grass.

'Where are you staying?' she asked.

'I don't know yet. But I noticed a nice-looking hotel on the way here. I'll probably book in there.'

'Oh you don't have to, Philip. We have lots of room at home. Mother and I would be delighted for you to stay with us.'

'I would like that very much, if your mother is agreeable.' Philip leaned a little towards her, and gave her a little peck on the cheek.

She pulled Philip towards her. She then demonstrated to Philip how to kiss. After about ten minutes Philip, all hot and bothered, had to surface for air.

That was the start! Madeleine had an insatiable appetite which had to be satisfied.

'Oh God!' groaned Philip under his breath. 'What I have to do for King and Country!' Then on reflection he added, 'But I like it!' He dared not allow himself to think of Fleur, Fleurette and Lucile. He had tried to ring Fleur's apartment in Paris, but the telephone was cut off. He had no idea where they might be. Thinking about them might impede the job in hand. Better thrust all thoughts of them from his mind until the war was over, he decided, and concentrate on what he was here to do.

Madeleine's mother made Philip very welcome. That evening he broached the subject of Germany, and the German soldiers strutting about the streets of St Palais.

'I detest them!' said Madame Renard. 'I would do anything to see the back of them.'

Madeleine, just as scathingly added her little bit. 'They walk about as if they own the place, as if they were God's gift to the world!'

That night Philip was quite happy to curl up all snugly in a nice clean bed. He envisaged a good night's sleep, but someone else had other ideas.

The night was quiet and conducive to sleep, and Philip was about to drift off when a sudden slight rustle broke the silence, as if a mouse was playing with silver paper. He closed his ears and turned over. Then he felt the edge of the bed clothes lift, then the almost dainty feel of a fairy slipping imperceptibly beside him.

'I'll give you three guesses,' whispered a sweet little voice.

Philip was beyond guessing games. 'I give up.'

Everything was silent. The world was asleep as Madeleine moulded herself into the contours of Philip's body, and so they slept in blissful peace.

It was the slight squeak of the door and the chink of cups that alerted Philip. Madeleine with the coffee, he thought. But no! He could feel Madeleine's body almost welded to him. Philip, deeply embarrassed, peeped from under the sheets to see Madame Renard placing a tray on the table.

'Good morning, Philip! Have you slept well?'

'Like the dead, Madame Renard!'

'Good!' she replied, and disappeared.

Philip, somewhat shocked, turned towards the half-asleep Madeleine.

'It was your mother, Madeleine! How embarrassed I am.'

'Don't worry, my love. Mother is a woman of the modern world. She knows everything. Nothing surprises her.'

They sipped their coffee and chatted about this and that in a leisurely fashion, then Madeleine gave Philip a passionate kiss and a cuddle. She then excused herself, saying, 'I must go and dress now, and open the restaurant. You can stay in bed as long as you like. Come into the restaurant for breakfast. We'll be able to chat during slack moments.'

Philip, now alone, became engrossed with the complexities of the job in hand. Now that he shared Madeleine's bed, having surrendered to her charm, he felt certain of her trust. Her distrust and loathing of the Germans reinforced that trust, both in Madeleine and her mother. Philip nevertheless decided to tread with caution. He had the address of Madame Pinson, which was the last, and most southerly, of the safe houses in the chain.

He had to make a start somewhere, and Madeleine seemed the obvious choice. He decided to try his luck and sound her out.

The restaurant was very popular with the locals, and sought after by the Germans. It was during a slack moment when Madeleine came and sat down for a breather that Philip took the opportunity.

'Do you, by any chance, know of a certain Madame Pinson, Madeleine?' he said.

'Certainly,' she replied. 'She comes in here most days, for her afternoon tea. I don't remember seeing her yesterday, so most likely she will be in today.'

30

It was the following afternoon that Madame Pinson finally appeared. Madeleine waved her to her usual table. Philip, as prearranged, was sitting quietly at the next table. He gave a friendly bow in acknowledgement to Madame Pinson's *'Bonjour, Monsieur.'*

'Good afternoon, Madame Pinson,' Madeleine greeted her. 'I trust you are well?'

'Certainly, Madeleine, and your mother, she is well?'

'Yes, as always.'

After a little interchange of conversation, Madeleine introduced her to Philip. They exchanged pleasantries for a while, then at a most convenient moment, and well out of earshot, Philip explained briefly who he was and suggested that they should meet.

It was arranged that Madeleine and Philip should cycle over to her house that evening.

It was quite dark as Madeleine pressed the doorbell. Madame Pinson beckoned them in, and locked the door. The three sat around the table, and Madame plied them with a glass of wine.

'Now then, Philip! Down to business,' she said.

Philip explained that he was there to replace the contact man who had been taken by the Gestapo. He wanted to know the full extent of the damage to the escape route.

Madame Pinson explained as much as she could. Apparently the German radio detection van, which had been very active of late, had finally pinpointed the source of transmission and captured the operator and the wireless set. It was a tragic loss and finally the operator paid the penalty and was shot. Nothing more had happened, which made one believe that the poor chap had resisted to the end, without breaking down.

The remainder of the escape route was intact, but without a radio it was impossible to get supplies for the resistance, and there was a lack of information.

'Well, Madame Pinson, we'll soon put that right! All I need is a place to work from, and a link to the underground movement. I intend to move around with my radio, to make tracking more difficult.'

'Leave the underground to me, Philip. I have connections. I'll get in touch with Madeleine as soon as I have made contact. It may take a day or two.'

It was impossible to guess what the Gestapo might have found out. Their methods of extracting information were so ingenious and sophisticated that it was beyond belief. That being so, Philip had to believe the worst: that they probably knew everything.

'We'll be in this together, Philip,' said Madeleine. 'When I think of the brave lads at the front, how can anyone, given the chance, deny helping them?'

'You're right, Madeleine. You are very brave! Thank you. But are you sure you have thought it through? It's extremely dangerous. In for a penny, in for a pound, as the saying goes. In other words, there's no drawing back.'

'I'm sure, Philip! I am not the kind of person to change my mind. I won't let you down, and neither will Madame Pinson. Our families are as one, lifelong friends.'

'That's right,' added Madame Pinson. 'We are as one family.'

Philip searched the faces of the two women and saw nothing but the strong determination to see it through, to the bitter end if necessary.

'Well,' he said, 'before going further, I think it only fair and proper to tell you a little about myself. I am trusting you implicitly, and what I am about to tell you is for your ears alone, and deadly secret. The safety of many people depends on it, both French and English. Are you both absolutely sure you still wish to be involved?'

'We are both dedicated to it,' they replied as one voice. 'So fire away,' added Madeleine.

'Well, first of all, I am French, born in Marseilles. My father is French, my mother English. Most of my life has been spent in France, though I have lived, and have been to school, in both England and Italy. I am a Colonel in the French army but seconded to the British Secret Service. As you know, Madame Pinson, our contact man has been taken by the Gestapo and probably shot.'

Madeleine and Philip returned to the restaurant. Philip was still a little apprehensive about Madeleine's immediate readiness to offer her help. Had she really considered the true gravity of being caught by the Gestapo? To put his mind at rest, he felt honour bound to ask her again. At the risk of an exasperated reply he repeated his question. 'Are you really sure Made—'

He was cut short by Madeleine's impatient reply.

'Not again, Philip! Yes! Yes! Yes!'

Philip was quietly rebuked and accepted her confirmation with a big hug and a flurry of kisses, to which she responded with interest.

Madame Renard had prepared a nice evening meal, in spite of the shortages of choice endured.

It was not until after the meal that Philip and Madeleine were able to discuss their plans further. Madame Renard insisted on clearing the table and washing up, a very nice gesture, or was it a ploy to get Madeleine married off?

Madame Pinson, true to her word, was back at the restaurant on the third day to say that everything was set up for a meeting with an official of the underground resistance movement at Madame Pinson's house at eight o'clock.

At eight on the dot, Madeleine pressed the bell, and Madame Pinson ushered them inside. 'This is really cloak-and-dagger stuff,' murmured Philip to himself, as he felt a tingle of excitement surge through his body. In the secret confines of Madame's lounge, Philip and Madeleine were introduced to the official, always referred to as 'Albert'.

Albert was one of the two men who had organized the escape route, which shepherded pilot and crews of the RAF shot down in enemy territory, and escaped POWs, along the route to Spain and freedom.

Madame Pinson introduced Philip. 'This is Colonel Philip Brodeau, born in Marseilles, belonging to the French 7th Army, but now seconded to the British Secret Service, and this is Madeleine Renard, a dear friend of ours who helps her mother to run a restaurant in St Palais. That is where I am able, from time to time, to pick up scraps of information from the Germans who frequent it.'

'I, too, come from Marseilles, Philip,' said Albert. 'I came here with my best friend to set up the escape route.' He added, 'It was his idea. You wouldn't by any chance be related to my late friend Charles Brodeau?'

The answer was plain to see. Philip's smiling face suddenly changed and plunged into the depths of despair. 'It was my father,' sobbed Philip, his eyes flooding with tears.

'I'm terribly sorry, Philip! How insensitive of me. I should have realized.'

'Don't worry, you weren't to know. I knew he wanted to play a more active part in the war than making tanks to be used by the Germans. So it doesn't come as too much of a surprise to know what he was doing. It is still a shock, but at least I know the worst, and that saves me a lot of worry. How did it happen?'

'I feel partly to blame. Your father was totally involved in the rescue operation – nothing was too much trouble or too dangerous. He often took terrible risks, and he was wearing himself out. It was I who persuaded him to take a complete break and rest. He had bought a little cottage in Maisons Blanches, the village in which he was born.'

'Oh, I didn't know that, Albert. He must have bought it since we lost touch with him.'

'Yes, you're right. He thought it was nicely placed for a safe house. Actually it was never used. Charles reluctantly took my advice to take a good rest, he was visibly at the end of his tether. The way he met his end was an outrage, and beneath the dignity of the honour he deserved,' said Albert, and went on to explain how it happened.

Charles had retired to his cottage in Maisons Blanches, where he slept for several days, only getting up to feed and wash and use the loo. Unbeknown to him, two German soldiers had their throats cut during the night. The German soldiers rounded up as many of the villagers as they could find, including poor Charles, who was totally unaware of what was going on. They were lined up and shot. One of Charles's cousins, who happened to be away, came back and somehow managed to get permission to give him a proper burial. He was buried between the graves of his mother and father, as was their wish.

'That is as much as I know, and I am sorry to be the bearer of such terrible news. Charles was my best friend, and his death is a great loss to me, to his friends, and to the escape movement.'

Perhaps because of Charles's friendship, Philip and Albert had an instant rapport. Philip was keen to know all about the underground resistance movement, their needs and how best he could help. Albert went to lengths to explain that the invasion of Europe was inevitable and could happen at any moment. The French resistance movement was ready to assist when the time came. Their greatest need was more arms, ammunition and explosives in order to play a major part in attacking the enemy rear, their supporting echelons, supply lines and communication systems, which could mean success or failure to the invading armies.

Philip immediately saw the wisdom of such a move, and its potential for shortening the war, and asked, 'Is it possible to land a light aircraft in this area? Is there a flat tract of land, preferably obscured by hills or forest, where it would be possible to land or make a drop, and are there still enough willing hands to hide and distribute it where it would be most useful when the time came?'

'Well,' he answered, 'there are lots of hills and woodland. I am sure such a place can be found. Can you leave it with me for a day or two? I'll ask around, and see what I can come up with.'

'Right!' said Philip. 'We'll leave it like that for now. As soon as you have a plan, get back to me, and I'll do my best to get it all coordinated with London.'

Albert arranged to contact Madame Pinson as soon as he had sorted out a plan. A week dragged by, and no message from Albert. Philip began to worry and feared the worst. Then at the end of the second week Albert turned up, all smiles and sweetness, to the relief of Madame Pinson, who lost no time in alerting Philip and Madeleine. A meeting was arranged.

It transpired that a suitable landing site had been found, moreover the site had been checked and the few obstacles cleared. Albert passed over the map reference, and informed Philip that enough men had been found to outline the runway with torchlight and cover the surrounding area with automatic fire, if needed. Everything was set, and now it was up to Philip to do his stuff on the transmitter and hope that the RAF and the Met Office would in their turn choose the right weather and make a success of it.

31

Since Philip had found out about his father's death, he had been in a state of depression. There was no way of letting his mother know of the dreadful news. He had no idea where Fleur, Fleurette and Lucile were living. All the possibilities were churning round and round in his mind. It was only the love and attention showered on him by Madeleine that saved him from going mad. He felt sometimes that his head would burst.

Now that everything was in place for the landing, it only remained now for Philip to send off a coded message to set everything in motion. This new activity concentrated Philip's mind on his job in hand.

That evening Philip put his personal difficulties behind him and set to work compiling a list of things needed to be flown in to make the French Resistance Movement a force to be reckoned with, also the location, map references, landing place and the system of runway illumination. Everything would be ready to receive the plane for three consecutive nights, to allow for weather conditions.

That night, as darkness approached, Philip and Madeleine retrieved the transmitter from its hiding place and travelled to a secret position to transmit. Armed men of the underground cordoned off a large area of the forest. The transmission was carried out without a hitch, and the transmitter rushed back to its hiding place.

Philip, Madeleine, and Albert had a rendezvous at Madame Pinson's house later that night. They were welcomed with the usual customary friendliness by Madame Pinson. A quiet discussion ensued, helped along by a drop of Madame Pinson's best wine, of which she was justly proud.

It was during the discussion that Albert suddenly interrupted the conversation and recalled that when he and Philip's father first drove in to St Palais, it was to call on Charles's daughter-in-law and her sister – so they must have been some sort of relatives to Philip, he continued, looking at Philip.

Philip was flabbergasted. The mounting flush of colour on his face, and the flashing sparkle in his eyes, said it all. He could not contain himself. 'Fleur! It must be Fleur, and Lucile,' he stammered.

'I don't know why I didn't make a connection,' moaned Madame Pinson. 'They moved into Annette's house opposite, which I take care of. How stupid of me,' she gasped sorrowfully.

'Can I go and see them, Madame?' he asked eagerly.

'Oh! I'm very sorry, Philipo, Annette came and took them to her house at Tourne Hemme. It's a small village some distance from Calais.'

Philip's mind flipped. He was speechless. It was like a slap in the face, to suddenly find your greatest treasure, only to have it snatched away before you even saw it.

Madame Pinson was then the recipient of a barrage of questions from Philip. How were they? Was Fleurette well? How long did they stay? The questions were endless, and Madame Pinson flogged herself mercilessly for not putting two and two together to come up with the right answer. Finally she was calmed down by Philip, who apologized for ranting so. A calm settled over the assembly.

It was disappointing news to Philip that Fleur had moved, particularly as their paths had almost met. At least he now knew where they were and that they were alive and well.

The tragic and horrific circumstances of Charles's death was a bitter pill to swallow. Philip worried about his mother, and thought of possible ways of letting her know.

Philip had become so involved with the underground that his mind whirled with half-formed thoughts about his personal worries. He had worried himself sick trying to conjure up some way to communicate the sad news to his mother, when all the time he had a way at his fingertips. It took Albert's logic to point the way.

'Why don't you write a letter to your mother?' he reasoned. 'Perhaps the pilot will kindly post it for you on his return to England.'

'Albert,' replied Philip, as though a great weight had suddenly been removed from his shoulders, 'you're a genius! Why couldn't I think of that?'

Philip, once again with a clear vision, set to work immediately to write his letter.

During the last radio contact with London, it had been agreed that Philip should transmit again in seven days' time for final instructions. Now the seven days were up. Charles and Albert had practised to perfection, with the men of the resistance, all the sequences leading up to the actual landing and the speedy turn-round of the plane. Hopefully all the cargo would disappear into the safety of the woods within minutes of landing. The boundaries of the forest would be alive with armed partisans, all ready with their lives to ensure a successful operation.

Philip and Madeleine had, once again, successfully done their little bit, and received their final instructions. The cargo contained all the things asked for, and the plane would be in the landing zone at 10.30; and the message ended, 'Good luck to everyone, and out!'

At 10 o'clock that night everything was in place. There was a mounting aura of expectancy as the vital hour approached. The sky was clear and starry. All ears were tuned to the slightest sound, and all eyes turned skywards, searching for the least twinkle of light that would herald the plane's approach. Each minute now felt like an hour, the expectation was so intense. The agreed time passed, necks were stiff and aching, and hopes fading, when somewhere out there among the stars came the faint steady throb of an aero engine. Aches and pains forgotten, the atmosphere became electrified. The rigorous training paid off. By the press of a button, two parallel lines of light appeared in the clearing, coinciding with the flashing intermittent light from the plane. Then the bright flare at the end of the runway was set off to point out the direction of the landing strip.

Within seconds, or so it seemed, the plane was down. As it taxied to a halt near the perimeter of the forest, anxious figures emerged from the gloom to bear away to safety the packages as quickly as they could be lowered from the plane. The operation was done as speedily and efficiently as ants carrying off grains of sugar.

The plane was quickly turned around, but not before Philip had had a quick word with the pilot of the Lysander and handed over his letter to his mother, to be posted in England.

In a matter of minutes the plane climbed steeply, to clear the trees and disappear the way it had come. The runway, and every trace of the activity, disappeared as though by magic, allowing the peace and tranquillity to return.

Philip was highly delighted that his first operation was so far successful and hoped with all his heart that the Lysander would land safely in England and his letter would reach his mother.

Slippery Edge Farm, like the quaint old village of Ashover, was quiet and strangely peaceful. Only the occasional flight of planes, and now and then the faint crump of falling bombs, and the replying rumble of ack-ack, gave any hint of the life-and-death struggle going on elsewhere.

Philip's mother felt more contented and secure now that Sammy was living at the farm. The arrangement suited both. Mary looked after Sammy, seeing that he was fed well and properly clothed. His bedroom was always clean and tidy, though it must be said that it was Mary's gentle but persistent persuading that finally paid off.

Mary felt more at ease and secure at night with a man in the house, and the cat and dog downstairs to give alarm of any intruder. Nothing unusual ever happened. Just occasionally the dog and cat would be alerted by the creaking of floorboards as one or the other tiptoed along the passage to seek solace and comfort. On such occasions the two animals would open their eyes, raise their heads skywards, look knowingly at one another – and would have tut-tutted if they could, but they couldn't, so they didn't – and went to sleep again.

It was a week or so after the successful air supply to the French underground that Posty Potter, the Ashover postman, dropped Philip's letter on the doormat of Slippery Edge Farm. It had become such an unusual event that Mary gathered it up in wonderment and curiosity, until she noted the handwriting. It was from Philip! Her heart skipped a beat. Her trembling hands eagerly opened the envelope to read the contents. In her anxiety her breath became laboured and her legs felt rubbery. She sat down to compose herself.

Dear Mother,

It is with such deep sadness that I write this letter. I have just found out that Dad was taken hostage by the Gestapo, from a cottage he had bought in Maisons Blanches, where we all spent a holiday together.

I cannot explain everything, but he was resting there. Unbeknown to him, two German soldiers had been killed. The village was raided, as a reprisal, and Dad, who was asleep in his cottage and unaware of what had happened, was taken with others and shot. His body was somehow retrieved by one of his cousins and buried in the little churchyard, between his parents. A headstone, prepared and inscribed some time ago, is now in place, between those of his parents.

I know this will come as a shock to you, and I am sorry not to be there to comfort and support you. I know that this letter will leave a lot of questions unanswered. I cannot say more! All will be explained one day.

I am keeping well, and longing for the day when we can be together again.

Goodbye, Mother

All my love

Philip xx

Although Mary for some time had had a premonition that Charles was dead, the confirmation of her fears did nothing to relieve the shock and sadness, tinged with guilt, remorse and regret. Her love for him was deep and abiding. It was the soul-destroying circumstances that had torn them apart for ever.

Mary gave vent to her sadness and drained herself of tears, and prayed for forgiveness.

After all the soul-searching and praying, she felt a lightness come over her, and the strength to accept her loss. By the time Sammy came in for his tea, Mary was quite composed and able to show him her letter.

Sammy put his arms around her in commiseration. 'I'm terribly sorry, love! You've always had a feeling that something had happened to him, but what a terrible way to go! And what a waste! At least now you know, and on the bright side you know that Philip is alive. When this terrible war is over I'll go with you to see Charles's grave, if you like. I would like to pay my last respects to him too. He was a nice man, Mary.'

'It's terrible not being able to write to Philip. I think he is in France doing secret and dangerous work.'

32

Back in France, Philip, Madeleine, Madame Pinson and Albert found themselves working and buzzing around like blue-arsed flies. They were becoming accustomed to flagging down the Lysander; the drill became expeditious and automatic.

With the passing of time, the Germans were almost in full flight and overwhelmed on every front. The saturation bombing by the American Flying Fortresses and the British Lancasters were having devastating effects on the German industry and its people. The German Army was flanked on all sides, and being pushed back to where they belonged, in Germany. Germany's capacity did not match Hitler's ambition. The Russians were on Germany's doorstep, leaving behind acres of German snowbound equipment of all kinds and the battalions of grotesque frozen corpses in equally grotesque attitudes.

The invasion of the continent, after the initial setbacks, had finally got the Boche on the run everywhere.

In a final attempt to change the course of the war, Germany used doodlebugs and rocket bombs. They were too few and too late. Everything was closing in on Germany. The amount of British and American aircraft being used caused a larger influx of shot-down aircrews using the escape routes, until they became blocked and eventually unnecessary.

Philip's Lysander drops played a great role in supplying with arms and explosives the underground and Maquis, who in turn ravaged the transport systems and supply routes and attacked the retreating army.

Now Philip's part in the war was virtually at an end. It was at this point that Philip's tug-of-war with his conscience began.

He was now free to travel northwards to Tourne Hemme to find Fleur, Fleurette and Lucile. But what about Madeleine? Madeleine had given so much to Philip. She had supported him through thick and thin. She had nursed and loved him through times of depression, when his father had been shot, and all the worry about Fleur, Fleurette and Lucile. She had laid her life on the line in helping Philip to send his messages. She never flinched or wavered in what she did, no matter how dangerous.

It would be hard to say goodbye. Madeleine and Philip were under no illusion about that. Philip had played straight with her, and for her part, she had gone along with it, knowing that their love affair had no future and would end as soon as Philip decided it was time to go.

Many things had happened in a relative short time. The American and British armies, in spite of strong, seemingly insurmountable coastal defences, had, after hard and costly attacks, broken through and caused a retreat from which the Germans never recovered. On the nineteenth of August 1944, there was a left-wing uprising in Paris. Hitler ordered General von Choltitz to raze Paris to a heap of rubble and to fight to the last man. The order of a madman, thought General von Choltitz, a more realistic man, who, on the twenty-fifth of August surrendered Paris and saved it from destruction.

Colonel Philip Pipkin-Brodeau now felt the time had come to say his goodbyes to Madeleine, her mother, Albert and Madame Pinson, and head for Maisons Blanches to pay homage to his father's grave. Afterwards he would continue his journey to Tourne Hemme, where he hoped to find Fleur, Fleurette and Lucile. Of course, with the liberation of Paris, it was just possible that they had moved back to their apartment in Paris.

Now, his mind made up, Philip broke the news to Madeleine. It was not unexpected, nevertheless Madeleine was brokenhearted, though she tried not to show it. 'Oh Philip! I know very well you must go. I shall be very sad all the same. We have only two more days together! We shall have to make the best of it, shan't we?'

They melted into one another's arms, neither, it seemed, inclined to part.

'We'll go and say your goodbyes tonight at Madame Pinson's. I'll see that Albert is there too! Then we shall have two whole days together, Philip. A lifetime in two days!'

That evening, helped along by a fantastic meal and copious amounts of wine, the four made it a memorable occasion.

'This must not be the end,' said Albert. 'These last months have been an endurance. We are lifelong friends. We must meet again.'

They gave one another addresses where they could be contacted, promised to write to one another and arranged to all meet up at some future date.

So much had happened that the parting was a bit emotional. Philip and Madeleine waved goodbye as they rode away on their bicycles.

For the next two days Madeleine was excused duty. Her mother was goodness itself. She went out of her way to make their last two days an unforgettably beautiful memory.

The morning of the departure, emotions threatened to bubble over and conversation became a little strained. There were no tears in parting. They had all been shed in private. Philip's car was waiting. They had a quick hug and a kiss, and he was off. Madeleine turned sadly away. There was no looking back. All that remained were fond memories.

It would be wrong to say that Colonel Philip was bereft of feelings. He felt much the same as Madeleine. Once, he even hesitated and eased the accelerator. He would never forget her. The thought of Fleur and Fleurette, often misted over by the activities of war, suddenly became clearer. He put his foot down and shot forward to new horizons.

Philip now knew what he wanted. Fleur and Fleurette were uppermost in his thoughts. His future and theirs would be forever fused together in love and happiness.

During the past few years Philip's life had meandered from one facet to another, dictated by the fortunes of war, all of which had left an indelible scar on his mind. He was constantly reminded of things he had done, both good and bad, in the name of King and Country. It was now that the real battle began – the battle of the mind. It was no easy battle. It was constant and invading, and interfered with his concentration. Only time and perseverance would conquer and obliterate the invading memories best forgotten.

After several hours at the wheel, he was overcome by fatigue, and sought to have a meal and refresh himself at the restaurant he was just about to pass. He pulled into a convenient space and entered. He gave a beaming smile to the flashy-eyed waitress who motioned him to a table. She at once warmed to his charm, and immediately acquiesced when Philip politely asked if it was first possible to have a wash, shave and brush-up.

'*Pas de problème, Monsieur!*' she said. '*Me suivez, s'il vous plaît!*' She led him to a *toilette des hommes*.

The meal, though basic, was wholesome and satisfying. He bade her a charming *au revoir* and left with a naughty feeling that little persuasion would have been necessary to have had his way with her. He brushed such thoughts aside. He had had a good meal, and a bottle of Beaujolais, and was not in the least in the mood for any hanky-panky. He felt more like sleep, which is exactly what he did on reaching his car.

Philip slept until early morning, when he woke up stiff and achy. He walked up and down to stretch his legs and revive his circulation. Feeling better, he made an early start, wishing to gobble up a few miles before stopping for breakfast.

There had been little sign of war, but now, every few miles bore increasing evidence of conflict. There were burnt-out vehicles, turretless tanks, others without tracks, an odd broken gun, and small areas with rifles stuck in the ground with a tin hat suspended from the butt – the temporary resting place of some poor mother's son.

Philip found the mile upon mile of havoc and carnage, and the smell of death, sickeningly revolting to his sensibilities.

It was night-time again as he hit the outskirts of Troyes. He found a small hotel and booked in for a meal and a good night's rest before visiting his father's grave.

Every few miles bore increasing evidence of conflict.

That night, in spite of a warm comfortable bed, the putrid stench of death lingered in his nostrils, and it was only the exhausting drive that eventually lulled him to sleep.

Philip slept on awhile the next morning, then worked his charms on Madame the proprietress to get a bath to freshen up for his next journey. After croissants and coffee, Philip tipped the waitress and took his leave.

As directed by Madame, he drove to Troyes' beautiful cathedral, then turned left, bought petrol and oil from a garage, then continued along the tree-lined road to Maisons Blanches. He faintly remembered the shady route from Troyes, but once he saw the cluster of white houses and the little church, the view, and his memory of it, clicked into place. He stopped the car and crossed over to the church gate, and as he entered he was overwhelmed by grief, his eyes welled with tears. As Albert had told him, his father's grave lay between those of his grandparents, and a headstone had already been erected. Tears streamed unashamedly down his face as he said a little prayer and sadly returned to his car.

He looked forlorn sitting there, his eyes and face awash with tears – a picture of grief and wretchedness. He sat there for an hour or so, lost in thoughts of times gone by. He realized how little time he had spent with his father, mostly because of his father's work. He thought of all the things he wanted to say to him, the places he wanted to show him, and the things they could have done together. Now those things would never happen. They were just unfulfilled dreams. He felt sad and lonely. He closed his eyes, and tasted the salt of his tears.

Philip painfully turned his thoughts to the future. He had a vision of Fleur and baby Fleurette. Fleurette must be going to school by now, he thought. Would she remember him? What would he say to her? All these thoughts flittered through his mind as he drove off to find out what the future held. One thing was for sure: he would never leave Fleur and Fleurette again. Wherever he went, they would be with him as a family.

He thrust all thoughts aside to concentrate on his driving. He still had a long, tiring journey to reach Tourne Hemme. He decided to skirt Paris and make for Rouen, where he would spend the night, so as to arrive at Tourne Hemme reasonably fresh. The journey took much longer than expected, owing to the huge concentrations of military vehicles, equipment and personnel moving from the ports to the battle areas.

From the few officers Philip was able to talk to during his frequent hold-ups, he was able to glean encouraging shreds of information. The passing troops gave the impression of a victorious army. They were flushed with eagerness to come to grips with the enemy. It appeared that the Germans were retreating on every front, often in disarray. No longer conquering heroes, they were fast losing the will to fight and beginning to feel the pangs of defeat. The thousand bomber raids were destroying German cities and the morale of both the population and the fighting forces.

Philip managed to cadge a fill-up of petrol and a couple of spare flimsies – 4-gallon sealed containers, which were poorly made and often leaked. The confidence and enthusiasm of the troops swept over him.

The artillery battery had stopped to replenish and have a meal, so Philip not only cadged the petrol, but muscled in on a plate of bully-beef stew and biscuits. He then wished the troops luck, drove to a quiet spot and settled down to sleep.

As tired as Philip was, sleep eluded him. The nearest he got to sleep was flashes of dreamy visions of Fleur – Fleur running to meet him, Fleur laughing, Fleur crying. Then he was surrounded by the three, all wanting attention, all excited.

Philip wasn't sure whether he had slept during his kaleidoscopic visions. All he knew was that he had more muscles than he knew about, and that every one ached like the very devil. He walked up and down, then disappeared behind a tree. Relieved, he returned to his car and set off with renewed excitement. This was his final lap to the loving arms of Fleur.

The sight of a welcoming café caught his eye.

Rubbing his hand over his chin decided him to try his luck again to get a shave and a clean-up. Philip had a way with pretty girls, and this one was no exception. Perhaps she was feeling benevolent, or taking pity on his hangdog appearance. With a coy smile she led him to a small, tidy shower room. He had a cold shave and a cold shower and returned to the dining room feeling refreshed, and did justice to a generous helping of ragout.

Striding out to his car, Philip felt on top of the world. His footsteps felt lighter. The war was going well for the Allies, and he was only a few miles from paradise – the love of his life! His excitement, his eagerness and his anticipation were hard to suppress.

Again on the main road, the car swept along at a lively pace. The vision of Fleur and their meeting was almost superimposed over his view of the passing scene.

PART VI
PEACE

PART VI

PEACE

33

Despite Philip's cracking speed, time passed at a snail's pace. It seemed an eternity before the car turned into the road leading to Tourne Hemme and the little cottage where Fleur and Philip had spent their lune de miel. Philip pulled up a hundred yards or so from the cottage. Someone was in the garden, hanging out washing. Philip wanted a few minutes to take in the view and compose himself for the meeting.

Now feeling calm and collected, Philip gave a couple of blasts on his horn, which caused a head to be raised over the garden fence. He gave a little wave. Then it happened! A little figure in white came out of the gate, running towards him. It was Fleurette, followed by another tall figure, also in white. Fleurette ran towards Philip's outstretched arms, calling '*Papa*'. He gathered her up to a barrage of wet kisses, supplemented by those of the other figure in white.

Philip, his eyes misty, held them both close to him, returning their kisses. 'Oh Fleur,' he said, trying to focus through his misty eyes. 'How I have longed for this moment!'

Before she could utter a word, he was smothering her with kisses and words of heartfelt passion.

'Philip!' she started breathlessly, but before she could utter another word Philip was holding her in a passionate embrace.

'Philip, I am Lucile!'

Philip held her at arm's length. He couldn't believe his eyes. She had grown into the image of Fleur.

'Oh Lucile, I'm so sorry! You are exactly as I remember Fleur.'

'Well, we have been taken for twins on many occasions,' she replied.

'Well then, where is she?'

'Come inside and I'll tell you,' she answered, taking Fleurette's hand.

Philip took the other hand. In a sort of swinging movement, Fleurette was propelled along in giant strides, much to her amusement. She bubbled over with laughter all the way home.

'Come inside, Philip,' Lucile repeated, and motioned Philip to a seat. 'Let me just see to Fleurette. I'll find her something to keep her busy, then we can talk.'

She returned with a brandy, which she knew was Philip's favourite tipple. She sat beside him as he sipped his drink and awaited her answer to his question.

'Philip,' she said tremulously, 'I have been dreading this day! I have some very sad news for you, and no easy way to tell you.' She held his hand. 'Fleur is dead, Philip! She was travelling by train from Calais. The train was shot up by rockets. She was one of the many killed. It should have been me! One of the villagers did a sort of communal shop each week – clothes, shoes etc. which weren't available locally. I feel terrible about it. It was my turn to go, but Fleur offered to go in my place while I looked after Fleurette.'

It was too much for Lucile; she sobbed her heart out in contrition and self-condemnation. Philip put his arms around her in sympathy and unhappiness.

'It wasn't your fault, Lucile dear!' encouraged Philip. 'It was the will of God, which moves in mysterious ways. Perhaps it was my punishment, for my wrongdoings. Oh, I'm not squeaky-clean, Lucile. It sometimes happens in wartime, in certain situations – the flesh weakens and animal instinct takes over, to be regretted later. It's an inexcusable human frailty.'

They clung together, supporting each other in their misery.

'I really don't know what to say,' said Philip, 'and even less, what to do. Thank you for being a mother to Fleurette – I couldn't have chosen a better one – but what am I to do?'

'Don't worry! There is plenty of time to think. When my parents were killed, Fleur became both mother and sister to me. She looked after me, she taught me, she loved me, she saw to my every need. I will do the same for Fleurette. I will be mother to her, for ever, if necessary. We are both very happy, she calls me her second mummy.'

Lucile was quite happy for Philip to stay as long as he liked, to adjust himself to his loss and to accustom himself to the new situation. She did her best to lighten his sadness. The three went out for long walks and picnics. They got along fine together.

After a month, Philip announced that he would go and report to the military headquarters to find out what his position was. Lucile had realized for some time that during Philip's periods of silence something was gyrating in his mind. On such occasions, she kept her silence and allowed him to work out his own salvation in peace.

Philip returned from headquarters with a relieved expression on his face. Paris was free and the war was in its final throes. He had been congratulated on his service and told to go home. He would be contacted at a later date, and in the meantime he was to enjoy himself.

Philip had always liked Lucile, and held her in high regard. She was pure and virtuous and a credit to Fleur, who had lavished unstintingly on her all the love and attention her mother would have given her, had she lived.

Now in full bloom, Lucile was so like Fleur in every way that it was almost beyond belief, and Philip suffered the torment of having to resist taking her in his arms. As time passed, he began to realize more and more that he wanted her.

One evening, after Fleurette was nicely tucked in bed, Philip motioned Lucile to sit beside him.

'I wish to discuss something with you Lucile.'

Lucile could see that his mind was in a turmoil, and that he was finding it difficult to express himself. She half suspected what was on his mind. She took his hands in hers and said gently, 'What is it, Philip dear?'

'You are so like Fleur, I think I am falling in love with you.'

'And I, in my own way, have always loved you from afar.'

'Oh Lucile,' he said, 'my thoughts are in a whirl! Fleurette is bonded to you. It would not be right for me to take her from you. She is so happy with you.'

Then Philip asked the question being tossed around in his mind. It was the only one that made any sense.

'Lucile dear, would you consider marrying me, so that we could be a family? Both Fleurette and I would be very happy. I am sure Fleur would have wished it. What do you say? Would you like to think about it?'

'There's no need! My answer is yes, darling. It's the best and happiest solution for us all.'

'Oh Lucile, you've made me very happy!' They clung together in a marathon kiss.

'I am sure Fleur would have wished it. She always said, in a joking, motherly way, that she would try out any prospective husband of mine, to make sure he was firing on all cylinders.'

They both collapsed in peals of laughter, as simultaneously they realized it would happen exactly as she had predicted.

That night, Philip went to his own bed, not wanting to put any pressure on Lucile, and, perhaps, to let her sleep on the idea and think it over carefully before coming to a definite decision.

It was all unnecessary. Lucile had made her mind up long ago. She had dreamt about it, hoped for it, and prayed that Philip would ask her to marry him. She was deliriously happy now that it had happened. If Philip thought he was going to have the bed to himself, he was mistaken. It wasn't long before light footsteps warned of a delightful intrusion. A fairylike figure slipped gently between the sheets and pressed itself against his body.

'I'm sorry, darling! I just had to come.'

'*Ça me donne beaucoup de plaisir, chérie.*' 'That makes me very happy, dear," replied Philip, snuggling close to her.

Thrilling to her touch, Philip turned towards her. They declared their love for each other and their devotion. They made love for the first time, then slipped peacefully into a wonderful relaxing sleep.

Morning broke with the patter of tiny feet, then the feel

of a squirmy little fairy wriggling for a snug position between them.

'You're asleep, *Papa*,' said Fleurette's quiet little voice, as she tickled Philip's ear and gave a cheeky smile.

'Not any more, little Fleurette!'

There was then a little game of 'find which hand it's in' – the ring supplied by Philip.

Fleurette then disappeared downstairs with Lucile–Maman – to make coffee for Papa. The three were very happy, and when the coffee and croissants arrived, they lingered awhile in bed. Philip and Lucile chattered and discussed plans. There was mutual agreement to marry as soon as possible, and with this in mind, the three made arrangements with Monsieur le Maire to marry as soon as possible.

The marriage was a quiet, simple affair, with Annette, Fleurette and Lucile's special friend from Vimereux, and a few new, local friends. Annette accompanied Fleurette, who took a great interest in the proceedings.

Although Paris was now liberated and free, Philip and Lucile decided to stay in Tourne Hemme for the time being, to allow the excitement and fervour to die down before returning to their apartment.

The Pipkin-Brodeaus, now a complete family, settled down to a quiet, contented life. Fleurette was a happy little girl, full of fun and playfulness and a delight to be with. She took much pleasure in showing off her daddy.

Philip was now able to write to his mother. He gave her the sad news of Fleur's tragic end, and the good news of his marriage to Lucile. 'Life must go on', he wrote. 'We shall never forget Fleur. We can talk about her with love and affection, and without embarrassment. Fleurette is a little beauty, with a little dimple, like yours. You'll love her! We'll be over to see you as soon as things get back to normal.'

In quiet moments Philip began to worry about getting a job, and wondered what he would like to do. He was very sporty but feared he had outlived his usefulness in that direction.

Running a business didn't appeal to him, neither did farm work. After running over in his mind all the different occupations he could think of, he came to the conclusion that he was useless. He would talk it over with Lucile. Perhaps together they could strike the right note, and come up with something worthwhile. Jobs weren't easy to come by. The economies and industries of the warring countries now had to revert to peacetime conditions, and make a workplace for the millions of servicemen and women returning to civilian life. It was difficult to keep pace with the speed at which the returning military forces came home. New jobs failed to be created quickly enough to supply the returning forces, consequently many found themselves without jobs to go to, or had to take a job far below their capabilities. It would take months, perhaps years, before things returned to normal.

One evening, after a lovely picnic by the riverside, with Fleurette safely tucked into bed and asleep, Lucile and Philip sat down to discuss the future. One thing they agreed on was that they would return to their apartment in Paris. That agreed, Philip's job had to be in Paris. What job, was now the question.

Between them, they covered every job from barrow boy to bank manager. It was a light-hearted conversation, and some of the jobs suggested were too hilarious to even contemplate.

'Now,' said Lucile, 'we have had a lot of fun with many impossible suggestions, let's consider real possibilities. Let me look at you in real terms. Apart from making love, for which I give you ten out of ten, what are your most assessable qualifications?'

'Well, I have the usual certificates of education from the Sorbonne, with an excellent report from the Principal. I was well sought after for sport, particularly for football and rugby; I never excelled in either, but I enjoyed playing.'

'What about your languages?' continued Lucile. 'Your French is impeccable, and what about your English, Italian, and German? As far as I can judge, you seem to be fluent in all four.'

'Yes, I was always in the top few for languages. I remember

one teacher suggesting that I should think seriously about taking up teaching. Then the war started, though I must say my languages came in useful during the hostilities.'

'Well there you are, Philip! That's the answer! Why not follow it up, and write to the Principal of the Sorbonne? What have you to lose?'

'Right. Well, that's settled. Now come here, and let me give you a big kiss.'

Philip sat down at once to write his letter. 'Nothing like the present, dear, to test the water.'

Next morning the three walked down to the village, where Fleurette was lifted up to drop the letter in the box.

'That should bring Papa good luck, *mon petit chou*,' remarked Lucile, putting her hands together and looking skywards in supplication.

34

Mary read it out to Sammy.

Down on Slippery Edge Farm in Ashover, Mary and Sammy were just having breakfast when Flash the second (old Flash having fretted himself to death after George and Sara's tragic accident) cocked his ears and gave a little woof to alert Mary that post had fluttered onto the mat.

'Save your legs, Mary,' said Sammy, going to retrieve the letter. 'It's from France,' he said, handing it over to her. 'I hope it's good news.'

Mary took the letter, turned it over curiously, loath to open it for fear of its contents. She gave a sigh, then her trembling fingers tore open the envelope and she read the awful news. Sammy could see from the anguish on her face that the news was bad. He put his arm around her in sympathy and support. Mary read it out to Sammy, both the good and the bad. The one could not eliminate the other. Both had to be absorbed individually. Mary did not know whether to laugh or cry. She did both in turn, in the comforting arms of Sammy. Sammy, in his own simple, uncomplicated way, was a pillar of strength and support to Mary; – always reliable, and always there.

'Come and sit down, lass, while I make us a cup of tea!'

Sammy always flew to the teapot, his first-aid treatment in any crisis. They sat down quietly together and sipped their tea in silent meditation, giving each other time to come to terms with the sad news. On top of the execution of Charles, it was hard for Mary to bear. She sought relief from her anguish in a flood of tears, while Sammy felt at a loss at what to do. He held her close and let the tears run their course.

'Now the war is over, perhaps we ought to think about a visit to Charles's grave, and perhaps we could fit in a visit to Philip and his family,' suggested Sammy.

Mary brightened up at the prospect. 'That would be nice, Sammy,' she replied, drying her tears. 'I feel that once I have seen his grave, I will be able to settle down and enjoy my life again. I really don't know what I would do without thee,' she added, giving Sammy a little squeeze. 'I really don't!'

'Right, Mary, I'll see to that. There's nothin' here to hold us back. I'll get in touch with that shipping company that goes from Dover to Calais, and you can write to Philip and tell him we're coming!'

Mary let Sammy take the initiative and only checked when he needed assurance about something. He booked their passage from Dover to Calais, and a train from Calais to Troyes.

And so it was that on the afternoon of a bright spring day, Mary and Sammy stepped off the train at Troyes. They booked in for the night at a nearby hotel, then, after buying a large bunch of mixed flowers, they took a taxi to Maisons Blanches. Mary brought Sammy's attention to the tree-lined route with its array of spring flowers and early blossoms along the hedgerows. Sammy, always the typical countryman, thrilled to the kaleidoscope of colours.

'Oh Mary, how grand it all is!' he enthused, giving her hand a little squeeze, and when the cluster of white cottages and the little church came into view, and the thought of the purpose of their visit, they were both reduced to tears.

'*Voilà, Monsieur, dame!*' announced the driver, bringing the taxi to a halt by the church gate. Sammy pulled out a handful of money to pay the fare. Francs and cents were far too complicated for him to deal with. He held out his hand to Mary, which brought a smile to the driver's face. Mary sorted out his change to pay the fare, plus a *petit pourboire*. The driver drove off with a satisfied smile on his face.

'Isn't it lovely and peaceful here, Mary! No wonder Charles thought so much about it. I remember he called it his little bit of paradise.'

Mary felt a catalogue of different emotions as she passed through the gate. Her emotions stirred as she came to rest in front of three graves. Charles's grave was in between those of his parents. When Mary saw the poignant verse that Charles had composed, and read to her whilst they were on holiday there, it was more than she could stand. Through the flood of tears streaming down her face she read, in a faltering voice, the heart-rending words

> If life goes on above the ground,
> Tis here you'll feel me, all around,
> And when your time comes, and you are free,
> Come join me here, where I wait for thee.
> We'll glide above, just thee and me,
> To find our world, where peace there'll be.

Sammy discreetly excused himself, saying that he would wait for her in the church. He understood her sorrows. It was private and personal to Mary and it was better to allow her to express her grief in her own private way. He was not a religious man or a regular churchgoer. He was a good man, honest and unsophisticated. He would do a good turn to anyone, but he wouldn't hurt a fly. He sat, head bowed, in church. It would be difficult to construe what was going on in his mind. Perhaps a little prayer learnt at his mother's knee? Whatever it was, it would be to the benefit of someone.

Mary knelt beside Charles's grave in prayer. She remembered the last time they stood together, on this very spot, and the promise she made to join him when her time came. She again quietly reiterated her promise. She kissed the tear-stained flowers and placed them in the vase of water, and uttered in a tremulous voice 'Goodbye, my love.' She walked slowly to the church and sat beside Sammy. They held hands in silence, neither wanting to disturb the peaceful stillness of the moment.

It was a beautiful day. Mary and Sammy chose to walk the few kilometres back to their hotel. The walk helped to calm their emotions, but brought on pangs of hunger.

The following morning, after a peaceful night's sleep, and a light breakfast of coffee and croissants, which did little to satisfy Sammy's voracious appetite, the two took their train back to Calais. On making enquiries at the station, it appeared that they had two hours to wait for a train to Tourne Hemme. This delighted Sammy no end. He said he was starving, and had a craving for a big plate of fish and chips. This amused

Mary, who secretly seconded his choice. They found a likely-looking café, where Mary ordered *poisson, frites et petits pois*, while Sammy gleefully rubbed his tum in anticipation. The two plates arrived, again to the amusement of Mary as she watched Sammy's face. It was a picture of amazement as he gazed at the huge pile of mini-sized chips and the smallest peas he had ever seen.

Those peas would take the booby prize in the Ashover Show, Mary,' he said, bringing a little light-heartedness to their sadness, and a touch of puzzlement to the face of the waitress.

During their journey to Tourne Hemme, Mary asked Sammy if he would do one last thing for her.

'What is it, Mary?' he asked.

'You know what it said on Charles's gravestone?'

'Yes.'

'Well, dear, I promised Charles to honour his wish. Would you do this last thing for me, when my time comes?'

'I promise it will be done as you wish, my dear,' he said, giving her a little kiss.

'Thank you, Sammy,' she replied, returning his kiss. 'You will be carrying out my last wish, and in turn, I shall be honouring Charles's last wish. A thousand thanks, Sammy my love,' she said, wrapping her arms around him in a big hug. 'You're wonderful, Sammy! What would I do without you?'

'When I think of all the things, and the life, you have given to me, there is nothing in this world I wouldn't do for you! You have been my salvation, Mary. Without you, my life would have been as nothing.'

'That's settled, then. Let's not dwell on it any longer, and let's enjoy the time left to us. Agreed?'

'Agreed, my love,' said Sammy. They sat close together enjoying the scenery with the river meandering through the lush pastures where cattle grazed contentedly.

'I really like travelling around,' he said. 'Since you came into my life, my eyes have been opened to the world around us. As a child Ashover Rock was the top of the world, over which I rarely strayed.'

'We'll travel more, Sammy! I'll take you to the Lake District for a start, then Scotland and Cornwall. After that, we'll go abroad and discover some of the wonders of the world.'

'Oh Mary! You really mean it, don't you?'

'You can bet on it, Sammy dear! There's nothing to stop us. We'll do it.'

There weren't many trains stopping at Tourne Hemme, so it was fairly easy for Lucile to judge which train would bring Mary and Sammy. They had hardly touched the platform before they were besieged by the open arms of Fleurette, followed by Lucile and Philip.

The cottage was quite near, and in no time at all the five were sitting around the table having tea, and, as one might expect, Fleurette pushed her chair close to Grandma, to which Grandma responded by putting an arm around her.

There was lots to talk about. Questions and answers flew back and forth across the table like a radio network. It wasn't until the teapot was empty and the plates of sandwiches and cakes began to look decimated that the babble of excited voices subsided to normal chit-chat.

The intended two-day stay soon stretched to a fortnight. It was a very happy time for everyone, but like all good things it eventually ended. There were lots of promises and plans for future visits and a few last-minute tearful kisses as the train slowly drew out of the station.

It was during Mary and Sammy's stay that Philip received a reply to his letter to the Principal of the Sorbonne, offering him an interview for a teaching post in the language department. Everyone was thrilled for Philip. He would be making use of what he was good at.

Mary and Sammy made the most of their return journey. They spent a night in Calais and crossed the Channel by day, so that they could enjoy the sea. On the boat they lashed out on an expensive meal, in the wake of Mary's suggestion that henceforth they were going to spend some of their hard-earned cash and enjoy themselves.

* * *

The following years, Mary and Sammy had the time of their lives. They spent holidays at lots of places they had only dreamt of or read about in the colourful holiday brochures.

It was after their never to be forgotten years of supreme happiness that Mary, in her eightieth year, fell ill and succumbed to pneumonia. As she lay there dying, Sammy put his head close to hers to catch her whispering voice.

'Don't cry, Sammy,' she whispered. 'Think of all the nice things we did together. Now give me a nice smile, Sammy dear!'

Sammy wiped away his tears and gave her one of his beaming smiles. Mary managed a half-smile in return as her face relaxed in peace.

Sammy was distraught. In his anguish, he held her close; his sobs and tears told of his deep love and respect for her. It took a while for him to come to terms with his loss. He wandered aimlessly around the house, deeply distressed and mumbling incoherently to himself.

It was in this disturbed state of mind that Robert and Sally found him.

'Whatever's the matter, Sammy?' Sally asked, putting her arms around him in a motherly way.

They half realized, and dreaded the answer. Through his sobs, he pointed upstairs and in a choking whisper said, 'Mary!'

Robert went upstairs while Sally gave Sammy a spot of brandy and tried to calm him down.

Both Robert and Sally knew of Mary's wish. Robert came down after a while. Sammy had calmed down, and with his permission Robert took charge of the situation. He got on the phone to De'ath the undertaker to make the necessary arrangements for a church funeral service and the transport of the coffin afterwards to Maisons Blanches, France. Robert explained that he would go over the details later when he came round. Then Robert phoned the doctor.

The sad news soon spread, followed by phone calls and

visitors. First came Doctor Swallow, followed by young De'ath the undertaker and a trail of sympathizers.

All the formalities were carried out quickly. Mary's body was taken to Maisons Blanches. Only Sammy and close family attended the burial.

Mary's coffin was already in the little church as the small gathering of relatives filed in. The service was reverent and brief. The mourners followed the pallbearers and assembled around the grave. The preacher said his few words of condolence, then the ritual ashes to ashes, dust to dust. There were sobs and tears as earth was dropped on the coffin. Then, as prearranged, the mourners filed through the gate, leaving Sammy a lone figure staring down onto the coffin, saying his own private goodbye. He kissed his posy of flowers and let them fall on the coffin. He then turned sadly away. He was helped through the gate by Sally and Robert, then joined by Philip, Lucile and Fleurette. This was now his family, and he knew he would never be alone, ever.

EPILOGUE

Sammy lived on, at Slippery Edge Farm. He never recovered from the loss of Mary. He died a year later, many said of a broken heart.

Colonel Robert and Sally Pipkin looked after Sammy until his death. He was buried next to his mother in Ashover churchyard.

Colonel Philip and Lucile Pipkin-Brodeau, with Fleurette, live happily in Paris. Philip is Professor of Languages at the Sorbonne. Fleurette grew into a living replica of Fleur, her natural mother.

As promised to the 'Sulmona Five' who blew up the explosives factory in Sulmona, Colonel Philip Pipkin-Brodeau organized a reunion for the five and their wives and families. The Colonel had the biggest surprise of his life when he was introduced by Major Ray Shorthouse to his wife Filomena and their son Filippo.

The reunion was a huge success, and no tales were told out of school! Although one or two eyebrows were raised, loyalty reigned, and Colonel Philip Pipkin-Brodeau secretly congratulated himself on a job well-done 'for King and Country'.